Praise for the Giulia Driscoll Mystery Series

"Giulia is a sympathetic, well-drawn character who has built a full life for herself after leaving the convent, but appealing touches of the former nun remain."

~oklist

"Driscoll's second solo turn a.   ffers a fun and fast read with a lot o.

~ıorary Journal

"Former nun and current private eye Giulia Driscoll tackles ghosts with the same wit and wisdom she uses to tackle crooks. Great fun."

– Terrie Farley Moran,
Agatha Award-Winning Author of the Read 'Em and Eat Mysteries

"Loweecey's characters are colorful without being caricatures, and once again we're lucky that Giulia Driscoll left the convent behind. She solves the crime with a happy mix of online savvy, humor and intelligence."

– Sheila Connolly,
New York Times Bestselling Author of *An Early Wake*

"How can you not love an author who quotes from the movies Airplane and Young Frankenstein? Giulia's recent marriage adds a delightful dash of romance, but the real appeal of this series is her genuine likability and fiery independent streak that could never be hidden behind a veil."

– *Kings River Life Magazine*

"Loweecey has once again crafted a delightful, sassy, smart tale that will send the hair on the back of your head skyward and keep your eyes glued to the page. I loved it!"

– Jessie Chandler,
Author of the Award-Winning Shay O'Hanlon Caper Series

Nun After The Other

The Giulia Driscoll Mystery Series
by Alice Loweecey

Novels

NUN TOO SOON (#1)
SECOND TO NUN (#2)
NUN BUT THE BRAVE (#3)
THE CLOCK STRIKES NUN (#4)
NUN AFTER THE OTHER (#5)

Short Stories

CHANGING HABITS
(prequel to NUN TOO SOON)

Nun After The Other

A
GIULIA DRISCOLL
MYSTERY

Alice Loweecey

HENERY PRESS

Copyright

NUN AFTER THE OTHER
A Giulia Driscoll Mystery
Part of the Henery Press Mystery Collection

First Edition | April 2018

Henery Press
www.henerypress.com

Trade Paperback ISBN-13: 978-1-63511-326-6
Digital epub ISBN-13: 978-1-63511-327-3
Kindle ISBN-13: 978-1-63511-328-0
Hardcover ISBN-13: 978-1-63511-329-7

Printed in the United States of America

Four other Oysters followed them,
And yet another four;
And thick and fast they came at last,
And more, and more, and more--
All hopping through the frothy waves,
And scrambling to the shore.

Through the Looking-Glass, and What Alice Found There

ACKNOWLEDGMENTS

Thanks to Rob Early for sharing his electrical expertise. Thanks to my cosplayers for this book: Barb Early, my Good Twin, the Head Honey of the Horror Honeys (where my dark heart truly belongs), and Steve Barber, my favorite Chihuahua rescuer. And as always: Thanks to Awesome Editor Rachel Jackson and my fellow Hens for all their support.

One

Giulia Driscoll, formerly Sister Mary Regina Coelis, ground a smoldering cigarette butt into the sidewalk.

"Why is there always one smoker who treats the park like an ashtray?"

Her husband dropped his empty Coke bottle into the nearest recycle bin. "Please take note of my effort to keep Cottonwood, Pennsylvania clean."

"As a good member of the police force should." She made a face. "We agreed no work talk on a date night."

Frank Driscoll tucked his wife's hand into his arm. "I won't mention the precinct again."

"And I won't mention the interesting ways a private investigator has to alter her usual methods of working now that I'm pregnant."

The bells on the First Presbyterian Church steeple began to chime ten p.m. Two pairs of teenagers ran around the park's central fountain, giggling and shrieking. A white-haired couple passed Frank and Giulia, discussing the relative merits of Dairy Queen Blizzards versus McDonald's McFlurries. Three of the teenagers picked up the fourth and tossed her into the fountain.

"Not my circus. Not my monkeys." Giulia patted her growing baby bump. "Zlatan votes for an Oreo Blizzard."

Frank steered them out of the park. "Zlatan's wish is my command."

They entered the sulfurous yellow pool of a streetlight. A Jeep blasting Blake Shelton's latest hit drove past.

Giulia said, "Everything about this idea of a date night each month on Zlatan's expected due date is great, except babies don't necessarily keep to schedules."

Frank stepped out of the light first. "As an uncle several times over I am painfully aware of this, but we have three and a half more months to convince Zlatan otherwise."

"He may rebel if we don't come up with a more mainstream name by his due date."

"If we could convince Ibrahimović, the great soccer player himself, to sponsor our first-born, it'd be worth it."

A shriek cut through his last word.

"Left," Giulia said. She was already running in and out of circles of light.

"One block over." Frank ran beside her. "Maybe two."

They cut left at the corner. The next street was too narrow to rate streetlights. High, frenzied barks joined the noise of their sneakers slapping the concrete. The barking got closer.

Giulia stopped Frank and listened over the sound of their breathing. "Ahead." She wanted to hear another scream. Another one meant a struggle. All she heard was the unseen dog.

They took off. A brown and white Chihuahua trailing a glittery blue leash appeared, yapping at such a rate its tiny mouth never seemed to close. Giulia grabbed for the leash, but the dog ran back and forth at their feet, whipping it out of her grasp.

Giulia took a step toward it. The barking ratcheted higher and the dog scampered back the way it came. As they followed, the chubby little dog ran so fast it appeared to hover. Its belly grazed the sidewalk at every other leap. It turned left into a street of boarded-up houses and stopped at a prostrate figure beneath a sputtering streetlight.

The little dog licked the figure's outflung hand, yapped in a higher register, and licked some more. Giulia knelt and searched for a pulse. Frank called 911.

"I need more light," Giulia said after he hung up.

The iPhone flashlight illuminated a rumpled black veil, black dress, and open-mouthed face. The pale blue eyes stared without blinking. Wrinkles covered the translucent skin, damp where the Chihuahua's darting tongue switched from the hand to the face.

"She's a nun," Frank said.

"She's dead," Giulia said.

Two

Giulia knelt on the sidewalk and said a silent prayer for the repose of the dead nun's soul. The dog resumed its barking conniption.

"Wallet's in the gutter," Frank said.

"Open?"

"Face down. Do you recognize her?"

Giulia finally hooked two fingers through the leash. "I don't know every nun within a fifty-mile radius."

"Worth a shot." He crouched in the street, nose all but touching the overturned wallet. "Can't see a thing. What kind of human waste goes after nuns?"

The Chihuahua ran from Giulia's ankles to Frank's. "One who needs a fix."

"Damn all pushers to...which circle of Hell is the worst?"

"Eighth circle, fifth bolgia. Eternity immersed in boiling tar. If they poke their head above the tar, demons claw them to pieces until they sink. Lather, rinse, and repeat forever." She caught Frank's look and heard the harsh edge to her voice. She stroked the dog. "How can something this small make so much noise?"

Lights flashed. A patrol car drove around the corner and headed for them.

Frank looked around. "Talk about a poster child for neighborhood revitalization."

Century-old houses lined both sides of the street. Only every third house possessed a complete set of intact windows. Once-graceful front porches sagged in the middle or were buttressed with two-by-fours. Postage-stamp areas of city "lawns" were bare of grass. Broken bottles and crumpled beer cans competed with weeds and torn sheets of newspaper. Shards of glass in the empty window frames caught the police car's red and blue lights, throwing gashes of color onto peeling paint and cracked woodwork.

The driver exited first. "Driscoll, aren't you supposed to be off duty?"

Frank attempted to look virtuous. "Sasha, the road to promotion is paved with overtime."

Banter ceased when both officers reached the sidewalk.

Sasha hissed a curse. "The scumbags have hit a new low."

Giulia's eyes refused to look away from the limp white hair sticking out from the skewed veil. "I checked for a pulse, but we didn't disturb anything."

Sasha inclined her head toward the police car and her partner reached inside for the microphone. With one finger stuck in his free ear, he relayed several requests.

"What's with the mutt?" Sasha reached for its head.

The Chihuahua jerked away from her, snatching the leash out of Giulia's loose grasp. It licked the dead nun's face, then looked up at the humans and barked like it was asking a favor. Giulia couldn't blame pregnancy hormones for the way the little dog's reactions squeezed her heart.

"We need forensics to take their pictures so I can get into the wallet," Frank said.

Lights flashed in the distance. An SUV drove past, followed a minute later by a Subaru wagon.

"At least we don't have to deal with nosy neighbors." Frank indicated the empty windows.

Sasha rubbed the dog's ears. "You think they'd come out to see what this one is so excited about? Not likely. My neighbors on either side have designer dogs. Poodles mixed with a canine perpetual motion machine, and they never shut up. The whole street ignores the noise like they're furry car alarms."

Ambulance lights appeared at the end of the street followed by two more cars. Sasha rubbed the dog's belly and Giulia used the distraction to wrap the leash around her wrist. Two EMTs reached the sidewalk first with the coroner and photographer on their heels. Frank's partner Nash VanHorne came straight over to Frank and

Giulia.

"Some date. What happened?"

"Heard a scream. Followed it but only got here in time to see this." Frank gestured at the nun's body, now being circled by the photographer under direction of the coroner.

The camera flashed. Everyone else waited. The Chihuahua made a dash for the coroner's ankles. Giulia yanked it back. It yipped but obeyed. Nash stepped in and placed evidence markers by the wallet and an overturned plastic cup with pink liquid oozing out of it. More pictures.

The photographer finished. The coroner knelt by the body and Frank dived for the wallet.

"Sister Mary Matilda Stapleton. Lives—" he checked the nearest street sign— "on this street." He turned his head toward the house behind them. "280. We want 386."

The coroner stood. "Heart. Nothing you didn't know already. I'll send you the technical version in the morning."

Frank didn't raise his head from the wallet. "No trauma?"

"Nothing from a surface examination. If you're thinking mugger, she may have died of fright at the sight of a weapon."

The EMTs lowered the gurney and lifted the body onto it. The Chihuahua leapt straight from the sidewalk onto the dead nun's stomach, yanking Giulia forward. She went with the momentum and scooped the barking beast into her arms again. It transferred its energy to her face and slobbered all over her cheeks and chin.

"You have a new friend," Sasha said.

"Thank you, no. A chameleon is more than enough."

"A what?" The radio in the police car crackled. Her partner picked up the mic, listened, and beckoned her over. "We have to go."

The ambulance pulled away. The coroner's car followed.

"I'll tell the nuns at the convent," Giulia said.

Nash exhaled. "I owe you one."

"Still scared of nuns?" Frank said.

"My abused knuckles have lifelong muscle memory."

Three

Giulia set the Chihuahua on the sidewalk. "Home, boy. Let's go home."

The little dog galloped to the limit of the leash. Giulia was ready this time. She took off at a slow jog which kept pace easily with its stumpy legs. Frank's longer stride matched Giulia's without the need to jog.

"300...308...314..." Frank read the house numbers as they passed. "These houses were show places once."

"I grew up in a neighborhood like this." Giulia pointed to the upcoming house on their left. "The scalloped brick porch looks like ours. The shabby outsides are deceptive. We could eat off our floors."

"344...348...When you and your brother weren't trashing the place."

"I neither admit nor deny the rumor that I spread wet Cheerios in the downstairs hall right where seven-year-old Salvatore liked to slide into the kitchen."

Frank chuckled. "Three Our Fathers and three Hail Marys as penance."

The Chihuahua dragged Giulia up a short, cracked sidewalk and sprang up two cement steps. A traditional statue of the Virgin Mary with open hands in blue dress and white veil was the only decoration in the weathered brown house's front yard. Four useless square windows in the front door were set too high to allow the person inside to see who was knocking. Two tall, narrow windows to the left of the door could be used as a fortress' first line of defense. Giulia rang the doorbell.

When footsteps reached Giulia's ears, the Chihuahua relaunched its vocal frenzy. The door opened on a gray-haired woman in brown slacks and short-sleeved white blouse who was already talking.

"Matilda, this hairy beast's barks are worse than a car alarm." She frowned at Giulia. "Who are you? Where's Sister Matilda?"

"Good evening. Is your Superior in?"

"Where else would she be at this time of night?"

Another woman entered the hall. She looked at the dog, at the nun, at Frank and Giulia.

"Where's Sister Matilda?"

Four

A large trestle table took up most of the convent's kitchen. Fourteen people could have fit around it with elbow room to spare. The six people who gathered at it kept to the end near the back door.

Giulia sipped plain Lipton tea. Two of the nuns laced their tea with brandy. The other two and Frank added whisky to their instant coffee.

The dog flopped onto a braided rug next to the refrigerator. A battery-operated wall clock with a miniature pendulum chimed twelve times.

The shriveled nun who'd answered the door blew her nose and tossed a third tissue into the corner wastebasket. Next to her, a middle-aged nun in a nurse's uniform worried a chip in her mug with a short fingernail. Even seated she towered over everyone except Frank.

Across from Giulia sat the Superior and a fourth nun, both with dark hair going gray. All four nuns would run through a tissue, toss it, sip their drinks, sniffle, and repeat the same pattern.

After several minutes of silence, the nurse shoved back her chair. The Chihuahua opened one eye and slapped its tail on the rug. The nun opened a plastic container on the counter. She returned with a plate piled with miniature scones, setting it in the center of the table with the napkins, salt and pepper shakers, and a tub of margarine.

"We're out of butter and despite the margarine we offer as good hosts, I suggest no one profanes the scones with it."

"Dip them in the coffee," the door warden said. She chose one studded with flakes of cinnamon and took her own advice.

Giulia chose a blueberry scone and nibbled it dry. She didn't need her all-natural assistant Sidney to tell her the yellow glop in the store-brand container was really chemicals masquerading as food.

The Superior ignored the scones and kept gazing at Giulia. "I remember you from the big reunion a few years ago. Did you leave the Order after the scandal? So many did."

The door warden's tea cup stopped before it reached her mouth. "I'm getting senile. We'd have recognized you with a veil on." She looked as though she was suppressing an urge to curse. "If you'd been closer, you would've taken out the thug before he killed Matilda."

The others performed the tennis match head swivel from Giulia to the doorkeeper and back again. The latter, whose name was Olive, drank her tea. "She's the former Community member who busted up the Motherhouse drug ring."

"At the reunion? That was you?" the fourth nun spread margarine on a plain scone. "The details were hushed up but everyone knows something about it."

Sister Olive launched into a colorful recap of Giulia's undercover stint in her old Motherhouse. Stars filled the eyes of her listeners. Giulia had to stop it before they expected her to be concealing a Wonder Woman suit beneath her too-tight pants.

"I assure you my work on that case was nothing out of the ordinary."

"You call stopping a drug-dealing priest and his minion the former Superior General, plus surviving a pipe bomb, ordinary?"

The nuns stared at Giulia with enraptured eyes. She had to take control of the story.

"The final moments were a little dramatic, but the pipe bomb surprised everyone. The days leading up to it were filled with routine interviews, cross-checking information, and trying to connect with a Swedish interpreter."

"With a what?"

"It only sounds chaotic." Giulia made a mental appointment for confession this Saturday for the mountain of lies she was telling. "When we discovered the priest and Superior General were using the Novices as drug mules, we contacted the narcotics department. They used their resources to confirm our information and make the arrests. The Swedish nun who bombed Nazis for the Danish resistance as a teenager had her own agenda. No one expected violence from her."

"No one expects..." the nurse began.

"The Spanish Inquisition," the other nuns finished.

"Why did she toss the pipe bomb?" the Superior said.

"It's complex and not applicable to the current situation."

"Good point," Sister Olive said. "What you've just proved is you know how to handle the extraordinary." She caught the eyes of the other nuns. "Victor Eagle killed Matilda."

"You're making a baseless accusation."

Sister Olive squared off against Sister Kathryn, her Superior. "How can you tell us that after the last four weeks?"

"We also have no proof—"

"No proof the CEO of Eagle Developers hired thugs to plaster the windows with smut? No proof his thugs spray-painted the graffiti? What about the phone calls? What about the stream of people at our door?"

"Stop this slander at once." The Superior's voice rang with the sharp authority of a teacher. "Have you forgotten how to behave in the presence of a guest?"

Frank shifted in his chair. Giulia applied pressure to his toes and poked the bears—that is, the nuns.

"Sister Kathryn, although the investigation into Sister Matilda's death is in its preliminary stages, we saw nothing to indicate an assault."

"Of course you didn't," Sister Olive said. "He's an expert at not getting caught."

"Sister Olive." Anger bled through the Superior's authority now, but when she turned toward Giulia politeness covered it. "Eagle Developers wants to renovate this block and the next one that way." She pointed north. "They acquired all the mortgages in arrears and bought out nearly everyone else."

"The infirm Sisters are used to this house." The tallest nun raised her cup, stared in surprise, and set it on the table. "Empty already. I'll never sleep tonight."

"You mean today," Sister Olive said.

Sister Kathryn rubbed her temples. "I keep having nightmares of us living under the Allen Street Bridge."

"That would make it difficult for us to keep the habits in the condition the Order expects," Sister Olive said. "Good thing only Matilda still wore it." She blinked, snatched a tissue, and muttered, "May he rot in Hell."

"Stop it this instant." Sister Kathryn took another tissue for herself.

Sister Olive rolled her shoulders back, adding a quarter inch to her height. "No. I've kept it in for weeks. We're Franciscans. We're committed to non-violence. We are the face of peace and forgiveness to the world. We obey." She slammed her cup on the table and coffee splashed out in an irregular circle. "They've been terrorizing us since the Feast of the Transfiguration."

"August sixth," Giulia whispered to Frank.

Sister Kathryn gripped the table. "I said we have no proof."

"What more do you need? Do you seriously think random teenagers are calling us in the middle of the night and hanging up? Or plastering our windows with pictures from dirty magazines?"

"We caught teenagers hiding in the back to scare us."

"Hired by Eagle. Offer your hourly employees a little overtime. Scare a nun out of her wimple for a bit of time and a half."

Frank tapped Giulia's ankle. She didn't need her newly trained psychic skills to know they both had the same thought about Sister Matilda's death. Scaring a nun was one thing. Scaring one of the oldest nuns they'd seen in awhile carried the added risk of a fatal heart attack. Giulia hadn't yet seen a ghost face to face, but she wished she could make Sister Matilda be her first.

The nurse broke her obsession with her coffee cup. "Do you think that's what happened to Matilda?"

Giulia temporized again. "The police may be able to share details as they proceed with their investigation."

Sister Olive dunked another scone. "In my youth we called that a snow job."

Sister Kathryn slammed the flat of one hand on the table. "Enough."

Giulia wondered exactly how much brandy the door warden had added to her coffee.

Sister Olive held the dripping triangle of pastry over her cup. "What is your professional opinion about Matilda's death?"

Frank answered. "Initial impressions can be deceiving. I've learned it's always better to wait for the expert's report."

Sister Olive's gaze could best be described as limpid. Giulia concentrated on her now-cold tea lest she laugh and tarnish her superhero image.

The nurse pushed back her chair. "It's quarter to one. I have to be up in four hours to give Sister Helena her meds."

"We all have to be up in a few hours." Sister Kathryn rubbed her temples. "Thank you for giving us the news about Sister Matilda. It was kind of you to bring Steve home."

The Chihuahua thumped its ratlike tail.

Sister Olive clamped her hand on Giulia's.

"You can't leave. We're hiring you."

Five

A moment of silence followed the doorkeeper's announcement.

Sister Kathryn detached Sister Olive's hand from Giulia's. Her mouth compressed into a thin, bloodless line. An impressed Giulia marveled at the Superior's reserves of self-control.

"Sister Olive, you do not have the authority to make such a decision."

"Then exercise your authority, Sister Superior. Patience and prayer won't keep us warm and dry when we're living under the Allen Street Bridge." The ingenuous expression returned. "James chapter two, verse sixteen."

The nurse returned from the study of her coffee dregs. "Olive is right. We need action. God helps those who help themselves."

The fourth nun murmured, "Dorothy, that's not in the Bible."

"I know, Diane," the nurse snapped. "Would you prefer Romans chapter eight, verse twenty-six? The Spirit helps us in our weakness?"

"Fine." Sister Olive stabbed the air in front of Giulia's nose. "Then the Spirit sent these detectives to help us in our weakness. Are we going to argue?"

"Who would dare presume in his heart to do such a thing?" Diane's lips writhed but a breathy giggle leaked out. "Esther chapter seven, verse five."

"We walk in obedience to his commands. Second John chapter one, verse six." The nurse ground the heels of her hands into her eyes. "Every day when I go upstairs the invalids ask me what's happening, what are we doing, where are we going to go? I'd like to be able to answer them."

Sister Diane turned on Sister Kathryn. "Dorothy and Olive are right. We need to fight fire with fire."

Their Superior stared into the distance for a moment. "Put away from thee a wayward mouth, and perverse lips put far from thee. Proverbs chapter four, verse twenty-four."

"A good wife girds her loins with strength."

The brown eyebrows of Dorothy met over her nose. "That's out of context."

Sister Diane shook her head. "I combined two verses. Both are in context as they relate to this discussion."

"We're not wives."

"We're Brides of Christ. It applies," Sister Olive said. "Let us rise up now and fight for our lives, for today things are not as they were before. First Maccabees chapter nine, verse forty-four." She gave Giulia a winning smile. "Who better to have as our champion than one of our own? She's no longer a nun, but once called, always chosen."

The bare idea of being sucked back into the convent made Giulia squeeze Frank's knee under the table to reassure herself of her married state. He returned the pressure.

Sister Kathryn aged twenty years as the quote war escalated. When the door warden finished her last quote, Kathryn gathered the cups. She brought them to the sink but instead of running water into them, she leaned on the edge as though only her locked elbows were keeping her upright.

"What if it was murder?" Sister Dorothy said.

"If it was, justice demands he can't get away with it," Sister Diane said.

"You can't let him throw us into the street," Sister Olive said.

The Superior said without turning around, "Ms. Driscoll, will you be available tomorrow after three?"

Giulia set her business card next to the napkins.

Six

At her desk late the next morning, Giulia yawned like a bear about to hibernate before peeking at the clock in her monitor's icon tray. Twenty to twelve. For the first time in her life, she contemplated purchasing a Red Bull.

To cancel thoughts of forbidden caffeine, she buzzed Zane.

"Yes, Ms. D.?"

"On second thought, I'm prying myself out of my chair."

Walking even the seven steps from her desk to her office door would keep her alert. Her admin waited with fingers suspended over keyboard.

Her assistant Sidney wagged her index finger at her. "You should know better than to hunt for dead bodies on a work night. Save those activities for the weekend."

Giulia yawned. "I never aspired to be a bad example. Zane, what can you give me on Eagle Developers?"

"Their trendy lofts are gorgeous and you have to sell your firstborn to pay the rent."

Sidney held up her phone. "I wouldn't kill to live here, but I know lots of people who would."

The photo on the screen showed a bright, open living space with tastefully arranged chairs and love seats. Sidney swiped and the living room became a tiled kitchen with gleaming chrome appliances. Another swipe and a bedroom with a king-sized bed and a balcony replaced the kitchen.

Giulia patted her stomach. "I would. Almost. But I prefer to keep my firstborn."

Zane read from his monitor. "The premier developer in

Cottonwood. Known for revitalizing run-down neighborhoods." Two clicks. "Their signature style incorporates luxury apartments and trendy businesses into repurposed buildings." Click. "They've also been the target of an investigation by the Commonwealth's Attorney General for bid-rigging and falsifying records."

The phone rang. Zane listened and hung up. "Mr. D. says he's officially assigned to the dead nun case."

"Aww," Sidney said. "You're working together just like you used to."

"Only if I agree to take on the living nuns' case. Could you spend fifteen minutes looking up housing assessments and recent sales in a four-block radius around 386 Erie Avenue?"

"No problem."

"Zane, please let me know what else you find. I'm going to walk around the block to wake myself up."

She returned with a passion fruit smoothie because not even extra caffeine was going to help today. Zane and Sidney looked up with identical expressions of chagrin.

"Are you prepared to hear *The Scoop* is hinting at an exposé of Eagle?" Zane spun his monitor.

Giulia pinched the bridge of her nose. "Of course they are. Well, maybe Cottonwood's homegrown *TMZ* can make our lives easier for a change."

The first teaser for *The Scoop*'s cable-access show was nothing more than fifteen seconds of deep, dark hints. Ken Kanning, the face and voice of *The Scoop*, used the second teaser to add a whiff of corruption to the hints. Pit Bull, Kanning's cameraman, created a montage of quick-cut shots of Eagle buildings, lawyers in courtrooms, and Victor Eagle's bald head with long ponytail shining in TV camera spotlights.

Giulia sipped her melting smoothie as the show's logo faded from the screen. "They don't have anything concrete."

"They're fishing." Sidney handed Giulia a printout and a pen. "In the past twelve months no house in the area sold for more than thirty thousand."

Giulia leaned over Zane's desk and wrote between the columns of figures. "Crime rate. Demographics. Turnover." She held out the pen.

"Whose pen did I pick up?"

Sidney and Zane laughed.

"You were right," he said.

"Told you," she said.

Sidney took the pen back from Giulia. "You're always reaching for someone's pen to write notes when we give you printouts. I figured it'd save time if we paired them up."

Giulia made a face at herself. "I'm not sure if I should worry about being predictable or thank you for anticipating my foibles." She counted the pens in Zane's holder. "Do we need to order supplies?"

The phone rang again. Giulia got out of Zane's face and aimed the printout at her in-bin.

"Ms. D., it's Vandermark Emergency Room."

Seven

Giulia folded time and space to reach the phone in Zane's outstretched hand while the sound of his last word still vibrated in the air. The only thought in her head was "Frank's been shot."

"Giulia Driscoll speaking."

"Giulia, honey, it's Aida. I know what you're thinking and you stop it right now. Your husband is not being ministered to by my capable hands."

Giulia clutched the back of Zane's client chair and sat. She remembered to give an okay signal to Zane and Sidney.

"I'm breathing again," Giulia said to her longtime friend.

"Good. Now I may have some bad news, so sit yourself down. Do you have a relative named Salvatore Falcone?"

"Six foot one, pot belly, curly brown hair, cross-shaped scar on left bicep?"

"That's him. He had an accident at work and they brought him here. The ambulance crew said his co-workers told them his name and went to lunch. Nobody offered to ride with him. The only things in his wallet were twenty bucks, pictures of three kids, and a few ID cards. We didn't know who to contact until I remembered your maiden name."

A "Salvatore Special" headache began to stab Giulia's temples. "He's my younger brother."

"His wallet looks like his wife started to reorganize it and got called away before she finished."

The way Sidney was staring, Giulia wondered if a monstrous vein was throbbing in her forehead. "The opposite, actually. He tried to clean his wife out of his wallet and his life."

A moment of silence. "As a responsible parent, he should know to have an emergency contact so his kids can be taken care of."

Years of anger bled into Giulia's voice. "He had no other contact information because he's specially protected by God Himself."

"Well then God's next employee review is going to be unsatisfactory." A moment of silence on her end, punctuated by the hospital intercom. "I'm sorry, honey. That was rude."

Giulia swallowed laughter. "No, it was funny. What happened to him?"

"I'd rather you come down here. It's complicated."

The moment of laughter evaporated. "All right. Give me half an hour."

"I knew you'd do the right thing. See you soon."

Giulia hung up and said to the anxiety on the faces of her staff, "Sorry, guys. I didn't mean to scare you. My brother's apparently done something worthy of workers' comp."

"Why didn't they call your sister-in-law?" Sidney's smooth forehead wrinkled. "They're doing okay with marriage counseling now, aren't they?"

"Define 'okay.' He purged her from his wallet. When they saw his last name the only person they thought to call was me." She rubbed her temples. "At least they didn't call the kids."

"You're going to see him? He does nothing but scream at you."

If Zane had been one of her nephews, she'd have patted his hand in encouragement. "You're speaking your mind. Higher Human Interaction Level achieved." She glowered at him a moment later. "Don't ruin it by getting embarrassed. Yes, I'm going. I'm overdue for one of his holier-than-thou lectures on my sinful life." Her smile was unsuccessful. "Maybe it will make him feel better. I'll be back by two, I hope."

Eight

Vandermark Memorial's Emergency Room parking lot at noon resembled the bumper car ride at the State Fair. The lot was too small, the asphalt cracked, the lines faded, and two adult males were playing musical chairs for the spot closest to the doors.

Giulia drove down the farthest aisle and parked in the second to last space. She took her time walking inside. The more buffering between her ears and Salvatore's self-righteous hate, the better.

She couldn't make the walk last long enough. The double doors into the emergency room whooshed open sooner than she wanted. She stepped into cool air saturated with public address system announcements, disinfectant, and several voices giving orders.

Giulia wished she were less familiar with the emergency room.

The nurse at the intake desk trapped the phone between her ear and shoulder to wave Giulia over. As she approached, the nurse stopped typing, thanked the caller, and hung up.

"Do I see a baby bump? I do."

Giulia's hand went to her belly. "I should've bought maternity clothes last month."

"They'll make it so much easier to breathe. I don't know why I waited so long to give in my first time." She pressed a button and said twice into the receiver, "Aida to intake desk."

The main doors slid open again and two EMTs wheeled in a stretcher. One carried an IV bag attached to a very unhappy old man.

"I'm supposed to be kicking my granddaughter's butt at chess, you quacks. There's nothing wrong with my heart. My wife's trying to give the kid an unfair advantage." He tried to yank out the IV, but both EMTs restrained his arms.

Giulia and the nurse grinned at each other. One of the EMTs slapped paperwork on the desk.

"Mild heart attack. Refused treatment until his wife put on a big weepy act. We need to get him into a room so a doctor can lay down the law." His voice pleaded even though his face showed no emotion.

The nurse tapped keys. "Seven's free." She pressed a different button and the doors marked "Hospital Staff Only" swung inward.

"You're a goddess."

"I keep forgetting my halo at home."

The EMTs wheeled the still-griping grandfather through the doors. A nurse in white pants and a Hello Kitty smock dodged the gurney and smothered Giulia in a hug. Since Aida could've been Serena Williams' body double, Giulia's five foot five frame never stood a chance.

"Honey, you're radiant."

Giulia wriggled her head back and looked up into the nurse's eyes. "Since when are you into Hello Kitty?"

Aida released Giulia. "Birthday present from my niece. The sick kids love it. Come on with me."

The doors closed behind them as they entered a wide hallway. The disinfectant was more overpowering back here. Machines beeped from every room. Two nurses and a doctor hustled into room seven behind the EMTs. The PA system paged doctor after doctor. Wheeled multi-tier carts stacked with supplies protruded from the walls.

Aida led Giulia to the end of the hall and turned left. "In here. He's hooked up to a roomful of machines. You know how intimidating it all can look, so take a breath."

Salvatore topped Giulia by eight inches, but the circle of beeping, ticking, dripping machines reduced him to Munchkin dimensions. The crib-style sides of the bed didn't help. Clear tape held IV tubes in his arm and more tape on his cheeks kept a fat breathing tube anchored to his mouth. His brown hair was mashed against the pillow and his tan merely made his sunken eyes appear corpselike. For the first time since he broke his leg playing football at age nine, he looked helpless.

Giulia's first thought was, At least he can't spew another hate-filled sermon at me. Her conscience prodded her the next second, but it also acknowledged the truth of her reaction.

Aida hushed her voice. "You never mentioned a brother."

"We don't exactly get along."

"While I wrap my head around someone not getting along with you of all people, you've figured out he's in a coma."

Giulia nodded. "What happened?"

"My favorite pair of EMTs brought him in so I got the scoop. He fell off a ladder and hit his head on a cement floor."

Giulia dragged her gaze from the machines. "They saw it happen?"

"No. His construction crew told them. He was on a ladder in a basement with his head in a drop ceiling. He had pieces of frayed wire in his hands and some idiot threw the old circuit breaker switch. He got a hundred twenty volts. He jerked away, which translates to falling backwards ten feet straight down."

Giulia cringed. "You said no one rode in the ambulance with him?"

Aida adjusted the IV drip and said to the EEG machine, "He doesn't seem to have many friends." She unhooked the clipboard from the foot of the bed and wrote a note.

The sun hit the brick wall opposite the window. Beneath the fluorescents illuminating the room, Salvatore's skin faded to the color of undercooked pie crust.

"He doesn't have any friends."

"Here." Aida handed her a scuffed black wallet. "I kept it for you to see before we put it in the safe."

Giulia opened the leather trifold. Twenty-three dollars, to be exact. His electrician's license. His driver's license with an eight-year-old photo. Giulia remembered the Fourth of July picnic when he passed it around for the family to see. Everyone laughed at his haircut. He'd done it himself to save money and botched it.

She shook off one of her last happy family memories and opened the side flap. Laminated prayer cards from their parents' funerals. Last year's school pictures of the kids. Their perfunctory smiles increased her anger.

"Is he divorced?"

Giulia choked. "Oh, no. That would be an offense against God."

Aida kept finding measurements to adjust. Giulia changed the subject. "Where was he working?"

"One of those redevelopment projects. Remember the Ben Franklin Hotel on Cardinal Boulevard?"

"That wreck? I thought it was condemned."

"Eagle Developers snapped it up. I heard it's going to be senior apartments."

The PA kept up its relentless paging. Between the hallway noise and Salvatore's machines, Giulia would've paid good money for three minutes of silence. She snapped shut the wallet.

"My brother is convinced he's a better Catholic than the Pope. His wife left him earlier this summer, but they're in counseling now. The kids..." Giulia looked with horror at a calendar on the wall. "When does school start?"

"Tomorrow. My nieces and nephews Skyped me last night to show me all their new clothes."

Giulia shuffled sideways between the bed and two machines to reach her brother's ears. "Salvatore, coma patients are supposed to be able to hear even if they can't respond. Listen up: I'm taking care of the kids for their sake, not to help you. Understand?"

She felt Aida's stare and turned with a smile. "My sister-in-law left her husband to join a Doomsday Prepper cult. She discovered the leader was brewing homemade hallucinogens and escaped to me for help. I might have judged her for deserting her children, but I know the lengths to which Salvatore Falcone can drive a rational human." She moved on. "The bit about unconscious people hearing what's said to them is the only fact I know about comas. What chance does he have?"

Aida pointed to the EEG machine. "His brain waves are quiescent right now, but earlier they spiked twice. Activity is always a good sign. His skull sustained a two-millimeter crack when his head hit the floor, but no brain swelling has occurred so far. The doctors want him to wake up before they open his head. A few bone slivers may have broken off."

Giulia stared at her silent brother. "Will he ever wake up?"

Aida put a comforting arm around Giulia's shoulders. "No one knows, and that's the truth. He could wake up tonight. He could stay like he is now for a week, two weeks, a month, six months."

Giulia leaned against her friend for a moment. "Family. You know what his situation means?"

"You're going to say a Novena for his recovery? It's called a Novena, right?"

With a short laugh, Giulia stood on her own feet. "He wouldn't accept it from me. No, it means this is my circus and these are my monkeys." She patted her belly. "Frank and I are about to get a crash course in kid wrangling."

Nine

Giulia called Frank from the Nunmobile and summarized the situation.

"*Cac naofa.*"

"I agree with the sentiment if not the language."

"'Holy shit' doesn't even qualify as objectionable language nowadays. Also, you're right. We can't leave the kids by themselves. What about your sister-in-law?"

"I'm not even sure where she lives. I'll call your brother tonight. Thank God he's also their marriage counselor."

Frank's voice became cheerful. "This will be our dress rehearsal for when we have a half-dozen kids of our own."

Giulia made a face at the phone. "Number one, let's make it through our initial offspring first. Number two, I know how good Catholic families think, so expect strong objections from me if everyone assumes one of our children is automatically earmarked for the clergy. We are not chained to the ways of our Italian and Irish ancestors."

"Yes, ma'am."

"I'll call you in a couple of hours."

Giulia waited for the post-lunch parking lot pinball game to end. An SUV missed clipping the bumper of a Lexus by the width of a human hair. The language from both drivers eclipsed Frank's mild Irish profanity.

When it became safe for responsible drivers to venture into the aisles, Giulia called the office.

"Guys, I won't be in for the rest of the day."

"Oh my God, what happened to your brother?" Sidney's voice echoed through Zane's speaker phone.

"He's in a coma."

"He can't yell at you then."

Giulia snorted. "Thank you for making me laugh. Correct. However, he hasn't let his wife near their kids since their one group marriage counseling session."

Zane muttered something Giulia couldn't make out.

"Zane?"

He cleared his throat. "I know you told us about how he goes on and on about how his wife broke all his Draconian rules so she isn't worthy and all that garbage. But isn't forgiveness supposed to be an important part of Catholicism?"

"It is."

Sidney jumped in. "Your brother pushed your sister-in-law to her limit and she walked, but she's got her head on straight now. The next step is supposed to be where they do the whole forgiveness thing and work at being a family again. Because kids."

Giulia conveyed her shrug in her voice. "In a perfect world, yes. In this world, not so much. My sister-in-law works in the front office of her church, but she lives in a studio apartment, if I remember correctly."

"You're taking the kids," Zane said.

"Three kids in your little Cape Cod?" Sidney said. "We give you permission to take tomorrow off."

"Not happening, but I have to drive them to school. They're all under fourteen and can't stay on their own. When I get them successfully started on their first day of the school year, I'll head to my sister-in-law's work to loop her in on the situation. Then I'll talk to our new clients." She worked out the timing in her head. "Maybe not in that order."

"So we're taking on the nuns as a client?" Zane said. "I also vote to sign up every client who wants us to hunt ghosts. Right, Sidney?"

Sidney's echo took on a shade of reproof. "Zane and I will be having a long talk after we hang up."

"Are you two reminding me what bickering siblings are like?" But Giulia smiled at the phone as she said it.

"Your hardworking staff is always ready to help."

"Perhaps I should look into boxing lessons for your Christmas presents."

To her surprise, neither of them laughed.

"Ms. D., what a great idea. My workout routine would benefit from a change up."

"Zane may be onto something." Sidney's voice was thoughtful. "Jessamine's too little for serious swimming and I'm way too young for Bingo Lady arms."

Giulia threw up her hands. "Zane, please send me an email so I don't forget. I'll see you tomorrow morning late."

She typed in Salvatore's address and began her journey to the Falcone circus.

Ten

The Falcones lived in an average two-story house on an average suburban street. Cottonwoods and maples lined both sides of the street. The houses varied only in their color of vinyl siding and the flowers planted to cloak the cement blocks of the basements. Chemically treated lawns added their unnatural shade of green to the mix. Kids played hockey in the street, basketball in the driveways, and minuscule chalk artists created masterpieces on the sidewalks.

Knowing what lurked behind her brother's beige siding, the comparison to the fallen robot-like planet in *A Wrinkle in Time* came to Giulia with too much ease.

She parked in the driveway. The sound of a lawnmower came from out back. Salvatore's house dared to differ only in its front door decoration. Other houses sported summery wreaths of flip flops or seashells or flowers. The Falcone door attacked the neighborhood with a three-foot tall bronze crucifix. Verdigris blossomed in Christ's armpits.

Giulia's first relief was not discovering a door knocker disguised as the crown of thorns. Her second was the normal ding-dong when she pressed the doorbell. She'd feared hearing the first notes of "O Sacred Head Surrounded."

Her eleven-year-old niece Cecilia opened the door wearing an adult-sized apron over a calf-length white skirt and high-necked shirt.

"Aunt Giulia? What are you doing here?"

"Are you going to invite me in?"

Cecilia hesitated. "I don't know if I should. Dad will have a cow."

Giulia put her hand on a non-crucifix part of the door and pushed. "I'm coming in anyway." Cecilia backed away as Giulia closed the door behind her.

The front hall was spotless. The air smelled of lemon furniture polish. A doily on a half-circle table appeared to be starched. The classic Veronica's Veil trick painting hung above the table. Facing it square, she saw the veil stained with blood and sweat. When she moved to one side, the tortured face of Christ appeared on the veil.

Giulia had always hated this painting. When she and Salvatore were small and visiting their grandmother's house, he'd creep into her room at night holding it in front of his face. She'd always known when he was in her room, even asleep. Yet every time she saw that haunted face of Christ looming over her in the moonlight, she'd shriek the house down.

One of the benefits of nuns giving up personal possessions: She was still Sister Mary Regina Coelis when their grandmother died. She couldn't inherit the painting.

Cecilia fidgeted with the doily. "Aunt Giulia, Dad keeps weird hours sometimes. He likes to make sure we're not wasting our time."

Giulia translated: Salvatore kept his kids in a constant state of fear.

A rail-thin boy a few inches shorter than Cecilia walked down from the second floor. "Cece, we need more floor polish." Carlo, the middle child, stopped on the bottom step. "Who are you?"

A second boy came into the hall from somewhere at the back of the house. Pasquale, the oldest by one year, was the only one with any meat on his bones. Giulia recognized the family body shape. His teenage growth spurt would kick in any day now.

All three kids were sweaty and red-faced. Strands of hair clung to their necks and foreheads. Grass clippings stuck to Pasquale's pants and shirt.

"Who are you?" Pasquale said.

Cecilia stepped between them. "She's Aunt Giulia, dummy. I showed you her webpage on the computers at school, remember?"

"Oh, yeah. Nice to finally meet you, Aunt Giulia, but you can't stay here. Dad won't even let us say your name in his house, so go away, okay?"

Carlo stayed on the bottom tread. "Yeah, Dad will freak out like he did last summer when Cecilia snuck over to your house after Mom ran away. He'll blame us for letting you in.'"

The misery in those few sentences brought Giulia closer to cursing than she'd ever been. "Guys, your dad was in an accident at work. He's in the hospital."

Salvatore's middle child shrugged.

His oldest child said, "Too bad for him."

His only daughter said, "Maybe he'll die and mom can come back."

Giulia put on her firm teacher face. "Listen up. I need everybody to pack a suitcase and a backpack. Put all your school supplies in the backpack and enough clothes and toiletries for a few days in the suitcase. Do you still have camping gear, specifically sleeping bags?"

Three pairs of eyes blinked at her.

Cecilia recovered first. "We're staying with you?"

Pasquale stepped forward and Cecilia shoved him back into a doorway. "Don't bring grass in here. Dad told me if he comes home one more time and finds anything on the floor I'm grounded."

Pasquale laughed as he backed away. "How is being grounded different from any other day?"

Carlo, free of any potential debris, stepped into Pasquale's place. "We're getting out of here?"

"Yes. You can't stay here by yourselves."

Pasquale said from the doorway, "You're not messing with us?"

Giulia ditched plans to break the news gently. "I'm not messing with you. Your father's in a coma and the hospital isn't sure when he'll wake up. You boys haven't seen me in six years, but I'm your aunt and you're coming home with me."

Cecilia leaped forward and squeezed Giulia. "Awesome!"

Giulia detached her. "No squeezing the pregnant lady."

Her niece's eyes got big. "We're going to have a cousin?"

"In a few months. Right now, everyone go pack."

As though they were released from playing a game of freeze tag, all three kids stampeded upstairs. Pasquale shed grass with every step.

Giulia went through the doorway he'd appeared in earlier. It led into the kitchen. On the counter, a dozen breaded chicken legs lay in two rows on a foil-covered cookie sheet. On a cutting board, half a head of lettuce crowded for space with a beefsteak tomato, a pepper, a can of black olives, and a cucumber. Next to the lettuce, a box of instant mashed potatoes.

Giulia opened the fridge and tossed the salad fixings in the crisper drawer. She pushed the drumsticks into two tight rows, folded the foil around them, and set the bundle in the freezer.

The milk and eggs in the fridge wouldn't expire for another week. She added the bread to the freezer. Everything else would survive a brief absence.

At least she didn't have to worry about a pet dog or cat. She shot the deadbolt on the back door and tested all the stove burners to make sure they were off.

Thumps and shouts filtered down from the second floor. Giulia walked to the foot of the stairs and shouted, "Where's the ironing board?"

Cecilia's voice: "In the cellar."

Giulia returned to the kitchen and opened the only other door. A switch illuminated wooden stairs and paneled walls. At the bottom Giulia spotted the iron and ironing board setup next to the dryer. She hoisted herself butt-first onto the dryer and unplugged the iron. Nothing else in the cellar needed unplugging or turning off.

The kids were still upstairs. She climbed to the second floor and stood in Pasquale and Carlo's doorway.

"Did your dressers explode?"

Both boys jerked around, fear in their eyes. "We're sorry. We'll clean it up right now."

For the second time in thirty minutes, Giulia experienced an overwhelming desire to return to the hospital and whack her brother on his fractured skull.

"Only bring what you'll need for a few days, remember? The weather's supposed to be in the seventies. Don't forget your phone chargers."

They did a double take worthy of a comedy team.

"We don't have phones anymore."

"Dad says they're a source of temptation."

They stuffed excess clothes any which way into the drawers and straightened their bedspreads. Giulia pointed to the bulging suitcases.

"Bag check time. Open up, please."

She refolded their white shirts. Carlo pulled his school shoes from under his bed. Pasquale found both their neckties.

"Nice work. Toothbrushes and deodorant?"

Carlo ran out of the room. Giulia said to Pasquale, "We only have one bed in our spare room. What about your sleeping bags?"

"Dad might have given them away. I'll look in the garage."

"I'll check on Cecilia. Meet you downstairs."

Like the boys' room, Cecilia's room looked more like a Catholic hotel room than a pre-teen's bedroom. A crucifix above the bed and a corner shrine to the Blessed Virgin Mary were the only decorations. A homemade rag rug covered a small section of floor in front of a sparse bookshelf. Giulia's glance took in Bible studies, lives of several saints, and homeschool-type study guides.

"Bag check." Giulia refolded Cecilia's school blouses. "You won't have to iron them tonight if you use this trick."

"I need my toothbrush."

"Carlo got them all."

"Yeah, right." She left and returned with a pink toothbrush.

This small instance of sibling rivalry pleased Giulia. It was the first sign of normal brother-sister interaction she'd seen in this repressed household.

The boys sat at the foot of the stairs with two suitcases, two backpacks, and two sleeping bags.

Cecilia rolled her eyes. "Okay, jerks, where'd you hide mine?"

"It's gone, Cece." Pasquale's frown aged him ten years. "Remember dad's Bible study last month?"

She leaned into the living room and took a Bible from a stand, flipping it open. Its cover proclaimed it a study edition. "The proper place of a Catholic woman is in the home or at church. Only the proper Catholic male, girded with the spiritual armor of God, should venture into the wilderness to gain the strength required to lead and protect his family." She shoved it back into place with enough force to bang the stand against the wall. "He is such a jerkface."

Giulia silently agreed but knew better than to lose a micron of her authority. "The decision is made, then. Cecilia gets the bed and you two share the floor. We have rugs, so it'll be a little better than camping."

The kids remained silent.

"Guys, I checked the stove and put the food away. The iron's unplugged. What else needs to be turned off?"

"Our alarms." Cecilia ran upstairs and returned a minute later.

"Nothing else technology related?"

"We don't have much technology anymore." Pasquale elbowed Carlo. "We'll lock the windows."

"Did you lock the garage when you put away the lawn mower?"

"Yes ma'am," Pasquale called from the living room.

"Cecilia, where's a house key?"

"I'll show you." She opened the front door. With her thumbnail she pulled open the side of Christ's footrest on the massive bronze crucifix. A nickel-plated key fit at an angle in the space.

"Clever."

Cecilia shrugged. "I guess."

Giulia gestured to the boys. "Let's go."

Cecilia ran inside and out again with her bags before the boys got theirs. She tossed them in the Nunmobile's trunk and jumped into the passenger seat. When the boys stowed their bags, Pasquale tried the handle. It didn't budge. Cecilia stuck out her tongue. Pasquale flipped her off.

"Hey."

Pasquale jerked ramrod-straight at Giulia's tone of voice.

"You're in my territory now. No language, verbal or otherwise. Got it?"

"Yes, ma'am."

"Good. In the car and buckle up. Carlo, please close the trunk."

When the odometer ticked past one mile from her brother's house, the tense atmosphere snapped.

"We're really leaving dad's house."

Giulia braked for a red light. "Obviously."

"Are you normal?"

"Do you have cable?"

"She has a gun, jerks." Cecilia poured scorn on her brothers. "She's a detective. She's normal. We're the freaks."

Eleven

The kids stood in Giulia's foyer with their bags, too quiet again. Their burst of excitement in the car had lasted only to the next stoplight. When Salvatore woke up, Giulia was going to take advantage of his obligation to her and flay him alive.

"Upstairs and turn left, you three. Come on."

The spare room was nothing fancy or deserving of a Pinterest spread. Leaf-green curtains, tan and white striped wallpaper, tan carpet, leaf-patterned bedspread.

"Ooh, pretty." Cecilia tossed her bags on the bed.

Pasquale and Carlo unrolled their sleeping bags.

"I call window," Pasquale said.

Carlo therefore spread his bag beneath the window. Pasquale dropped his bag on top of Carlo's. Carlo picked up the bag and shoved it into his brother's stomach.

"Stop behaving like brats, you brats," Cecilia said, hands on hips.

Giulia's hands came down on her nephews' shoulders. "Hey. My house. My rules. Rule number two: No fighting. I don't have the time or patience for it." She released them. "You'll shoot rock-paper-scissors for the window. Best of three. Go."

The boys hesitated.

"I expect to be obeyed."

They shot the fastest three rounds Giulia had ever seen. Pasquale won. Giulia herded them back downstairs, wondering how to get Carlo to talk to her. After that one sentence in the car, he'd shut down.

"Kitchen facing you. Living room to the right. Game closet is this door on the left, but it's off limits until Uncle Frank gives the okay. It's his space. Come into the kitchen with me."

They followed like ducks, chose Cokes to drink, and returned to the living room. A minute later they clustered around the TV watching back episodes of *Agents of S.H.I.E.L.D.*

At 6:32 the next morning, Giulia turned on the spare room light, stepped between Carlo's arm and Pasquale's head, and opened the curtains.

"School is in session."

Three jacks-in-the-box popped up.

"Yes, Dad." Covers fell away before any of them were actually awake.

Giulia moved away from the window so they could see her face. "You're at Aunt Giulia's. We only have one shower. Pasquale, you're first. You have five minutes each."

Giulia waited in the hall. They each made it in less than six minutes. Giulia gave reluctant props to her brother for keeping the kids efficient in the mornings.

"Do you guys need help with your neckties?"

"No, ma'am, they're clip-ons."

"Breakfast will be ready in fifteen minutes."

Fourteen minutes later, the kids were sitting at the table sipping orange juice. Giulia set plates with English muffins, eggs, and bacon in front of them. Frank slid into the head chair and Giulia set him a plate with twice the amount of food plus a cup of coffee. Instead of his fork, Frank picked up his phone and put it on speaker.

"Mom? I want you to know I never appreciated you enough growing up."

His mother's voice said, "I wish I had a tape recorder handy."

Giulia said from the stove, "I'm the witness."

Frank's mother said, "Why the sudden homage from my youngest son at seven o'clock in the morning?"

"Giulia's niece and nephews are staying with us for a few days. They're thirteen, twelve, and eleven. In the space of half an hour, starting at six thirty, she has everyone in the house sitting at the table eating a home-cooked breakfast." He winked at Giulia. "I'm not worthy."

"You are quite right," his mother said. "Now hang up and eat your breakfast while it's hot."

"Yes, Mom."

Giulia brought her own breakfast to the table, minus bacon. She and little Zlatan needed to talk. First he restricted coffee. Now he was making her regret eating bacon.

Over the rim of her first allowed pregnancy coffee of the day, she saw three pairs of eyes staring at her and Frank.

"Is there egg in my hair?"

Cecilia said to her brothers in a perfect imitation of mansplaining, "You see? This is how normal families interact."

"No sh—um, no kidding." Pasquale became very interested in his eggs.

In between small bites thanks to Zlatan's rearranging of her internal organs, Giulia began her prepared speech. "Here's the way this is going to work. You know your mom and dad have started marriage counseling, right?"

"Yeah." Pasquale spoke with muffin in his mouth. Giulia gave him a pointed look. He swallowed, coughed, reached for his orange juice, and chased down the mouthful. "Yes, ma'am. Dad told us before his first appointment."

"Get real," Cecilia said with an empty mouth. "What he did was give us another lecture about the proper state of a true Catholic marriage. Remember when he came home? He used the counseling to try to make us think he should be wearing a halo for even talking to Mom."

Pasquale muttered into his orange juice.

Giulia didn't ask. "I know your dad told you to keep quiet about your home situation. As much as I hate lying, I want you not to let anyone at school know what's happening now."

"Why?" Cecilia said.

"Because the school will call CPS and we'll get separated, dummy."

Cecilia stuck out her tongue at Pasquale. "Guess what, dummy, we're at a relative's house so they won't care."

Giulia wished she possessed a full-size stop sign. "They will care. They'll find out about your mom's problems back in July. When they talk to the hospital about your dad they could very well decide you'd be better off in foster care."

Cecilia stopped shoveling in food. "But Aunt Giulia, why wouldn't they let us keep staying with you?"

Frank said, "They have rules. They might not think it's good for all three of you to be squeezed into one small room here. In the end we might get temporary custody, but you'd have to go through the whole Child Protective Services process first."

"Bureaucracy sucks." Pasquale finished his bacon.

"Whoa." Frank pointed out the back door. "The chameleon lassoed the biggest black fly I've ever seen."

Carlo raised his head for the first time. "The what?"

"Chameleon. Aunt Giulia got it from one of her clients."

"Can I see?" Carlo's chair tilted at a dangerous angle, but he caught it before the crash.

"Me too?" Cecilia and Pasquale said.

"I'll get the dishes." Frank stacked empty plates.

Giulia led the way through the central garden path to the three-foot square chameleon cage.

Cecilia poked her arm. "Uncle Frank does dishes?"

Giulia wondered how long it would take these kids to unlearn her brother's indoctrination.

"What's his name?" Carlo squatted nose to nose with the chameleon.

"He's a she, and it's Scarlett." She explained the lizard's eating and drinking habits. Carlo asked most of the questions, his perpetual frown lightening.

"It's seven thirty," Frank called from the doorway.

Giulia separated Cecilia from Pasquale and asked how much school lunches cost. When Pasquale gave the same figure, she handed out lunch money. To prevent another fight, she arranged the Nunmobile seating herself.

"One of us will pick you up. Look for either of these cars as close to the main doors as we can park."

Frank kissed her. "I'm buying you a Wonder Woman nightshirt."

Twelve

Giulia rang the convent doorbell at 8:20 instead of her planned eight o'clock because dropping the kids at school involved NASCAR-level driving skills. Every single parent in the queue needed to spend their lunch hour in the confessional. She nearly shouted this advice out the Nunmobile's window at a mother putting on mascara while cutting off two other cars. Investigating a possibly shady developer would be relaxing.

The door opened and the little brown and white Chihuahua limped to the threshold.

Giulia squatted on the stoop. "You poor thing. What happened to you?" She rubbed the pointy ears. The dog licked her hands. She looked up at Sister Olive. "He was fine last night."

The nun smirked at her. "You fell for it. Steve, you're a furry con artist." She tapped the little dog in its head and he ran into the house on four good legs. "Most dogs can sit up, roll over, and play dead. Steve knows how to fake a limp to get sympathy when he meets new people."

Giulia laughed. After all the strain and craziness of the last thirty-six hours, a Chihuahua devious enough to solicit extra attention with a phony injury was the funniest thing she'd ever seen. She laughed until she hiccupped.

Sister Olive brought her back to the kitchen and poured her a glass of water. "Drink it all without stopping."

Giulia complied. She'd used this remedy before. The hiccups gave up after a last half-hearted attempt. "Thank you. Did you teach your dog that trick?"

Sister Olive affected shock. "What kind of Franciscan would teach an animal to lie? No. He's a rescue. We discovered his talent when

Kathryn brought him home and he pulled it on Matilda. She loved it." Her lips pinched together and she inhaled sharply. "He was Matilda's dog from that moment. The rest of us were demoted to stand-ins when he needed extra attention."

Steve sat at Sister Olive's feet and yipped. She scooped him up. "Come on. I'll take you for a walk."

"Wait," Giulia said. "I'd like to speak to everyone in the house."

"Kathryn and Diane are gone. They teach."

"Can we try calling your Superior?"

Sister Olive looked at the clock. "Kathryn's first class starts at nine fifteen. She teaches music. Diane's in classes straight through to two forty-five. Let me get Dorothy. She should be done feeding the invalids breakfast upstairs."

Giulia dialed Sister Kathryn's school office number and put her on speaker in the center of the kitchen table. "There is an initial ground rule: Driscoll Investigations does not interfere with an active police case."

"In other words, Matilda's murder," Sister Olive said.

Giulia didn't acknowledge the interruption. "It is our understanding you wish us to investigate harassment and other illegal practices, possibly initiated by Eagle Developers, as they relate to the potential buyout of your convent with regard to your continued occupation here."

Kathryn's voice took on a shade of amusement. "You make it sound so clinical."

"Someone's got to be objective. We sure aren't."

Giulia ignored this interruption too. "We have a reduced fee schedule because of your circumstances." She listed the hourly rates.

"That much?" The Superior's voice cringed.

"It's not too bad," Sister Olive said.

"We don't know how long the investigation will take."

Six-foot-tall Sister Dorothy leaned in from the end of the table to reach the speaker. "Maybe we can ask the Head of the Order."

Sister Olive pushed her face between Giulia and Dorothy. "Because they've been so responsive to our pleas for help up to now."

"Sisters." After wrangling her niece and nephews, Giulia was not about to referee a convent of bickering nuns. "We can work out a payment plan if our fees are acceptable."

Sister Olive took the phone. "Ms. Driscoll isn't going to send her jackbooted thugs to shake us down."

Sister Dorothy said in her calm voice, "Eagle Developers has that market cornered."

A school bell and the sounds of hundreds of feet and voices came from the speaker. Sister Kathryn spoke above it. "Ms. Driscoll, please draw up a contract. I'll sign it this evening."

The call ended. The doorbell rang.

Sister Olive said, "I hope it's one of those teenage thugs."

Sister Dorothy said in the same even voice, "Why?"

"Think about it." Sister Olive's voice exhibited extreme control. "We have a witness here who can intimidate those delinquents. The battle could finally turn in our favor."

She hurried to the door, Steve the Chihuahua trotting next to her. When the door opened he barked like he was channeling his inner German Shepherd.

"Good morning," Frank said. "May I speak to your Superior, please?"

Thirteen

Giulia scrambled from her chair into the hall to capture Steve's performance on video.

The whimper. The raised paw. The shivery acceptance of sympathetic pets. Sister Olive's laughter. Steve's unashamed retreat on four working legs.

"Please come in, Detective. Sister Kathryn is at work, but Sister Dorothy and I will be happy to help you."

The house phone rang. Sister Olive lifted the receiver from its wall mount. "Convent of the Assumption...Yes, Sister...What perfect timing. A detective is here and wants to talk to you...I'll tell him."

She hung up and said to Frank, "The school where Kathryn and Diane teach had a water main break. Everyone's been dismissed. She should be here in half an hour. I'll get Dorothy."

After she climbed the stairs Frank joined Giulia in the kitchen. "Are you officially here?"

"I am. Contract execution tonight. What did the medical examiner say?"

"We're still waiting."

The two nuns entered the kitchen. "This is Sister Dorothy, who takes care of our infirm sisters. Ms. Driscoll, I'll show you around so Detective Driscoll can have some space. Detective, you should have time to interview both of us before Sister Kathryn returns."

Giulia and Frank shared a glance which conveyed, "We've both dealt with this type of nun before. We'll save time and grief if we let her orchestrate for now."

Olive led Giulia in to the front parlor. The three windows—two facing front, one on the side—lit the faded wallpaper too well. Several joins were starting to split. The couch and chairs needed their cushions re-stuffed, but the floor and bookcases gleamed.

Giulia clogged her phone with pictures.

"Why are you doing that?"

"When I meet with Eagle Developers, I may need evidence to back up my counter offer on the buyout."

Olive raised her gray eyebrows. "I knew you were a good decision."

Worn forest-green carpeting covered the stairs to the second floor, offset by brown wallpaper with beige fleurs-de-lis. The railing was not as polished as the parlor floor.

"For better gripping," Sister Olive said. "The second floor is for our invalids. It's easier for Dorothy, too. Only one flight of stairs to carry trays up and down."

The wide hallway accommodated a desk at one end. Two of the three doors were open. A muffled moan or wail came at regular intervals from behind the closed door.

"This is Sister Helena."

They entered a bright, airy room with a window fan moving the warm air. A hospital bed filled two-thirds of it, a nightstand with a tray of prescription bottles next to the bed. Pale yellow walls and flowered wallpaper offset the same green carpet.

The woman in the bed grimaced at Giulia. Under a sheet her arms and legs bent in on themselves. Her head leaned on her left shoulder. Her clear hazel eyes and short brown hair made her appear no more than forty, but her shriveled body could have been twice that age.

She tried to speak, but Giulia couldn't understand her. A dribble of saliva trickled from the corner of her mouth. Sister Olive plucked a tissue from a box on the nightstand and cleaned the invalid's chin with a gentleness that surprised Giulia.

Her voice, however, retained all its snark. "Helena, remember the drug bust scandal at the Motherhouse three years ago?"

The drooping eyelids opened.

"Who could forget it, right? This is the detective who broke it wide open. Now she's working for us."

Another grimace. Sister Olive was right there with the tissue.

"You threw the pipe bomb?"

Giulia and Sister Olive turned. A tiny, plump nun blocked the doorway with a wheelchair. From the waist up she resembled Mrs. Santa Claus. Thick orthopedic shoes and atrophied legs in surgical support hose explained the wheelchair.

"I survived the pipe bomb." Giulia held out her hand. "I'm Giulia Driscoll with Driscoll Investigations."

"I'm Eugenie. I remember now. This contraption gets me the best seats in the house, including church. Some little old nun threw the bomb. You came out of the chapel vestry looking like something out of the evening news." She included the other two nuns in her concluding remark: "The students back in my teaching days would've called her badass."

A garbled noise came from Sister Helena's mouth.

"Helena, I charge you to say a Rosary for my vile soul."

"I always do." The words weren't clear, but this time Giulia caught their import.

"Come on." Mrs. Santa Claus spun her wheelchair and rolled down the hall. "I want to talk to you. Olive, you're not needed."

Fourteen

Sister Eugenie's room revealed the truer state of the old house and the nuns' finances. Where the walls and curtains in Sister Helena's room were in excellent repair, in here the paint was chipped in the upper corners and a blotch of mold discolored a lower corner. The mismatched curtains and bedspread had been mended so often the stitches resembled an M.C. Escher staircase.

"Sit on the bed. I don't need chairs and nobody visits me anyway."

Mrs. Santa Claus in a plain black skirt and green blouse wheeled herself to the bed and blocked Giulia in.

"Olive will drag you into Agatha's room in a minute, so I have to talk fast. Olive doesn't trust me. It's mutual. She's got it in for Eagle Developers, but she's wrong. Eagle isn't the sole cause of our grief. The Superior General of the Order is in lockstep with Eagle to toss us into the street. It's cheaper."

Giulia chose Polite Smile Number Four, the one which covered her racing thoughts as she tried to talk her way out of the room. Being trapped was one of her few phobias. "I'm not investigating the head of the Order this time. I don't know the current Superior General, but can she be as bad as the last one?"

"Sister Fabian the drug dealer and priest's mistress?" Sister Eugenie cackled. "At least she kept things interesting. No, the current Superior takes her vows seriously. Especially the Vow of Poverty. When she dies, they'll carve on her grave 'I recycled. This headstone is pre-owned.'" A wink. "I have friends on the fringe of her inner circle. She wants the money Eagle's offering for this termite trap, and she wants to shove us into the cheapest digs possible. She really can't dump us into oncoming traffic. Bad press."

"Eugenie, you're going to give Ms. Driscoll claustrophobia." Sister Olive dragged the wheelchair away from Giulia.

Giulia stepped away from the bed. "I should finish going over the rest of the house."

"Come see me before you leave." Sister Eugenie made a face at Sister Olive's back.

Sister Olive paused with her hand on the knob of the only closed door. She raised her voice above the intermittent groans coming from behind it. "Eugenie likes to needle me. She'll exaggerate to get a bigger reaction."

Giulia had not missed the dubious joy of convent politics.

"Sister Agatha's Alzheimer's is extremely advanced. We don't know why she moans some days and not others."

"Does she have lucid spells?" The sounds were heart-wrenching one moment and the wails of a dungeon-dwelling ghost the next.

"Every so often. Her triggers change. She may not even realize we're in the room."

She opened the door. The noise rolled over them. The woman in the twin bed could've been anywhere between fifty and eighty years old. Gray hairs straggled out from under the loose, old-fashioned wimple on her head. The crow's feet in the corners of her closed eyes and the lines radiating from her open mouth gave no age indication. Giulia had met forty-year-old tanning addicts with more wrinkles.

"Sister Agatha? We have a visitor."

The moans stopped but the eyes remained closed.

"Sister Agatha? It's Sister Olive."

"Would she respond to the dog?" Giulia said.

Sister Olive shook her head. "On her worst days she screams when we put Steve on her bed. We don't like to risk it."

The curtains, walls, and bedspread were in a state of repair halfway between Sister Helena's room and Sister Eugenie's room. Giulia knew without a doubt that the majority of repair funds were spent on the invalids' rooms.

Another low moan came from the bed. Sister Olive touched Giulia's arm. "It's one of her unresponsive days. Maybe she'll be better the next time you're here."

Sister Dorothy's head appeared at the top of the stairwell. "Olive,

Detective Driscoll would like to speak with you."

"Not more than I want to talk to him." She pointed to Giulia as she passed Sister Dorothy on the stairs. "Helena and Eugenie are in good shape. Ms. Driscoll's ready for the third floor. I hope you hid your bodice rippers. We don't want to give a former Franciscan a poor opinion of our minimal leisure time."

The nurse's smile resembled an extreme version of Giulia's Polite Smile Number Two, the one where she briefly considers stabbing someone with a letter opener. The nun dropped it when the door warden reached the first floor.

"Ms. Driscoll, please allow me a minute to check on our infirm Sisters for myself."

The minute expanded to five between the three rooms. The sounds from Sister Agatha's room increased and decreased as the door opened and closed.

Sister Dorothy returned to Giulia with a genuine smile. "Our rooms are expected to be quite plain, but you're free to inspect anything you want."

Giulia followed her up more flattened-carpet stairs. "I remember certain rules too well. I won't invade your privacy."

They entered the first room to the right of the stairs. "This is my space. Sister Kathryn is at the back of the house, Sister Diane is next to me, and Sister Olive has the front. There's also a spare room squeezed in between mine and the outside wall. Sister Bartholomew sleeps there when she makes her monthly visit to home base."

Dingy room followed dingy room, in the sense of peeling wallpaper or paint, flaking ceilings, and carpets worn to the pads. Those spots were covered with a chair in one room, a nightstand in another. Every room was spotless. The curtains in Sister Kathryn's room were free of mended spots. Those curtains were the only sign of the Superior's elevated status.

Footsteps with an echo came up the stairs. Sister Olive popped onto the third-floor hall, Steve the Chihuahua scrambling up behind her.

"Dorothy, Helena needs her ten o'clock meds."

Sister Dorothy yanked up her sleeve and checked her watch. "Jesus, Mary, and Joseph. I'm sorry, Ms. Driscoll. Olive, we finished this floor."

"I'll take over. Come on, Ms. Driscoll. Now that you know the intimate details of our hedonistic lives, I'll take you to where the madwoman hides in the attic."

Giulia stooped to rub the Chihuahua's tummy. "Should I have looked for a stash of Gothic romances in your room?"

Sister Olive's laugh was the first response Giulia had heard from her which was neither sarcastic nor belligerent.

"My guilty pleasure is Zane Grey westerns. I know you saw them." She opened a narrow door at the end of the hall. "The nice thing about old houses is real stairs to the attic, not one of those pull-down ladders and a trap door."

The doorbell rang and Steve deserted them for fresh victims.

"Attention hog."

Two bulbs lit the attic, but the sun shining through the windows at either end made artificial light unnecessary. Steamer trunks and sheet-covered furniture took up most of the floor space.

"I expected more dust up here," Giulia said.

"Training never fades." Sister Olive ran a thumb across the top of a broken bookshelf. "No one's been up here for a couple of months. It's due for another cleaning."

Giulia wandered the attic, getting a feel for what the Sisters considered too unsightly to be seen downstairs. Sister Olive provided running commentary.

"The trunk with the flower découpage is Sister Helena's. She loves frilly decorations. The single positive aspect to her disease is she's spared the daily harassment from Eagle and his minions. And don't you give me any pious claptrap about God afflicting her with ALS to bring her closer to His suffering or to give us all an example of holy resignation." She slapped a dust cover. "This place is a dump, but it's our dump. We've been helping the neighborhood for twenty years. Come to the cellar with me."

As Giulia passed the open doors on the second floor she caught the faintest whiff of cigarette smoke. Odd that nuns living at this level of poverty found money for cigarettes.

The moans continued unabated behind the closed door. In Sister Helena's room, Sister Dorothy massaged the woman's atrophied muscles. At the end of the hall, Sister Eugenie slumped in her chair, staring out the window at the beautiful September day.

Giulia scowled at herself. Who was she to point a finger at these women? As secret vices go, an occasional cigarette didn't rate a second glance.

Fifteen

Frank and Sister Kathryn sat at the kitchen table. Frank took notes on an old-fashioned flip pad. Steve the Chihuahua dropped a rawhide bone next to his water bowl and loped over to Sister Olive.

"Come on, freeloader. Earn your keep."

The dog bounced down wooden slat steps illuminated by a single bulb set high on one wall. The stairs were newer than Giulia had expected, but the cellar itself lived down to her expectations. A furnace from the dark ages lurked in one corner. Three twelve-inch windows requiring a stepladder to reach were covered by petite midnight-blue curtains spangled with sequins. The curtains allowed in slivers of light around their edges, illuminating persistent cobwebs.

Ancient whitewash peeled away from the walls in chunks. Rust speckled the bottom of the hot water heater. The dog abandoned them to nose behind the furnace. Square laundry baskets sat on two tables. Peeling Linoleum on the tabletops matched the squares of Linoleum on the floor. Their curling corners gave glimpses of a packed dirt sub-floor, reminding Giulia of cool summer afternoons at her favorite aunt's house.

The dryer buzzed the end of a cycle. Sister Olive pulled a chain above one table and lit another bulb. "Reason number five why we belong here." She emptied the dryer and began folding a pair of jeans. Giulia turned the sleeves of a windbreaker right side in.

"Thanks. We're the unofficial laundromat for the street people. Sister Bartholomew brings the clothes and picks them up."

A second windbreaker in Giulia's hands hovered above the table. "Sister Bartholomew who was a Canonical Novice four years ago? The one who comes from a long line of mechanics?"

Sister Olive paused this time. "You know her?" She made an impatient sound. "Where's my brain? Of course you know her. You helped her survive the Community's Great Scandal."

Steve's sharp little teeth began shredding a stack of newspapers in shades ranging from off-white to ivory to yellow pirate teeth.

"Steve! Stop it!" Sister Olive reached for a plastic jar of Milk-Bones on a high shelf and rattled it. The dog abandoned the papers and sat up like a meerkat at her feet. He took the bribe behind the hot water heater to consume it in private.

"We keep the papers to donate to the local animal shelter fundraising drive, but we missed it this year. Steve thinks they're his personal chew toy tower." She shook out an oversized knitted sweater. "If Kathryn hasn't told you yet, we've had two break-ins in the last four months. Two we know about, that is."

"Did you report them to the police?"

"Of course, but they don't care. We lost a batch of clothes from the dryer the first time. Total value approximately sixty dollars. It would cost more to complete the paperwork." She snapped the hem straight on a t-shirt. "We got Steve the next day. We knew he wouldn't be any use in home defense, but he's a great alarm system when he's not distracted by treats."

Giulia began to pair up socks. "What about the second break-in?"

"Three weeks ago. Steve woke up Diane first. She got me and Dorothy. We huddled together at the top of the stairs like teenagers in a horror movie. Nobody wanted to be the first to go down. When we heard noises from the front parlor Diane said she could get to the baseball bat."

"Why didn't you call 911?"

Olive insulted Giulia's intelligence with a glance. "The only phone is in the front hall. Dorothy and I stayed on the bottom step while Diane got the bat, then we followed her into the parlor. A teenager in ragged jeans and a black t-shirt was pawing through our bookshelf. God knows what she thought we were hiding."

Giulia finished the socks. "She was looking for money hidden in a hollowed-out book."

Olive's laugh was harsh. "Only an addict with a completely fried brain would think a bunch of nuns living in a house like this would be hoarders. She was an addict, by the way."

"Her brain wasn't too fried if she read Victorian penny dreadfuls as a hobby."

"Read what?"

"Short, cheap books known for their shock factor. I recall an entire series about misers who lived in abject poverty, but after they died people found money hidden throughout their houses. Where do you want the socks?"

"In the blue milk crate. Diane didn't crack the book hunting thief's skull, in case you're wondering. Steve ran between our legs and dug his teeth into her jeans. She screamed and saw the bat and passed out cold." Olive wrinkled her nose. "I'm surprised she didn't pass out from her own body odor."

"Perhaps you should've gotten a traditional guard dog. A Rottweiler or a German Shepherd."

"Hold this for me, please." Olive handed Giulia a brown milk crate and filled it with folded shirts. "Large dogs are too expensive to feed and maintain. Bart knows a vet in training who checked out Steve for free to make sure he was healthy. Besides, we didn't want to risk a trained attack dog inflicting harm on anyone, not even a home invader."

The nun stacked filled milk crates along the back of the folding table. "You listen to me now, Ms. Driscoll. We have a duty to help the needy. Eagle Developers doesn't care about our duty. Why should they? You have to find a solution which won't interfere with our mission." She hefted the last crate, piled with jeans. "And make sure you pin Matilda's murder on them while you're at it."

Sixteen

Giulia took her interview turn at the kitchen table. Even though less than forty-eight hours had passed, Sister Kathryn looked like she hadn't slept in days.

"Detective Driscoll covered everything. I don't know what else you could ask me."

All lead-ins should be so easy. "Do Sister Olive's views on Eagle Developers represent all of you?"

She got a crooked smile in return. "You've proved me wrong with one sentence. No. Sister Olive's views are mostly her own. The more venom she indulges, though, the more some of us are coming around to her views." She fiddled with the napkin holder. "Matilda's funeral is tomorrow. She had no living relatives. She has no one to seek justice for her."

Giulia put a hand on the fidgeting ones. "Yes, she does."

Sister Kathryn started to cry. "I'm sorry," she gulped between sobs. "I should be setting an example of resignation. Or hope. Or whatever it is we're supposed to project when a nun passes."

Giulia, who never cursed, with difficulty refrained from saying "Bull—." Instead, she shook out a napkin and held it to Sister Kathryn's nose. The nun honked into it as though Giulia was her mother. After soaking a second napkin with tears she took a deep breath and sat up.

"Sister Olive has some justification for her opinions. Eagle is relentless. I'm given to understand such tactics are their standard." She recited a list of actions which could be construed as harassment. "In a way, the worst is sending the neighbors to us to tell us how terrific the buyout money is and how much better they're living now. After they leave, I feel like I'm betraying the Sisters by not using my authority to take the offer and somehow find us a new place on my own."

"The Order will take the money and decide where you'll be living?"

Kathryn shook her head. "Yes and no. We have jobs, so they more or less ignored us until Eagle swooped in." She stood and tossed the napkins in the trash. "There's not enough room for us all in the Motherhouse. They've agreed to allow us enough from the buyout to find a new place, but it has to meet with their approval."

"What are the chances they approve anything in better shape than this house?"

"Less than ten percent. I see you still possess the skepticism required to negotiate with the Superior General. You'll need it."

When Giulia drove past the empty coffee shop, the sign on the door confirmed it was closed. It kept odd hours: five a.m. to ten a.m., six p.m. to eleven p.m. She left herself a voice memo to talk to the owner tomorrow morning. He was the only other resident in the two-block radius who hadn't caved to Eagle.

She continued to her next stop: The church where her sister-in-law was secretary.

The thin woman with limp hair sitting at a weathered picnic table looked nothing like the skeletal LSA addict who'd fainted on Driscoll Investigations' office floor two months earlier.

Since today was the first day of school, Giulia thought she knew the reason for Anne's air of sitting in the midst of day three of a three-day rainstorm without an umbrella.

The lawn muffled Giulia's approach. Anne started when Giulia sat across from her, her half-eaten apple bouncing on her flattened lunch bag.

"Giulia? Why are you here? What's wrong?"

Giulia smiled at her. "You sound like my mother used to when I called her any time other than Saturday morning."

Anne's face fell into its usual lines. "My grandmother used to say the same thing to my mother."

"Guilt. It's in Italian DNA." Giulia waited a beat, then gave up on trying to get Anne to smile. "I need your help."

The statement roused her. "My help? Why?"

"Salvatore's in the hospital."

The thin lips compressed into virtual invisibility.

Giulia indulged a moment of wickedness. "Are you trying to figure out how a good Catholic wife should react?"

Anne's lips writhed for an instant. "What did he do?"

Perhaps a good wife would've asked "What happened to him?" but such an equation required a good husband to balance it.

"He touched a faulty wire and fell off a ladder. He's in a coma."

Anne reached for her apple. "His company has good insurance."

Because she liked planning surprises, Giulia rejoiced at Anne's missing the mark. "What time do you get off work?"

"Four thirty." Her lips vanished again. "Look, I'm not going to visit him in the hospital. One, I don't have a car. Two, I need time to put on rhino hide before I get near him. You know how he wields his self-righteous malice. Three—"

"Anne. I'll pick you up at your apartment around five. I could use a little help with the kids."

The import of Giulia's words swept the lines from Anne's face. Her hands shook. The lunch bag rattled.

"My kids are staying with you?"

"If you ask them, they'll probably say they're staying with our cable TV."

It was a weak joke, but Giulia wasn't dense enough to think it caused Anne's tears. She reached into her messenger bag and handed over a travel pack of tissues. When Anne wiped her blotched face with the third tissue, Giulia stood.

"I have to get back to work. Five o'clock, give or take."

Anne clutched at her. "You're giving me access to my kids again. How can I thank you?"

"Don't be silly. We're family."

Seventeen

Giulia entered the office carrying a gyro salad and a can of caffeine-free Coke. She pointed at Sidney with the Coke. "Do not say one word."

Sidney put on the pious innocence of a stained-glass saint. "Who am I to comment on your lack of attendance at your own workplace?"

Giulia set the takeout container on the table under the window. "I thought you were going to chastise me about the chemicals in the Coke and the marinated lamb."

"You went into Pittsburgh?"

"No. Our favorite Greek restaurant opened a satellite place in Cottonwood last week."

Sidney snatched a pen and paper. "Where? I would kill for their potatoes. As in, right now."

Giulia gave her the address. "It's after one. I was sure you both had already eaten." She stabbed lettuce, tomato, and meat with a flimsy plastic fork. "Next time I'll buy lunch for the office."

"Deal."

Zane rose from behind the printer, dust on his knees. "Souvlaaakiii...."

Giulia swallowed before her salad went down the wrong pipe. "Much better than braaaiiins..."

He fist-bumped Giulia from across the room. "One day your offspring and Jessamine will go on a date and spend the entire time trying to find common movie ground. Also, the printer's fixed."

"You're a treasure. And then they'll go to the Garden of Delight for dessert." She popped the tab on the Coke. "Where Jessamine will initiate him into the wonders of life without processed sugar."

"If she hasn't already done so at least fifty times before."

Sidney said, "You don't need a crystal ball to predict that. Eat your lunch. The baby needs nourishment."

"So does his mom." Giulia popped a cherry tomato covered in tzatziki sauce into her mouth.

Zane turned his monitor toward the windows. "Can you see anything?"

Giulia squinted. "No. Too much glare. If you don't mind me eating in front of you, I'll come over there."

"Adversity breeds character. Calvin and Hobbes."

"The game is afoot. Sherlock Holmes." She set her lunch on the corner of his desk.

"I'll remind you of this moment when it's time for my annual review." He opened a spreadsheet on his screen. "If Cottonwood ever gets on the revitalization wagon, Eagle Developers will be driving it. No, Eagle will probably own the wagon."

"One of my rich cousins lives in an Eagle condo," Sidney said. "It cost enough to put Jessamine through four years at Carnegie Mellon."

"I hope it's spectacular." Giulia dug through the salad for another tomato.

"It's intimidating. I was terrified Jessamine would spit up on the Berber carpets." Sidney wrinkled her nose. "My cousin followed us around with a lint roller in case we shed any stray alpaca fibers. A movie star could've lived in the place. No, thanks."

"One of Eagle's slogans is 'We're the future of Cottonwood,'" Zane said. "I wouldn't like to try to prove them wrong. Look at their acquisition pattern over the past six years." He walked Giulia through the research as she finished eating. "In summary, they're progressive, ruthless, forward-thinking, not above bribery, and have been caught dealing on the fringes."

Sidney groaned. "Did you really say 'forward-thinking'?"

Giulia said, "Are they fringe enough to terrorize a houseful of elderly and infirm nuns?"

Zane chewed his inner left cheek. "Possibly."

Eighteen

Giulia returned home with her sister-in-law at five to six. When she opened the door from the garage, her niece and oldest nephew were six inches away from the TV screen watching reruns of *Samurai Jack*. There was no sign of Carlo. For a panicked moment she feared he'd run away.

Cecilia turned her head when Giulia closed the door a second time with a bang.

"Mom?" She jumped up and tackled Anne at a run.

"Mom!" Pasquale did the same.

"Mom?" Carlo came running in from the garden. When he landed on Pasquale, the whole pile of Falcones crashed to the floor.

"Mom, where'd you come from?"

"We miss you so much."

"Pasquale has a new girlfriend."

"Cecilia learned a new swear word."

Carlo remained silent as he clung to his mother's neck.

Anne said through blubbery tears, "Guys, I can't breathe."

As one, her kids leaped off. All three helped their mother to her feet. As soon as she was vertical, Carlo latched onto her waist. Pasquale stretched one arm up around her shoulders. Cecilia nestled in between Pasquale and Anne.

Giulia passed a tissue to Anne and closed the screen door to the garden.

"Are you staying here with us?"

"School started today."

"I got Sister Mary Margaret for homeroom."

"I got Sister Brigid. Remember how she ragged on Pasquale from

September to Christmas?"

The kids' words tumbled over each other. Their mother somehow squeezed in one-word answers around her huge smile and the tissues Giulia kept handing her. The floods showed no signs of slowing when Frank opened the garage door bearing three large pizza boxes.

"Supper has arrived."

Giulia kissed him. "You are the best husband on the planet."

"Tell my mother, please."

"I'll make salad." Giulia raised her voice. "Supper in eight minutes. Please return your mother to her autonomous state before then."

Silence reigned for two full seconds as the kids turned puzzled faces to Giulia.

"She means un-cling so we can eat." Anne held them closer. "I can go hungry."

"So can we." The alternating recaps of school resumed.

In the kitchen, Giulia ripped lettuce and sliced tomatoes. "I vote we wait a few years between pregnancies."

Frank set out plates and napkins. "Instant parentage isn't my lifestyle choice either."

"Could you get the salad dressings out of the fridge? I'll get drink orders."

Despite their stated disdain for food, the siren call of pizza lured all Falcones into the kitchen. Once seated, however, not one hand moved toward the food. Giulia needed only five seconds for enlightenment. She caught Frank's eye. "Grace, please."

To his credit, Frank took the hint. Giulia had developed a distaste for vocal prayer after a decade of it in the convent, and Frank had been pleased to eschew it with her.

Pasquale spoke up when Frank finished. "Dad says grace because he's the oldest male in the house, but, um, this is your house."

Giulia smiled at him. "Pepperoni or sausage or both together?"

Another moment of silence.

Cecilia held out her plate. "I'll take a slice of the combo, please." She inhaled like a chocoholic in the Hershey factory. "Get with it, you guys. We watched TV. We're eating takeout pizza. Uncle Frank might let us play video games later." She took a delicate bite of her pizza.

"This is normal."

"Normal includes vegetables." Giulia scooped salad into bowls and dealt one to each child like a hand of cards. "Choose your dressing."

Nineteen

After supper Cecilia and Giulia volunteered for dish duty. Frank challenged Pasquale to a game of *Halo*. Carlo dragged his mother out to the garden to see the chameleon.

All but the forks were dry when the doorbell rang.

Cecilia flapped the dish towel. "Go ahead, Aunt Giulia. I'll finish these."

Distracted by Frank and Pasquale's shouts from the gaming closet too small to be called a room, Giulia opened the door without checking first.

"Giulia!" A crunchy granola hippie from the 1970s stood on the threshold. She wore a tie-dyed t-shirt and jeans old enough for the bottom hems to have dissolved into fringe. Puka shells clacked at the ends of her pale brown braids. "I'm sorry Crankenstein is taking up your whole driveway." She stepped over the threshold and enveloped Giulia in tie-dye and shells. "It's been ages since we had face time."

A moment later she saw Frank and switched the hug to him without interfering with his on-screen alien slaughter. "Kids? Not yours yet, right?"

Giulia said, "Sister Bartholomew, let me introduce you to my sister-in-law Anne Falcone and her children."

Frank paused the game. Carlo and Cecilia detached themselves from their mother and all three kids became model Catholic school pupils in the presence of a nun.

After the third "Good evening, Sister Bartholomew," the crunchy granola hippie laughed. "You can call me Sister Bart."

Cecilia reached for one of the braids. "Where did you get those? Are they beads? Can you show me how to put them in my hair?"

"Cecilia. Where are your manners?" Anne's voice was sharp.

Cecilia collapsed into the cowed drudge Giulia had seen in Salvatore's house. "I beg your pardon, Sister."

The young nun glanced at the Falcones and her infectious smile glowed on the room. "Mrs. Falcone, I love it when students don't create an invisible bubble around me. Cecilia, they're shells. You can find them at craft stores or flea markets. After I give Giulia all the news I'll show you how to attach them. Did you know Giulia saved my bacon a few years ago? Really and truly. She was the absolute master Sherlock. In disguise and everything."

"Bart, have you eaten supper?" Giulia never liked extravagant praise.

"Not exactly."

Giulia's facial expression harked back to her years of cross-examining students. "That would be no. I'll bring you pizza and a salad."

"Ooh, I haven't had pizza in months. Our budget doesn't allow for takeout."

Carlo spoke up, startling Giulia. "Sister Bart, have you seen the chameleon?"

"The what? You have a lizard?"

A tight shake of the head. "Not us. Aunt Giulia does. Come on."

He took Bart's hand and led her into the garden. The early evening sunlight lit everything with a golden glow. Scarlett perched on the branches in her openwork cage with green either beginning to creep over her blobby skull armor or beginning to fade off it. Giulia still had difficulty telling the difference.

Carlo launched into a chameleon documentary. He described its feeding habits, how it differed from other types of chameleons, why and when it changed colors. All without taking even a breath for Bart to comment.

Giulia reheated three slices of pizza in the toaster oven and marveled at the difference between Carlo reunited with his mother versus Carlo without her.

"Where did you learn all that?" Giulia asked him when she called them in so Bart could eat.

"Looked it up during study hall. Is there any pizza left?"

Giulia halved the remaining slices. Everyone else discovered the need for more pizza. They stood around the table to eat, bringing back memories of Giulia's childhood, when everything good happened in the kitchen.

"Aunt Giulia, are you supposed to be eating for two now?" Cecilia offered her the narrow triangle of pepperoni and cheese she'd taken. "You can have this."

"Hold it." Bart swallowed, coughed, held up a hand, and caught her breath. "Eating for two means only one thing."

"It does."

"Awesome!" Bart jumped behind Giulia and squeezed.

"Sister Bart, you'll squish the baby."

Bart freed Giulia's ribcage. "You're right, Cecilia. Thank you. Wow, everything's changed for both of us. Have I told you what I do for a living now?"

"Something involving an RV in our driveway?"

"The detective strikes again." She spoke between bites of her third slice. "Turns out I'm something like the Homeless Whisperer. I wheedle food and overstocked supplies and pass them on to the street folks. Stores can't sell the stuff past the expiration dates but who's going to turn up their nose at day-old chocolate chip muffins? I charm them out of aspirin and pain reliever creams and antacids too. At first when I showed up at the service doors of bakeries and groceries and drug stores I had a whole speech prepared. Manufacturers ship expired stock to third-world countries, I said, but here I am ready to haul the stuff away plus give them an immediate tax write-off. They had to check with the manager and make a few phone calls the first two times, but now they even help me load the boxes into Crankenstein."

"You drive around alone?"

Bart grinned at Giulia. "You sound like my mother. I live in my RV but I'm not naïve. I've got some wicked skills with a baseball bat and I keep pepper spray on me day and night. Junkies tried to break in a couple of years ago, but I broke their arms. Word got around, and besides, the street people know I'm there to help. Plus no one's going to score crack pawning a few pairs of jeans and a beat-up frying pan."

Giulia refilled glasses. "Don't you carry car repair tools, Sister Pit Jockey?"

Bart laughed again. "Like I said, I'm not clueless. Never keep anything in your vehicle worth stealing. My tool box is stashed at the convent."

"You can fix cars?" Pasquale's voice took on a tinge of adoration.

Bart and Pasquale shut out the rest of the room as they discussed the merits of four- versus six-cylinder engines with regard to gas mileage and acceleration efficiency. Anne helped Frank clean the second wave of dishes. Giulia dumped the empty pizza boxes in the garbage tote, reveling in Sister Bart the vibrant, happy-go-lucky, busy nun. She remembered too well Sister Bart the Novice a few years back: Drugged and under the control of an evil priest and the equally heinous Superior General, sneaking into the bathroom to cut herself. Giulia would've gladly washed and waxed the RV in the driveway all by herself in gratitude.

When she returned, the group had moved to the living room. Frank offered Carlo his choice of *Assassin's Creed* or *Call of Duty*.

Giulia tapped Pasquale and Cecilia on their shoulders. "I need Sister Bart to myself for a little bit, please."

Anne's oldest and youngest planted her between them on the couch.

"Come give me the tour of Crankenstein," Giulia said to Bart.

Twenty

An ancient baby blue Roadtrek Popular blocked off three-quarters of their driveway. Giulia walked its circuit. "If you painted it green and added giant vinyl flowers, you'd have your own Mystery Machine."

Bart patted its rear bumper. "I know, right? I considered the Scooby-Doo color scheme for half a second, but fun and cool equals conspicuous. Nobody gives my anonymous, well-used home a second glance."

Giulia said as Bart opened the back door, "Have you heard about Sister Matilda?"

"She's why I'm here. But first you must enter my personal castle."

Boxes of pharmaceutical supplies crowded milk crates piled with cans of nuts and soup that lined the castle's back entrance. A small, square sink on the left with cupboards above and below faced a narrow drop desk with an antiquated laptop on the right. Shelves above the desk groaned under a Bible, a Franciscan Omnibus, what looked like a complete collection of Agatha Christie paperbacks, cookbooks, and spiral bound car repair manuals. Homemade flowered curtains covered all the windows. An artist's easel and a fishing tackle box of painting supplies sat in the passenger seat up front.

"Bed? Toilet? Shower?" Giulia said.

Bart opened a door next to the desk and pointed out the concealed bed. "Nothing like those five by nine paper-thin cells they stuffed us in at the Motherhouse, is it?"

"It's better than any Tiny House I've been in. This is a home."

Bart squeezed Giulia with more gentleness this time. "I was hoping you'd see it like I do. Kathryn likes to make sure I remember I'm still part of the Community, so I bunk at the convent one week a month. She's a good Superior, so I never tell her how much that week makes me love tooling around in Crankenstein even more."

Giulia's fingers made a locking motion on her lips. "I'll never tell."

"You're the best nun I've ever known."

"Ex-nun." She rested a hand on her belly.

"Good point. Shove one of those crates over and sit your pregnant self down. There's pencils and paper in the desk. I put word out that I needed dirt on Eagle Developers and boy did my people come through. Would you like the good stuff or the bad to start?"

"The good. I'd like to balance what I've learned so far."

Bart perched on the edge of the sink. "There's more good than bad, to be honest, which I should, being a Franciscan and all. They're one of the biggest local employers and they walk the tightrope of hiring both union and non-union employees."

"On the same projects?"

"Ha ha ha, are you kidding? *The Scoop* would be all over the fistfights like a rash and they'd finally eclipse the real news. No, Eagle keeps both sides far apart, and I mean far. This week, for example. The hotel renovations on the north side are union, but the landscaping projects on the west and south sides aren't." She watched the pencil fly. "Want me to slow down?"

Giulia made a face at her. "If I had a dollar for every time someone asked me that, the baby's college fund would be well on its way. Thank you, no. I can keep up."

"I should've figured. Okay. Eagle also won some award three years running for hiring and promoting women. Eagle's right-hand man is a woman and she's the power behind winning the award. My street folks get a lot of under the counter work from them and they always listen for bits of information that could lead to more work."

Giulia shook out her fingers. "This isn't fitting in with what your fellow Sisters have been telling me."

Another laugh. "You've been getting the Sister Olive Special Broadcast. If she was younger, I'd swear Eagle himself ditched her at the altar twenty years ago to marry his now ex-trophy wife."

Giulia joined in the laugh. "If I were ever to turn to the dark side, I'd try to work the topic of jilted brides into my next conversation with Sister Olive."

"Only if I can be there to listen." Bart slid off the sink to straighten one of the curtains. "Now for the bad. He undercuts buyout prices when he can. You might call that good business."

"Considering he targets poor older neighborhoods, I'd call it borderline evil."

"As would the people dishing the dirt for me. One of them took an Eagle offer and snorted every cent of the payment. He's better now because he can't afford any more coke."

Giulia looked around the RV's interior. "Where exactly do you keep the baseball bat?"

Bart pointed to the side door. "It's ready to grab before I touch the deadbolt. But we aren't talking about me. We're playing Good Developer-Bad Developer. There are rumors he pays at-risk kids to hassle holdouts."

"Sister Olive has more than hinted they're at the center of a harassment campaign." She started a second piece of paper.

"You won't hear me arguing. My people tell me our place has set a record for the longest holdout and the rumor is Eagle is stepping up his game. You know they buy out entire blocks of mortgages at a time?"

Giulia nodded. "He chooses places banks are eager to unload, as long as the area is close to a positive feature to draw in new residents. In your case, the park fountain."

"Bingo. We have no leverage. We're three months behind on the mortgage. Eagle did us a favor without realizing it."

"By taking over your mortgage before the bank foreclosed?" Giulia looked over at her. "I'm quite sure he did realize it."

Frank stuck his head in the open door. "Carlo's planning to kidnap the lizard, Pasquale's kicking my butt in *Halo*, and Cecilia is trying to convince her mother to raid your dresser for nail polish and have a girls' night in. Help."

Twenty-One

Giulia and Frank on the couch put their heads together with Anne in the corner chair. Bart sat on the floor with the kids, telling them funny stories of her life driving around in Crankenstein.

"Please, please can you keep them here until Sunday morning?" Anne clasped her hands. "I work a half day on Saturdays and I can't afford to take any time off. I'll take a bus to the hospital Saturday afternoon and pick up the minivan, pack up my stuff, and move back into the house. I don't want to disrupt their first week of school, even if it's only two days."

Cecilia butted in with a key hooked to a stretchy spiral wristband on her outstretched palm. "Here. Dad changed the locks, so you'll need this even if you have your old key, which you don't, right?"

Frank stared at Cecilia. "He changed the locks? *Go dtachta an diabhal é.*"

Giulia caught his eyes and angled hers toward the kids. "Language, please."

Cecilia planted herself in front of Frank. "What did you say? What does it mean? Is it like holy shit? Will you teach it to me?"

Giulia and Anne said as one, "Stop swearing." Then they laughed.

All the Falcone offspring stopped cold. They maintained a startled tableau for a solid three seconds before Cecilia squeezed her mother in a scrawny-armed bear hug. The boys said to Bart's puzzled look, "We haven't heard Mom laugh in ages."

Frank said, "It means 'May the devil choke him.'"

Cecilia looked disappointed.

Giulia brought the discussion back to practicalities. "All right, you three. We have a plan."

Anne said, "I'll call the school to get you all on the bus starting Monday."

Giulia made an annoyed noise. "I should've thought. Salvatore's minivan keys are in the hospital with his wallet and clothes. The minivan is still at the hotel his company was renovating."

"That's all right. The hospital's on a bus route. I hope there's one close to his work site."

Giulia pulled up the bus schedule on her phone. "No...maybe...no. Maybe...yes. How does this one look?"

Anne studied the map on Giulia's screen. "Yes. This route won't interfere with my work schedule. Could you print it out for me?" She held up a basic TracFone. "No internet access on this." While the schedule printed, Anne continued. "I'll pick up the minivan on Saturday, then get my things and make a grocery run. You three will stay here tomorrow and Saturday and I'll be here Sunday morning to bring you back home. I think we'll celebrate with homemade Oreos."

Her children said nothing for a moment.

"I thought you liked my cooking?" Anne's voice wavered.

Pasquale said, "Are you really coming back home?"

"At least until your father gets out of the hospital."

Carlo said in a voice much too old for age twelve, "I hope he never gets out."

Giulia kept herself from showing any reaction. From the corners of her eyes, she saw Frank and Bart not reacting in the same manner.

Cecilia must have picked up on the friction in the room, because she cuffed her middle brother. "Pay attention to what's important, dummy. Homemade Oreos again."

Carlo rubbed the back of his head. "If Dad saw you swat me, you'd end up saying a Rosary on your knees in the cellar."

She stuck out her tongue at him. "Dad's not here."

Pasquale, one inch shorter than Cecilia but three inches taller than Carlo, clamped a hand on each of their heads. "You're both morons. Mom's coming home." He turned their faces toward his. "Get it now? Mom is coming home."

Carlo grabbed his mother's hands and pulled her into the middle of the room. "Mom's coming home. Mom's coming home." They danced her in a circle as they sang.

To Giulia's mental catalogue of Reasons to Beat Salvatore with a Wooden Ruler, she added borderline mental abuse. Sidney's psychologist husband Olivier would have been able to tell if a line had been crossed.

Frank murmured, "If you were Supergirl, your heat vision would've burned a hole through the wall and fried our diva lizard on its way to your brother's hospital room."

Giulia's vertebrae didn't relax. "Notice how they're acting like kids now?"

"Instead of rage-filled time bombs in kid suits?"

"You did notice."

The kitchen clock chimed. Anne stopped the dance. "School night. Time to get ready for bed."

After polite "good nights" to the other adults, the rejuvenated Falcones pounded upstairs and dragged their mother with them. Cecilia ordered the boys to straighten their sleeping bags in a higher version of her mother's voice.

Bart said from her cross-legged position on the floor, "I'm headed back to Chez Dilapidation tonight. Crankenstein needs some TLC and I need to be on hand for Matilda's funeral. You know it's tomorrow, right?"

Giulia pushed her hands against the small of her back. "Sister Kathryn told me."

"Nobody will be there besides us now that the Pittsburgh Motherhouse is no more. She was the oldest nun in Cottonwood." Her ebullience faded. "One of the good points of being Catholic: We're allowed to be glad there's a Hell waiting for people who kill little old nuns." She moved from the floor to the couch and patted Giulia's belly. "Whatever you do, don't name her Bartholomew. However, if she's a he, I would be thrilled and honored if you named him after me. Oh, before I forget. Can you bring Cecilia to the convent tomorrow after school? The bedridden nuns could use some cheering up."

Because Giulia liked Bart, she didn't slap her hand away. "Only if they don't teach her new ways to curse."

Twenty-Two

Giulia leaned on Zane's desk at nine thirty Friday morning. "I know Eagle has a Midas Touch. What I'm saying is it may be deserved."

Zane enlarged one of the spreadsheets. "My Advanced Statistics professor at MIT spent an entire semester teaching us to vivisect results like these."

Giulia pointed to three different cells. "Their success is not fabricated."

"Not all of it. They build actual buildings where actual people live. But see these charts here and here?" He pointed to different cells. "Their growth projections are a little too symmetrical."

She pointed to a different chart. "Not here."

"It doesn't take a statistics genius to insert realistic data on purpose to give verisimilitude to the unrealistic."

Giulia inclined her head. "I bow to your superior analytic brain cells."

Sidney picked up her phone. "Neil? It's Sidney. Have you got five minutes?...Awesome. Let me put you on hold." She pressed a button. "Giulia, Eagle bought out my cousin's dry-cleaning business two years ago. He's on three."

In her office, Giulia set up pen and paper before picking up.

"Ms. Driscoll, I've heard so much about you. What can I help you with?"

Volubility and perkiness ran in Sidney's family. Neil's story was the opposite of the nuns' experience.

"Remember the strip mall out toward Oakdale? It hadn't been renovated since Elvis hit number one with 'Heartbreak Hotel.' I had a core of loyal clientele, but I was squeaking by every month. Eagle called all twelve of us into a meeting and showed us what they wanted to turn the mall into. Then they offered us about three-quarters of the assessed value for our businesses."

"Did you consider the offer fair?" Giulia wrote and talked at the same time.

"Most of us did. The antique shop and the yarn shop kibitzed, but their bank reps had long talks with them and they caved within a week."

"Wait a second. Didn't construction on the new build come to a screeching halt last spring?"

"I heard it did. Something about zoning restrictions. Eagle paid us sixty days after we signed the agreements, which is all I cared about. You might have heard rumors about them. Oh, and there was that investigation when the Attorney General for our fine commonwealth was up for reelection."

Giulia allowed her voice to convey her smile. "Would you be implying the Attorney General's motives weren't pure?" She tore off a new sheet and wrote in big letters: AG investigation of ED.

His answering smile came through. "Perish the thought."

When Giulia hung up from him, she drove to the coffee shop one block over from the convent. If there had been a morning rush, it was over. Two older men and one woman sat one per bistro table, scrolling through their phones. A thirty-something man behind the counter was wiping down the aerators.

"Welcome to the Coffee Break. What can I brew for you?" White lettering on his brown apron proclaimed: "Powered by caffeine."

"A large dark roast with..." she scanned the syrup bottles. "I've never seen Baked Alaska syrup before."

He smiled, revealing hockey teeth. "It's my own creation. So are the Bananas Foster and Baklava." His smooth brow furrowed. "I never noticed all my signature syrups begin with the letter B. My shrink is going to have a field day."

"My assistant's husband is a psychologist. I've picked up several useful terms. I'd like to try the Baked Alaska, please."

The first sip demanded she close her eyes to appreciate the taste without distractions. "I will post a glowing review on Yelp when I get back to the office."

The hockey teeth reappeared. "I appreciate the offer, but there isn't much point. I'm not sure we'll be here long enough for a review to make a difference."

Giulia savored another sip. "Coffee this perfect deserves honesty in return. I'm a private investigator looking into Eagle Developers' buyout of the neighborhood."

A humorless laugh. "The nuns in the next block and my place are the last holdouts. Eagle's people are strong-arming me to sell. The little old nun who walked her dog at dark o'clock every morning said they're getting the same treatment."

One of the men set his cup and saucer on the dish cart and left. The other began a too-loud conversation on his phone: "I don't care what she said yesterday."

Giulia leaned on the counter. "I'm sorry to tell you she was found dead late Tuesday night."

He nodded. "I know. The police were on the stoop when I opened on Wednesday. Wanted to know if I'd seen anyone suspicious, heard anything out of the ordinary, the usual." He tossed the towel beneath the counter. "She was a fun old lady. Her scenery-chewing dog was the star of the neighborhood."

The one-sided conversation at the corner table heated up. "She'd sell her mother's organs for the chance to go viral. Triple-check anything she says. Then check it again."

"I wouldn't want to interview with him," the owner whispered. "One applicant lied on their resume two years ago and now he says there isn't an honest person in the state."

"And people think only bartenders get their customers' woes poured into their ears." She sipped again. "Not even an unwanted public conversation can detract from this coffee."

"You give me hope. Eagle upped their game last week and I'm tired of fighting. The neighborhood was emptying out slowly but surely even before Eagle swooped in." More hockey teeth. "See what I did there? I don't have the money for this month's mortgage payment or to renew the service contract on my steel mistress here." He patted the coffee machine.

"I'm sorry your business won't make it." Giulia inclined her head toward the cell phone over-sharer. "Any objections if I wash his mouth out with soap?"

"His vocabulary has been circling the drain since I opened, but he's one of my most loyal customers."

"I'll close my ears. What will you do next?"

"Spend a few years working for The Man. Eagle's offer plus what I'll net for selling the equipment and fixtures will pay off most of my debts. My goal is to have my own place again in five years."

The woman glared at the over-sharer and left without bringing her cup to the dirty dish caddy.

"I'm not sure what else I can tell you about Eagle. I don't like them much, but their offer is fair. Do you know what the nuns plan to do?"

"They've dug in their heels for now."

"Good for them." He made a wry face. "In principle, I mean. In reality, what chance do any of us have against the Eagle juggernaut?"

The over-sharer set his cup and plate in the caddy and walked past them, still on the phone. "Don't waste your time on him. Trust me. I golf with his last employer."

Giulia threw up one hand in defeat. "I should learn to golf."

"Business clichés exist for a reason. You know what I'll miss the most? Talking to the little old nun while I opened up every morning and closed every night. They're all living below the poverty line, so I invented a discount smoothie for her. She refused to take a freebie. I'd fill a medium cup halfway with the day's flavor and charge her a buck fifty. We pretended she was my unofficial taste tester."

Three old men entered the shop together.

"Here's my card." Giulia passed one across the counter. "Let me know when you're in business for yourself again. I have to try your other syrups."

Twenty-Three

Giulia sat in her car to record a voice memo of the conversation, and to give herself some quality alone time with her coffee. Frank called as she dictated her summary thoughts.

"Hey, babe. How did you make out at middle school NASCAR this morning?"

"Thanks to my aggressive driving, I only committed two venial sins. The other drivers will need to go to confession as well."

His laughter mixed with his partner's.

"Dear, please tell me when you have me on speaker."

"Right. Sorry."

"Sorry, Giulia," his partner said. "Make Frank pay for it later."

"Please don't corrupt my wife."

Giulia said in a thoughtful voice, "No one's tried to corrupt me...yet."

Nash said, "That thumping sound you hear is your husband beating his head against the dashboard."

"Dear, before you knock yourself unconscious, why did you call?"

A long-suffering sigh. "Autopsy results. There's no evidence to contradict what we all thought. She died of a heart attack. It might take an act of God to discover proof the attack was caused by an attempted mugging. However..."

Giulia opened the Notes function and typed while he talked. "There's a however?"

"When I interviewed the nuns yesterday morning, I asked about the dead nun's habits. Shut up, Nash. I'm not making a joke. She walked the dog early and late every day no matter the weather. She never changed her pattern, which could give weight to a planned attack."

"A desperate junkie?"

"For example. Everyone knew the nuns were barely scraping by, so the chance she had more than ten bucks on her was slim."

Nash's voice: "When you gotta have a fix, you gotta have a fix."

"How desperate do you have to be to think a little old nun is going to have enough cash for heroin, meth, or crack?" Giulia sipped coffee, recognizing the irony of her own obsession. "Have there been any similar muggings in the area?"

"That would be the however. Eleven in the three-block radius in the past eight weeks. The neighborhood ought to have a poor return on investment for crime, but the statistics indicate there's something we don't know yet."

"You know the nuns think someone from Eagle Developers did it to scare them into selling."

Nash started his own phone conversation in a low voice. Frank took Giulia off speaker. "They told me so at great length."

"What does your gut say?"

"It says you make a great breakfast."

"Frank."

"Okay. Chances it was a random junkie or an organized band of junkies: Ninety-five percent. Chances it was Eagle: Five percent."

"So low?"

"Yes."

Giulia tapped her steering wheel. "I'm not going to argue with your experience."

"But you're not happy."

"More like I was allowing the client to influence my ideas. I know better." She set the coffee in the cup holder. "I think it's time to lie."

Twenty-Four

At twelve fifteen Giulia locked herself in a bathroom stall on the first floor of Cottonwood's biggest glass office building. Every business with an excellent opinion of itself fought for space in the five-story reflector mirror. Eagle Developers occupied one-quarter of the top floor.

Before Giulia could don her persona of web reporter, she had to work magic with safety pins. Her navy-blue interview suit, the only suit she owned, did not accommodate little Zlatan. A trip to a department store's maternity section could no longer be postponed. She opened the pack of safety pins she'd bought en route and hooked four together. When she pinned them to the waistband of the skirt and turned it around, she could almost sit. She added two more and tried again. There. The skirt fell in unattractive lines, but she could breathe.

"Zlatan, you are cramping my style."

The baby didn't even kick in response.

She stood at the bathroom mirror to refresh her makeup. First she reapplied bubblegum-pink lipstick and checked her pink-glitter eye shadow and overdone mascara. Next she took a plastic baggie from her pocket and inserted narrow rolls of cotton against her bottom gum lines. Last she pulled her blonde wig back with a pink band and set heavy-framed glasses with clear lenses on her nose. Thank you hipsters for this useful trend.

The elevator repeated the solid glass theme, this time with spiderweb-thin gold lines meandering through the glass. The gold threads in the maroon carpet of the fifth-floor hall led her feet to Eagle Developers' main door, also glass.

The large open space accommodated three desks with enough room in the center to drop Driscoll Investigations' entire office. A discreet printer stand was nestled behind the desk furthest form the door.

As expected, Giulia's safety-pinned skirt tried to drag her bodily out of the room in humiliation at the sight of the clothes of the two women and one man at the desks. But after surviving the spectacular Dahlia dress creations last month, Giulia would never again be intimidated by designer garments.

"Welcome to Eagle Developers." The receptionist's glasses were the real thing.

"Good afternoon. I'm Maria Falcone. I have a twelve fifteen appointment with Mr. Eagle." For this character, she pitched her voice a little higher in addition to the vocal distortion of the cotton rolls.

The receptionist typed and read her screen. "Yes. Mr. Eagle is finishing up with his eleven thirty."

The door facing Giulia opened as she spoke. A young female photographer with a real camera, the kind with detachable lenses, exited with a bearded man pocketing a micro cassette recorder.

A round man shorter than Giulia was shaking their hands. Bald on top, a brown ponytail reached halfway down his back. "Thanks for coming. Always happy to talk to the press. No bad publicity, that's my motto."

"We'll let your office know when the article will run." The reporter didn't pause on his way out. Giulia caught him wiping his hand on the shirt beneath his jacket.

Eagle advanced on Giulia, hand outstretched. "Come on in. Ms. Falcone, right? Perfect timing, perfect. We'll treat the local interview I just finished as dress rehearsal. I'm Victor Eagle, of course, CEO of Eagle Developers. This is my right-hand woman, Barbara Beech. Barb, this is Ms. Falcone from the online division of *USA Today*."

Next to Beech, Eagle could've posed for Mr. Potato Head. This though Beech was an inch shorter than Eagle. Her upswept platinum hair gave the illusion of height. Her shadow plaid suit had the indefinable lines of expert personal tailoring. Her eyes, like Eagle's, were blue. But hers were was the color of glaciers. His were Smurf-skin blue.

Despite the glacier, Beech's welcoming smile reached all the way to her eyes. "Good afternoon. We're pleased to meet you."

Giulia held up her phone, already recording. "Thank you for fitting me in. To be honest, I don't actually work for *USA Today* yet. I'm still a freelancer. I'm pitching a series on influential women in up-and-coming businesses to break into USA Today. My photos won't be as perfect as the ones from the last photographer, but I'm a solo operator." The cotton rolls were sucking all the moisture from her mouth but she didn't dare ask for a glass of water. For all she knew, the rolls would absorb the liquid and *floomp* her cheeks into twice their size.

Eagle beckoned her to the wall behind his simpler than expected desk. "We all started out somewhere." The small framed photograph showed a younger Eagle in front of a real estate agent's sign—Salesman of the Month: Victor Eagle. "This is me at age eighteen. First real job. Forced to find one because I had to get married to the ex, if you know what I mean. But I wasn't going to let one mistake sabotage my life plan. In six years I opened my own branch. Five years after that we were the top sellers in the state. By the time the ex and I called it quits, I'd saved enough to start Eagle Developers. While putting two kids through Catholic school, I might add." He walked her past a series of photographs arranged like an artist's gallery show. "Here's my favorite: Barb and me on the day we formed our partnership."

Beech stepped into Eagle's performance as though on cue. "I was managing my own satellite office for the competition. Victor approached me because I was cutting into his sales."

A belly laugh from Eagle. "I will categorically deny those words ever came out of my mouth."

"If it makes you happy, Victor." The look they shared indicated a level of comfort seldom achieved between two alpha personalities. "Victor proved his salesmanship when he convinced me we could take over the world as partners. I sold my office and we set up shop together."

Eagle winked at Giulia. "More shops than one, if you get my meaning. But you know what? We discovered we're better in the boardroom than the bedroom. So here we are, twelve years after we started our joint venture, poised to make Cottonwood the jewel of Pennsylvania."

Beech's wry expression also conveyed affection. "It's true. I believe the current term for it is 'adulting.'"

At first Giulia wondered what type of reaction they wanted from their unnecessary revelation. There was no profit in telling intimate details to a nobody freelancer. "I've seen a lot of your redevelopment work. You know how to design living spaces people want to own."

Eagle picked up his phone. "Amy, write this down: We create living spaces you'll want to own." He hung up. "Great slogan. Think of this interview when you see it in our ads."

Giulia played along. "I won't even ask for royalties."

She catalogued their body language. They stood too close in this day of no physical contact whatsoever in the workplace. They slipped into the occasional "couples" gesture: A hand touching an elbow. Beech straightening Eagle's collar. Much better to explain their level of intimacy outright than let Giulia speculate à la *The Scoop*.

"I will ask what first gave you the idea to focus on older, run-down neighborhoods."

Eagle grinned like a carnival barker. "Would you believe me if I told you it was my dear, sweet grandmother?" When Giulia gave him an "I didn't fall off a turnip truck yesterday" look, he held out both hands, still grinning. "You can't blame me for trying out heartwarming copy on a cub reporter."

Beech cut in. "It was my ex-mother-in-law. She could have been on the *Hoarders* TV show. Of the many reasons I divorced my ex, the way he ignored his mother was in the top five. The charmer got in a fight with an entire motorcycle gang about a year after we split and somehow his Dynasty Green 1964 Mustang failed to negotiate a turn in the West Virginia mountains. His lawyers tracked me down for the reading of the will, and when his mother showed up, I saw the equivalent of a leprechaun riding a unicorn—a lawyer rendered speechless."

Giulia murmured "Oh, wow," which served its purpose of encouragement.

"The poor woman looked like Miss Havisham's skeleton and kept demanding the keys to her son's house." She closed her eyes for a moment. "Two days later my ex-brother-in-law called and begged me to meet him at his mother's house. Half the houses on the street were boarded up. None of the others had a complete set of windows. This was a neighborhood once known for its antebellum-style architecture."

Eagle appeared not to like being out of the spotlight for too long. "She called me. I contacted some of my people and we swooped to the rescue. After the chaos she shared her inspiration: Buy up these blocks and turn them into prime living spaces again." He flung his arms wide. "And Eagle Developers began its journey to greatness. No, to legendary status."

"At least within the real estate redevelopment world." Beech shook her head with an indulgent smile.

"Are the residents generally happy to be relieved of the burden of living in deteriorating neighborhoods?" Only Giulia's years of undercover experience enabled her to mouth such platitudes without breaking character.

Eagle rolled his Smurf eyes. "You've been watching those teasers from *The Scoop*." His voice soured when he said the show's name. "I don't waste my time on their scandal-mongering but my rivals take great joy in tweeting the links at me. Eagle Developers knows how to maintain goodwill. We pay a fair price for the properties and the residents get to move out of their shit holes."

Giulia smiled. "I think I'll rephrase that for the article."

Eagle possessed an infectious belly laugh. "Sounds like your reporting will make up for *The Scoop*."

Beech stepped in. "Before you pose a careful question about the State Attorney General's attempt to use us as a stepping stone to get himself re-elected, the only charge he managed to stick to us was underbidding on certain low-profile projects."

"Our government needs to remember it represents the entire commonwealth, not just the capital city." Eagle stood next to his wall of windows. "Get a picture of us here. See the symbolism? We're looking forward to the day Cottonwood is the showcase of Pennsylvania. We're leading the charge."

Giulia complied.

Twenty-Five

The best part of Giulia's day was getting out of the makeup and skirt. The second best was her niece and nephews not bickering on the drive from school to home. She left the boys playing the latest *Assassin's Creed* and headed to the convent with Cecilia.

Steve the Chihuahua did not disappoint. He limped. He turned big, soulful eyes up to Cecilia. She sat on the stoop and took him into her arms, cooing and petting him. Sister Olive laughed and explained Steve's ruse in the same gentle voice she used with Sister Helena.

"You little weasel." Cecilia put her hands on the dog's face and touched her nose to his. "You live with the Sisters and you think it's okay to lie to people? They should make you do charity work with abandoned cats as penance."

Steve licked her face. Cecilia turned flat on her back and the dog plopped its four-pound self onto her chest. For the first time, Giulia heard Cecilia giggle like the young girl she was.

Sister Olive gave Steve thirty seconds before freeing Cecilia. She deposited the dog onto the hall floor and swatted its behind. Steve yipped and returned to the kitchen.

Bart appeared in the hall. "Hey, Cecilia. I'm so glad you came. The Sisters are looking forward to your visit."

Cecilia held up a manila folder. "I painted some pictures for them in art class."

"You're terrific. Did you forget I never showed you yesterday how to braid puka shells into your hair? We'll have a makeover session after your visit."

Polite Cecilia followed Bart upstairs. Giulia marveled at the transformation.

Sister Olive returned to her usual self. "Come with me."

Giulia followed her down to the cellar, wondering what conspiracy theory evidence was about to be revealed. All the windows broken? Oil-based paint splashed in the washer and dryer? A disheveled teenager tied to the hot water heater?

The nun stalked to the ragged stack of newspapers. "Look."

Two dead rats lay on the floor against the wall.

Giulia went with the straight line. "You set out powerful rat poison."

"We don't use poison because of Steve. You should know that. We've never had a rat in this house. Not even a mouse, because some big, nasty cats roam the neighborhood. Eagle's thugs planted these dead creatures to scare us out."

"How would a saboteur enter the house unnoticed to deposit the rats?"

"You think this old place is air tight? The windows only latch when they feel like it. The floor only looks solid. If I were twenty years younger, I'd crawl into every dark corner down here. I'd bet you anything I'd find a brand new hole in the foundation or a suspicious mound of dirt between two peeling pieces of Linoleum."

Always the professional, Giulia refrained from the obvious comment. The door warden would not appreciate knowing her continual harping on Eagle was having the opposite of its intended effect.

"Sister Olive."

They both turned. Sister Kathryn stood on the bottom step, arms crossed and eyebrows merged into a single disapproving line.

"I was showing our detective the latest gift from—"

"We have no proof the rats are connected to anything other than hungry rodents searching for their next meal."

"We have circumstantial proof. Have you forgotten our last two break-ins?"

"Those were perpetrated by drug addicts looking for money."

"Addicts don't target houses like ours on their own."

"Olive—"

"The rats were planted."

"If you cannot control your unguarded lips I will place you under a vow of silence."

Her subordinate breathed in slowly and heavily. Giulia sympathized with Olive's inner conflict, as she'd had too many similar conflicts back in the day.

Olive said a measured voice, "But you keep your head in all situations, endure hardship, and discharge all the duties of your ministry."

For one second, Giulia thought the Superior was going to slap the door warden. Her nostrils flared. "Be subject to your masters in everything, try to please them, do not talk back to them."

Tension crackled in the air.

"If you were more interested in listening to what we're saying instead of hiding behind your brick wall of authority—"

"If you had any recollection of taking a vow of obedience—"

"A superior is supposed to look after the welfare of her charges."

"Which is exactly what I've been doing all these years."

"The situation has changed. You're supposed to adjust with it."

"I've been adjusting since the day I was appointed Superior of this cross to bear."

"Now you're saying we're your personal crosses?"

Giulia walked between them and up the stairs. Much more of this and she'd want to inaugurate DI's often discussed fifteen percent grief upcharge to the bill, and the nuns couldn't afford it.

Bart and Cecilia weren't in any of the invalid nuns' rooms, so Giulia climbed to the third floor. She followed the sound of conversation to the spare bedroom and got a snootful of cigarette smoke.

"Bart, what are you doing?"

Bart and Cecilia looked up from the bed. Cecilia's hair had been pulled into a partial braid over one shoulder. Bart's fingers were on Cecilia's, threading shells on the loose strands.

"We're ornamenting Cecilia's hair."

"Why are you sneaking cigarettes in the presence of a minor?"

Bart's baffled expression took Giulia aback. "No one smokes here. It's too expensive."

"Smoking will kill you, Aunt Giulia. Everybody knows that. It tastes gross, too." Cecilia's cheeks burned bright red as the words left her mouth.

Giulia didn't bother to roll her eyes. "Tried it in the gym locker room to play tough?"

"Maybe." A small voice.

"I tried in fifth grade. It cured me forever."

"Third grade for me," Bart said. "One of my dad's friends who hung around the gas station let me sneak a puff of an unfiltered Lucky. Disgusting."

Cecilia's eyes and mouth turned into miniature hula hoops.

Giulia softened. "Nuns are human too."

Bart chuckled. "Yes we are. Are you saying you smelled cigarette smoke in the hall or something?"

"Yes. Twice now."

"Someone must be smoking outside and it's blowing through the windows."

Cecilia bounced. "Maybe it's a ghost or something. This is a really old house. Wouldn't a ghost be cool?"

"There's no such thing as ghosts." Giulia controlled her own urge to blush, since she was parroting Sidney rather than expressing her own thoughts.

"Who used to live here, Sister Bart?" Cecilia's voice turned ghoulish. "Maybe there was a murder. Ooh! Maybe there's a dead body buried in the cellar."

Bart finished Cecilia's braid. "We had the cellar floor fixed a few years ago, but maybe there's a secret passage we don't know about."

"The ghost could hide in the passage and make scary noises." Cecilia stood to peer into the tiny mirror next to the dresser. "This is awesome. Thanks, Sister Bart."

Bart winked at Giulia. "I could take Steve up into the attic in the middle of the night. Animals are supposed to be able to sense ghosts."

"Where is he now?" Cecilia ran to the door. "Aunt Giulia, I don't smell anything. Do you? Hey, ghost! Come visit us!"

Giulia glared at Bart. "There is no ghost in this house. Let me prove it to you." She took out her phone and opened the EMF app.

"WEEoooWEEoooWeeoooweeooo..."

Giulia stared at her screen as the jarring sounds faded into silence.

Cecilia glommed onto Giulia's arm. "What's that? What does the noise mean? It sounds like a siren. Is it calling ghosts? Do they answer?"

Bart approached Giulia's phone with slow steps. "Is that a ghost-hunting app?"

Giulia nodded, adjusting the settings. She closed the app, shut off her phone, waited ten seconds, and restarted it. This time when she opened the app, it remained silent.

"Sorry, Cecilia. No ghosts here. Only electronic interference."

Her niece rewarded her with an epic pout. "I've never seen a ghost. It would've been cool."

Twenty-Six

After dinner, when the kids were all at the kitchen table with their homework, Giulia sprung her latest idea on Frank.

"The Attorney General's office?"

Giulia pecked him on the nose. "You are adorable when you're mystified. When the current state Attorney General was running for reelection, he investigated Eagle Developers. Either Eagle is more honest than some people think, or they hired phenomenal lawyers. I'm betting on the latter."

"Because?"

"The Attorney General managed to make only one minor infraction stick. If I've lived a good life, there will be a disgruntled paralegal who expected to use the Eagle case as their boost up the state ladder. I want to convince this person to help me."

Frank's mouth crimped. "You're ringing a bell…" He went to his gaming closet. "Have you seen my iPad?"

She followed him in and pulled it from between *Super Mario* and *The Legend of Zelda*. "Have you considered bringing your games into the twenty-first century?"

He clutched his chest. "You want me to give up my classic discs for a shadow life of online gaming? Never. Old school all the way, baby."

She shook her head. "Forget I said anything."

He stroked the stacks of jewel cases. "Shh. It's okay. Don't listen to her. I'll spend quality time with you when the kids are in bed." He looked around the shelves. "Uh, charger?"

Giulia held up her left hand, cord dangling from her index finger.

"I'm not worthy."

"Far be it from me to argue."

He booted the tablet. The homework session became much too loud. Giulia swooped into the kitchen, physically separated Pasquale and Carlo by the hair, cut Cecilia's smug snarkiness off at the knees,and enlightening each in turn on grammar, algebra, and earth science.

Several minutes later, Frank said, "Aha." Half a minute after that: "Oh, really?" In another two minutes: "Could you stop being right all the time?"

Giulia held an expression of sainted innocence until Frank noticed it.

"Yes, dear. Okay, because Eagle is a local company, your friendly neighborhood detectives were called to give evidence."

"You?" Giulia said.

"No. I was running DI then. Nash was driving a patrol car and fielded some calls from people Eagle was trying to buy out."

Giulia leaned forward. "Could I ask you to ruin his Friday night?"

Frank gave her the side-eye. "Please. Everyone likes you. My boss still wants you to work for him. Of course Nash will help you." He opened his phone to call Nash. "Besides, he's re-grouting his bathroom this weekend. He'll love the interruption...Nash? Frank. Punched a hole in the tile yet?" He laughed. "Wash your hands and find your laptop, would you? The wife needs a favor."

He put the phone on speaker and Giulia explained what she was looking for.

"That was a couple of years ago. I don't remember what I had for breakfast yesterday."

"Two Egg McMuffins and an extra-large coffee with three sugars," Frank said.

"Geez, Driscoll, why don't you just Instagram my life?" Keyboard clicks underscored his words. "Hold on, I'm plowing through my reports."

Giulia said, "I really appreciate your help, Nash. Without you, I'd have to wait until Monday to put in a request for the trial transcripts. Who knows how long the bureaucracy would hold it up?"

"Consider me your personal Freedom of Information Act." More clicks. "Okay. Two years ago we got a series of complaints about Eagle harassing people who were dragging their heels on his buyout offers."

Giulia sat up. "Eagle himself?"

"I don't know. One old couple, two old men, and one single mother. They all described a similar pattern of phone calls. They couldn't prove anything specific against Eagle—the company, not the guy—but when the AG's office launched its investigation into unethical practices, they were extremely thorough."

Giulia wrote bullet points on a smaller sized legal pad. "Marvelous."

"Yeah, but you want a contact. I remember half a name. Something like a butler. Jeeves, but not Jeeves. It began with J, though." Clicks. "Driscoll, our email sort function sucks."

"Is this where I say 'first world problems'?"

"Screw you. Sorry, Giulia."

"Frank has that effect on people."

Nash laughed. Frank pulled a 'sad clown' face and made Giulia laugh.

"Nash, he's pretending to be deeply hurt by our cruel words."

"Not even the rawest police academy grad would fall for his act...Here it is. Man, my brain isn't with it today. Jeremy Butler, assistant to the Attorney General. He was something like third assistant. He got his teeth into the probe like a terrier into a rat."

"Please tell me you have his email."

"Better than that. I have his cell number. He kept after me for more information so he could leapfrog over assistants one and two."

Giulia's pen hovered over the paper. "Since Eagle emerged with the barest smudge on its reputation, I hope Jeremy Butler is still seething with resentment."

Nash spelled out the email and phone number. "He used to call me after hours to dig for more Eagle dirt. The email is part of the public documents. Good thing no one ever wants to read them. Talk about dull."

"Nash, you and your girlfriend are invited for sauce and cannolis any Sunday you care to name."

Twenty-Seven

"Aunt Giulia, we'll clean your house, okay?"

Giulia stared down at her niece and nephews. "Cecilia, you guys did the breakfast dishes."

"Yeah, but you're, like, wicked busy," Pasquale said. "Besides, you're doing all the cooking. Uncle Frank's getting the lawn mower from the garage, right?"

"Yes, but—"

"Cool. I'll mow."

Carlo said, "Cece, I'll vacuum if you dust."

"Okay, I'll start the laundry."

They scattered. Frank came through from the garage a minute later.

"The free labor is an unexpected benefit. Easiest Saturday morning I've had in awhile."

"I'd still rather start with one offspring at a time." Giulia picked up her notes from last night's phone call. "I'm off to cajole an attorney."

She closed herself in their bedroom and dialed the former third assistant to the Attorney General.

"Butler speaking."

"Good morning, Mr. Butler. I'm calling on behalf of Driscoll Investigations."

"I don't represent wife beaters, child abusers, or people who think the Spice Girls have more talent than The Supremes. You have five minutes."

Giulia chose her words to trigger the maximum knee-jerk response. "Our client may be the target of systematic harassment by Eagle Developers as part of a neighborhood redevelopment project."

The tenor voice on the other end cast doubt upon Eagle's parentage, Eagle's manly parts, and the microscopic dimensions of Eagle's principles.

Giulia waited for him to run down. "Mr. Butler, I'd like to meet with you to pick your brain about Eagle Developers."

"You think a rinky-dink private detective agency can bring him down when the AG's office couldn't?"

Giulia remembered that she had yet to meet a lawyer who didn't irritate her worse than a case of poison ivy. "Mr. Butler, are you available to—"

"Hell, yes. What time is it? Nine thirty? Let me check my calendar. Oh, wait, it's Saturday. How soon can you get here? Where are you?"

"Cottonwood."

"Eagle's home base? You'd better come to me. I won't guarantee my veneer of civility if I happen to see the butterball in person."

"I'm happy to accommodate you if you'll give me your address."

"Oh, yeah. I moved last year. I'm in Oakmont now. Got a practice of my own and meet clients on the golf course. It's the life. Can you be at Casey's by one? I'm booked solid next week with depositions and pretrial work."

"I'll be there."

"Bring your appetite. I'll buy you lunch. Anything to help shoot Eagle down."

Twenty-Eight

When Giulia slid into the restaurant booth opposite Jeremy Butler, Esq., she understood why Frank's partner remembered him as "Jeeves." He was as out of place in a modern American restaurant as a starched upper-crust butler would be.

He shook her hand. "Nice to meet you. Go ahead and get it out of your system."

"I beg your pardon?"

He snapped open his menu. "I look like every movie butler from every British costume drama ever filmed."

Giulia gave him a friendly smile. "I've been compared to a poodle by people with more manageable hair."

"My sister has hair so straight you could use it as a plumb bob. Sorry, you told me your company's name but I don't remember yours."

"Giulia Driscoll." She opened her menu.

"Your own business? Nice. I opened mine after I left the AG's office. Because I'm not stupid, I didn't tell him what I thought of the flaccidity of his spine."

The waitress arrived with glasses of water as the piped-in classical music changed to Vivaldi's *The Four Seasons*. Giulia had been forced to wear worse outfits as a waitress than a frilly white apron over a mustard-yellow uniform. When the waitress left with their orders, Giulia placed her phone on the table.

"I'd like to record our conversation. I find it less intrusive than taking notes."

Butler shrugged. "Doesn't bother me as long as we lay some ground rules." When Giulia pressed the record button, Butler the lawyer appeared within the Steelers sweatshirt and jeans. "You can't use anything from this meeting in a legal case unless you bring me in as an adjunct. I want partial credit for taking Eagle down and I want to see his face when it happens."

Giulia made a mental note never to bring Butler and Sister Olive together. Their combined vindictiveness might cause an explosion which would level a city block.

"I accept your conditions. Here are mine."

Their lunch specials arrived. Giulia averted her eyes from Butler's double bacon burger. She couldn't put it off any longer. The balance of her pregnancy would have to be burger-free. Little Zlatan was sending NO NO NO signals at the aroma.

Zlatan was, however, all about tomatoes and cheese. She took a bite of her grilled cheese with tomato and everything in her sighed with contentment. She made another note to herself: Ask Sidney if her psychologist husband had written a paper on the conflation of mother-baby desires in the second trimester.

She got herself back on point. "Harassment may be proved without your evidence and the case settled out of court. If Eagle Developers takes it to court, we agree with your earlier stipulations." He opened his mouth but she continued. "Your fee will have to be negotiated separately with our client."

He paused with the burger halfway to his mouth. "Are you kidding? You get Eagle into a courtroom and my services are pro bono." The burger reached its destination. "Since you bothered to track me down, you know about the fiasco in Harrisburg."

Giulia nibbled a corner of her sandwich. "I know the basics. What will help me is more knowledge of the charges your former office brought against Eagle."

Butler held up his burger. "Food. Eagle knows people, which is the way to get things done. Everybody cultivates the right names to get on a bid list." Another bite disappeared into his mouth, followed by a swig of Coke. "Eagle got himself access to the decision makers. He treated them to meals at restaurants where the check equals a week's worth of groceries."

Giulia led him on. "That's not illegal."

He bared his long teeth. "It is if you charge those meals to your state expense account."

"Oh, dear."

"Yeah. We found thousands of dollars in improper charges. Not only fancy restaurants, but fast food. He claimed his people worked twelve- to eighteen-hour days on projects and feeding them on the account allowed them to keep on deadline."

He signaled for a refill.

The waitress stopped at their booth with an overloaded tray of Cokes, waters, and coffees. As she set down Butler's drink and picked up the empty, a woman pushing a stroller fumbled her baby's bottle and lunged for it. The stroller clipped the waitress' ankles, the tray tilted, and in dreamlike slow motion three cups of steaming coffee and four filled with iced beverages crashed onto their table.

Several things happened at once. Giulia snatched her phone away from the flood, waterproof case or not. Butler must have been a yoga practitioner, because in one smooth motion he was standing on the vinyl bench, last bite of burger inviolate in his hand. The tray followed the cups onto the table. The coffee cups shattered. The plastic glasses bounced left, right, forward, and backward. The mixed hot and iced flood streamed to the back of the booth on Butler's side and drained off the corner.

"Are you okay? Are you burned? Do you need ice?" The waitress called over her shoulder, "Jacky! Towels!"

Giulia checked her clothes. Only a few splatters. Butler's showed the same. Two bus boys popped up on either side of the waitress armed with broom, dustpan, gray dish bucket, and an armful of towels.

"We're fine," Giulia said. "We were almost finished anyway." As she squeezed past the cleaning operation she heard laughter and applause from nearby diners.

She raised her voice. "Did your mothers teach you to make fun of other people's accidents?"

The applause dwindled and died. The laughter too. The scrape of broken glass and the squelching of soaked towels were the only sounds for a long moment. Then a different waitress banged open the door from the kitchen and the other patrons returned in silence to their food.

Giulia's waitress smiled. "Thanks."

"Been there."

"The booth behind you is clear. I'll bring dessert on the house."

They sat. Giulia set her phone on the dry surface. "We were talking about padded expense accounts."

Twenty-Nine

Butler waved away her words. "We're moving on to bid-rigging and bribes."

Giulia smiled sweetly at the twenty-something couple passing them, who had been among the loudest applauders. They didn't meet her eyes.

"Numbers?" she said to Butler.

"Two hundred thousand in bribes to state suppliers. Twenty-five thousand in donations to the governor's reelection campaign. Magically, two no-bid contracts were awarded to Eagle."

A plate with slices of cake and pie arrived. They both requested decaf.

Giulia said, "With such an abundance of evidence, how did the AG's office not obtain a conviction?"

Butler's face could have curdled the milk in his coffee. "Technically, we did. Two counts of underbidding on state contracts, not the magical ones. One fifteen-thousand-dollar fine and one successful reelection campaign." He stabbed a fork into a slice of chocolate cake. "Eagle reached into his deep pockets and put together a team of lawyers that could've gotten Lucifer out on parole. I took notes. They twisted witness's words. They manipulated the jurors' minds. They painted a halo on Eagle's shiny head and it stuck."

Giulia convinced Zlatan that cherry pie was almost as good as strawberry. "Did they play the 'Eagle creates jobs and boosts the economy' card?"

"You got it. The governor sent us a polite letter of commendation for our efforts." He caught the waitress's eye. "Check, please. Working for the AG went to hell. My blood pressure shot up and I was mainlining antacids. I called two of my law school buds and we went indie. Doing pretty well now, if I do say so myself."

The waitress stopped by. "No charge. Sorry about the mess."

"Thanks." He finished his coffee. "I won't ask you for details on Eagle's latest games."

"I wouldn't give them to you."

"You PIs are all alike." He tossed three dollars on the table.

Giulia added a five. "Thank you for your information."

"Remember, get Eagle into court and I'm all yours."

Polite Smile Number One was her only answer.

Thirty

"Frank, tell me why all lawyers make me look for a trail of slime in their wake?"

Giulia sat on the edge of the tub, soaking her feet. The kids had joined the street soccer game and a casserole was in the oven.

"They're not all like that." Frank sat behind her, hands on her belly. "Was that a kick?"

"I didn't feel it."

"Maybe he's giving me a dad-only special."

She swished her feet in the water. "Butler's data dovetails with everything the nuns have been saying."

"Not surprised. Eagle didn't rise to the top by running his company as a charity."

"I'm too tired to make a speech about how honest businesses also succeed."

"Consider it given." A pause. "Now that was a kick."

She suppressed a sigh. "I didn't feel it."

"Your feet are distracting you."

The front door banged. "Is supper ready? We're starving?"

"What time is it?"

Frank checked his watch. "Twenty after five."

"Ten minutes," Giulia called. She drained the water and dried off. "Fair warning: I'm going to be nagging you for important details about your half of this project."

He handed her fresh socks. "My half?"

"Autopsy results. Criminal activity stats."

He kissed her. "The romance has not yet gone out of our marriage."

Thirty-One

The ringing phone dragged Giulia up from a dream of the invalid nuns living under a bridge begging for candy canes to hang on a dead Christmas tree they found while dumpster diving.

"H'lo?"

"He's dead." The voice on the other end was breathy with panic. "He's dead."

Giulia snapped awake. "Bart? What happened?"

"He's dead. He's in the cellar. Oh, God."

"What? Who's dead?"

"I don't know. I don't know. Oh, God, his face was—it was all—"

"Bart, I'll be there in fifteen minutes. Do you hear me?"

"Yes."

"Say it back to me."

"You'll be here in fifteen minutes." Bart's voice came through a smidge steadier. "The fire's out."

"What fire?"

"The cellar was on fire when I found him."

"Call 911 right now." She was out of bed and opening her dresser drawers when Frank joined her.

"What's up?"

"Someone broke into the convent. Bart doesn't know who, but she thinks he's dead. She's panicking. I'm going over there now."

Frank stepped out of his pajama bottoms. "I'll come with you."

They stopped moving and said at the same time: "The kids."

"You stay," Frank said. "If they need someone they're more used to you."

"No. You have to stay. I can get into any room in the convent. You can't without a chaperone."

"*Och i gcuntas Dé.* You're right."

She pecked his nose. "I love it when you say that. Do I love what you said before it?"

"I said 'Oh, for God's sake.' Does it meet with your approval?"

"Teach it to Cecilia, please. Don't wait up. This could take awhile."

Red and blue lights from police cars, fire trucks, and ambulances threw rotating colors over the empty houses on the nuns' block. Giulia found a parking spot five houses down from the convent.

Despite the neighborhood being a ghost town, a couple dozen living people crowded the sidewalk. They kept a few hundred feet away from the emergency vehicles, speculating and pointing and taking pictures with their phones. Giulia skirted the edge of the gawkers and stepped over a firehose.

Two firefighters were hosing down the side of the house. Several voices yelled instructions back and forth over the sound of the water. The radios in the police cars squawked. Giulia worked her way to the front door around the equipment crisscrossing the sidewalk and street. A uniformed police officer was interviewing Sister Olive. Steve was nowhere in sight.

Sister Olive reached out an imperious hand as soon as she caught sight of Giulia. The officer blocked her access with one arm.

"I'll have to ask you to stay behind the barriers, ma'am. This is an active crime scene."

He appeared to be unacquainted with Sister Olive.

"Officer, Ms. Driscoll is our advocate. We insist she be present during every interview."

When he turned to look at Giulia, his face rang a vague bell. "Sorry, Ms. Driscoll. I didn't realize it was you. You're a lawyer too?"

She smiled at him. "I'm not. They've retained me as their Private Investigator."

Two different local news vans screeched to a stop before they hit the fire truck on one side and the knot of spectators on the other.

"Which means we require her advice in tonight's situation." Sister Olive pulled Giulia into the hall. The officer squeezed himself in before the door warden performed her duty by shutting out the night.

"I'd lock it if I could, but the firefighters need access. Come on, you have to see what happened."

The officer followed them downstairs, trying to finish his interview with Sister Olive. It wasn't working.

The few cellar lights appeared much brighter with no daylight to compete against. At first, all Giulia saw was two inches of water sloshing around the floor. The farther downstairs she came, more of the activity became visible. A forensics team gathered samples in test tubes and envelopes. An older woman with a camera took pictures of something on the wall by the hot water heater. An odd stink hit Giulia's nose. It wasn't gasoline or kerosene or the smoke from a candle wick, but something had started a fire.

"Look." Olive pointed to the window next to the hot water heater.

Giulia saw the difference in the stack of newspapers first. It was charred and smoking. Mingled with it were pieces of cardboard boxes, frayed sheeting material, and the warped end of a plastic water bottle. Her eyes traveled up to the open window. Hanging half-in, half-out of the window was a pudgy a man or woman in a long-sleeved black shirt. Well, the burned remnants of a long-sleeved shirt. White detritus clung to the few parts of the body, the wall, and the water heater not yet drowned from the fire hose. Half of his or her hair had been fried off, including the visible eyebrow.

As had half the face. Giulia swallowed hard several times. She didn't recall when the young officer behind her had stopped expostulating.

"Why—" She cleared her throat. "Why try to burn down a convent?"

The camera flashed. A firefighter clomped downstairs and brushed past with an "Excuse me."

Olive said in Giulia's ear, "You're not thinking."

The forensics team started packing up. The photographer looked around the cellar and spied the uniformed officer. "We're all finished here. Found his wallet. Fell out of his pants. The detectives here yet?"

"I don't know. I'll tell the coroner you're done." He ascended to the first floor at a rapid clip.

Giulia forced herself to stop staring at the torched, weeping eye.

Without that distraction, she studied the shape of the body and the remains of a long brown ponytail on a bald head.

Victor Eagle turned out not to be as savvy as his publicity implied. She turned away and said to Olive, "We have to talk."

Thirty-Two

Frank and Nash came down the stairs as Giulia and Sister Olive came up.

"I called your sister-in-law. She picked up the minivan yesterday so she was able to drive to our place. She's bunking on the couch."

Giulia jerked a thumb over her shoulder. "It's not pretty down there."

Frank stared hard at his wife. "You okay?"

"I'm still vertical."

He continued downstairs. Giulia took the lead and headed for the kitchen. Bart and a different uniformed officer sat at the table. The teakettle shrieked on the stove. Giulia turned off the gas and found mugs and the box of tea bags. She poured water over the bags and pushed one mug into Bart's hands. The young nun's trembling hands clutched the warm stoneware without looking down at it.

Olive took a mug for herself and handed another to Giulia before scooting a chair next to Bart. The door warden said nothing as Bart leaned against her. For Bart's sake, Giulia didn't relieve her own stress by pointing out to Olive her irascible mask was slipping.

A third uniformed officer manning the front door yelled before slamming it shut, "Get off the lawn or we'll arrest you for obstructing an investigation."

His voice got louder as he approached the kitchen. "Three news trucks blocking the street now. There're more people outside than live in a five-block radius from here. I expect food trucks to pull up next. Andy, give me a hand, will you?"

When he left the room, Giulia reached across the table and touched Bart's hands. "You found the body?"

Bart raised her head. "I'm a light sleeper. Even though everyone on the streets knows me, there's always a chance some random junkie will decide Crankenstein looks beat up on purpose to hide gobs of cash, like I told you." Her voice trembled along with her hands. "I heard a voice. I couldn't tell if it was a man or a woman. I picked up the baseball bat we keep by the back door."

"Why?"

Olive said, "You're not thinking again."

Bart kneaded the mug. "Diane and I are the stars of the annual Catholic Charities softball game. Either of us can break an arm or a kneecap."

"Disabling a criminal doesn't contravene our principles of non-violence." Sister Olive plucked the tea bag from Bart's mug and pushed the mug and Bart's hands to Bart's lips.

Bart looked at her hands like they belonged to someone else but sipped the hot liquid. "I checked this floor first, but all the doors and windows were locked."

Two EMTs carried a stretcher into the house and down to the cellar. Everyone at the table turned to watch their progress. More voices reached the kitchen through the open front door, but their words were unintelligible. A firefighter stomped through the hall and stopped in the kitchen doorway.

"Would you Sisters have a ladder we could use?"

"I'll show you where we keep it." Olive led him to a utility closet off the kitchen and he carried a step ladder down to the cellar.

Bart couldn't seem to look away even after the ladder vanished. "When I didn't find anything, I opened the cellar door. I smelled something burning so I ran for the fire extinguisher under the kitchen sink." She shuddered. Sister Olive took the mug from her hands as it tipped. "I saw flames under the window and emptied the extinguisher onto them. I didn't see him right away."

Giulia said in a quiet voice, "Did you check to see if he was alive?"

Bart gasped, giggled, and lost it. She rocked back and forth in the wooden chair, laughing and hiccupping. Tears ran down her face.

Giulia went to the sink and poured a small glass of water. With the dish towel in her left hand, she returned to the table and dashed the water in Bart's face. Bart gave a louder gasp, hiccupped once more, and the laughter stopped. She stared up at Giulia through beaded eyelashes. Giulia handed her the dish towel.

As Bart wiped her face in silence, Giulia heard a voice outside the kitchen door. She hadn't paid any attention to the door and now saw it was ajar. As she sidled along the far wall, the opening revealed Ken Kanning's eyes shining in the moonlight. He spoke in an undertone at a rapid clip, his smooth voice promising delightful scandal to *The Scoop*'s viewers. Pit Bull, *The Scoop*'s cameraman, adjusted its light as Giulia watched.

She did not slam the door because slamming it would've ramped up Kanning's "fox hunting chickens" method of reporting. Instead, she shut and locked it as though she were merely trying to keep out the night air. As an added precaution, she checked that all the blinds in the kitchen were closed.

"What are you doing?" Olive said.

"*The Scoop* is lurking outside."

"Who?" Bart said.

"Really? I love their show." Olive turned toward the door, but its small curtains were drawn.

Giulia fist-bumped a befuddled Bart. To Olive, she said, "We'll have to agree to disagree."

"But you were great on the Doomsday Cult episode."

Loud noises came from the front hall. Giulia put her forehead on the table. "Faster than a slamming door. More powerful than a restraining order. Able to leap any barrier in a single bound." Scuffling sounds joined the voices in the hall. "It's a skunk. It's a leech."

Ken Kanning and Pit Bull leapt into the kitchen.

"It's *The Scoop*," Olive said.

Sister Agatha's wails billowed down the stairs, cutting off all conversation.

Thirty-Three

"*The Scoop* never sleeps! Despite the misguided efforts of flatfoot cops and firemen with nothing better to do, we're in the Convent of the Assumption in the dead of night—literally."

Kanning gestured and Pit Bull swung the camera to the kitchen clock, then back to his boss.

Even in the dead of night Kanning's hair radiated perfection. His teeth stopped just short of gleaming. His button-down shirt, open at the collar, conveyed the impression of a pressured executive working overtime for the good of the project.

"These women of God have been dragged from their ceaseless prayers by Criminals In Our Midst." He gestured again and Pit Bull aimed the camera at Sister Olive's open mouth. "Sister, could you tell our faithful Scoopers what's happening?"

Dorothy came running down the stairs. "Is there any cocoa left?" She skidded to a stop as the camera's light hit her full in the face. One hand went up to smooth her hair.

"I'll make some." Bart pushed herself up from the table.

Olive snapped out of her stupor. "I'll tell you what got us out of our beds in the middle of the night. Victor Eagle himself is stuck in our cellar window like Winnie the Pooh. He tried to burn us out of our home but set himself on fire instead."

Kanning threw off sparks like a Fourth of July firecracker. His hair stood on end for an instant before he oozed closer to the table.

Dorothy said, "You're Ken Kanning."

The Smile beamed on her. "I am, Sister. *The Scoop* is here to champion the underdog and to do our part to ensure might doesn't automatically equal right."

Sister Olive applauded. Giulia suppressed a groan.

"We watch your show whenever we get the chance." Another wail from the second floor interrupted Dorothy. She closed her eyes for a moment.

Bart waved a plastic tray with penguins dancing around the edge. "Two minutes until the water boils."

Kanning's gaze flicked to Bart and back to Olive. He took Bart's abandoned chair and aimed the microphone at the door warden. "Sister—?"

"Olive. I've been a Franciscan for fifty-three years. That's Sister Dorothy, who takes care of our invalid Sisters. At the sink is Sister Bartholomew." She straightened her posture. "What do you know about Eagle Developers buying out this entire block and the next for its latest whim?"

Kanning lapped it up. He gestured for Dorothy to sit with them and she came like a star-struck teenager with a backstage pass.

Giulia helped Bart scoop—no, spoon, a much better word—cocoa into four mugs. The instant steam escaped the kettle's spout, Bart shut off the gas.

"I don't want to interfere with the news," she whispered.

"They're not the news." Giulia matched her whisper. She didn't want Kanning the lamprey glomming onto still-shaken Bart. She stirred the cocoa until it dissolved.

Bart brought out the milk and added a little to each mug. "Helps us pretend it's not the extra-thin bargain basement kind."

The other nuns were telling Kanning about Sister Matilda's sudden death when the EMTs brought the intruder's body up from the cellar. Giulia said a silent prayer of thanks the face was covered.

Bart shuddered and turned away. When she faced the room again, the tray was in her hands. It shook a bit as she stepped forward. Giulia relieved her of it before disaster occurred.

"Sister Dorothy, the cocoa's ready. Would you like me to bring it upstairs?"

Kanning's eyes tried to bore holes into Giulia as his unspoken questions dive-bombed her: Why are you here? Who's your client? Can I trick you into giving something away because it's late and you're probably tired?

Dorothy ran a hand through her hair again. "I'll take it."

Kanning slithered in. "Let me, please."

Olive shook her head. "This is a convent."

Dorothy sagged. "He's a visitor. It's been done before."

Kanning lit up like a slot machine with a jackpot. "We're preparing a show on Eagle Developers. Sister Olive's given us some incredibly useful information, but we can never have enough of the human element." He leaned on the table, closing the short distance between himself and his target. "If you'll allow us some brief footage of your bedridden nuns, we're certain to gain sympathy for your cause."

"What a great idea." Olive beamed at Pit Bull, since Kanning's attention wasn't on her.

A third wail reached them, longer and louder than the others. Dorothy winced. "Let me make sure everyone's properly dressed."

Kathryn opened the back door. "Sister Bartholomew, the detectives want to talk to you." The briefest pause. "I asked the police to keep reporters out of our house."

Pit Bull lowered the camera. Kanning dialed his charm meter up to nine. "Sister, we're *The Scoop*. We're so much more than the mainstream news."

Giulia watched the Superior's expression also become "fangirl" for a moment before resuming its authority. "Mr. Kanning, I would have preferred to meet you under less trying circumstances."

Olive interrupted. "He's already got his eyes on Eagle. He's on our side. Wait until you hear his plans."

Giulia nudged Bart. "Get out while he's distracted. The detectives are Frank and his partner. You'll be fine. Go."

Bart went. Dorothy came to the foot of the stairs. "You can come up now."

Giulia handed Kanning the cocoa tray. When he and Pit Bull were out of sight, she said to the Superior, "I'll keep an eye on them, but they're not stupid. They'll treat the Sisters with respect because it will make good television."

She ran upstairs. Pit Bull's camera panned the stairwell and the hall. Kanning carried the tray of mugs like an offering into Helena's room. Dorothy glanced around and muttered, "At least Olive kept out of it this time."

"This is Ken Kanning and his cameraman, Sister Helena. They're the TV show called *The Scoop*."

The bedridden nun's eyes widened and her mouth worked itself into an upward grimace.

"They'd like to interview us as part of an episode on that developer."

Garbled sounds came from Helena's mouth. The nurse dipped a teaspoon into one of the mugs and held it to her charge's lips to drink.

Ken Kanning proceeded to do the impossible: Impress Giulia. He modulated his voice into a semblance of gentleness and asked very few questions. Dorothy translated the replies, but Kanning appeared to win Helena's heart by maintaining eye contact with her as though he understood every syllable. At the end of the interview, he took her knotted hand with a courtly gesture.

Giulia caught Dorothy's eye and pointed to herself, then to Kanning. The nurse nodded.

"Mr. Kanning," Giulia said, "let me introduce you to the second of the three retired Sisters."

Kanning blew all the ground he'd gained by winking at Giulia like they were a team. Eugenie forestalled any reaction from Giulia by wheeling herself into the hall.

"Ken Kanning in our convent? You, Ms. Driscoll, take our picture. I'm going to frame it when you send me a print of it." She bumped Kanning's legs with the chair. "Come down here next to me, Mr. Kanning. You're the only celebrity I've ever met."

The Scoop never turned down a fan's request. Eugenie's smile rivaled Kanning's in brilliance. Giulia took three shots with her phone, just in case.

"Now all of you come into my room so the noise doesn't disturb us. Don't worry about the proprieties, you men. I'm too old and you're too famous for anyone to think inappropriate thoughts about us."

Giulia joined *The Scoop* in the bedroom. The combination of Sister Agatha's wails, the fire truck's idling engine, and various shouts from the emergency personnel still on the grounds made conversation difficult. She closed the window.

Pit Bull took an establishing shot of the room before he and Kanning each got down on one knee.

Eugenie wasted no time. "First of all, why are you wasting your lives in Cottonwood? You need to go national. *TMZ* is celebrity gossip. You're real news. You're ripe for a larger audience."

Giulia was certain only the remaining ambient noise kept her from hearing Kanning purr. Eugenie and Olive were joined at the hip when it came to Eagle Developers, and Kanning got his easiest interview of the night. Eugenie started with Sister Matilda's death and backtracked through the harassment stories. Kanning interjected an occasional syllable and let the conspiracy theories flow.

The fire truck drove away at the same time Dorothy appeared in the doorway.

"Mr. Kanning, it's nearly three a.m. and our Sisters need their rest."

He took the hint and concluded the interview.

"Don't forget to print out the picture," Sister Eugenie said to Giulia.

"I'll bring it later today."

Kanning invaded Giulia's personal space. "Who's the dead guy? Or is it a dead woman? A renegade nun trying to torch the place out of revenge?" He said over his shoulder to his cameraman, "Bull, we may want to add a terrorist angle to the intro."

Dorothy joined them in the hallway, rubbing her bloodshot eyes. Her face had a gray tinge. Giulia wished she could order the nun to bed and take over *Scoop*-wrangling duties.

"Thank you for your help, Ms. Driscoll." She led them to the door at the end of the hall. "Mr. Kanning, let me explain about our third invalid. Sister Agatha has advanced Alzheimer's. In addition to the usual symptoms, it manifests vocally." She raised her voice over the moans coming from the other side of the door. "Tonight's events have unsettled her. She may not be able to address you." Her hand grasped the doorknob. "If this is the case, please follow my lead in exiting the room."

"We'll take our cue from you, Sister."

Ken Kanning had never sounded so compliant. Giulia turned her head to hide a smile.

When Sister Dorothy opened the door the moans hit them with physical force. The camera's light made a wide circle on the pillow. The bedridden nun's eyes narrowed to slits.

"Is it possible to dim your light?" Dorothy hurried around to the other side of the bed and shielded her charge's face.

"Sure. Sorry about that." Pit Bull lowered the camera and adjusted the settings.

The moans stopped as the invalid pushed her nurse's hands away. Pit Bull raised the camera to his shoulder.

Sister Agatha said in a clear voice, "Clarence Finch, why did you desecrate your body with tattoos?"

Thirty-Four

Giulia and Ken Kanning stared at Pit Bull. Pit Bull and Sister Dorothy stared at Sister Agatha.

Pit Bull broke the tableau first. "You're *that* Sister Agatha?"

A fresh groan started and stopped. The watery eyes blinked and opened wider. "Clarence, why haven't I seen you in church for a month?"

Pit Bull aimed a helpless look at the nurse.

"She's been like this for the last four years." Sister Dorothy kept her voice low.

Kanning never wasted time recovering from a surprise. "Bull, you know her?"

"She was my sixth-grade teacher."

Sister Agatha was still staring at Pit Bull. "Well, young man? I'm waiting for your answer."

In a voice nothing like his usual efficient responses, Pit Bull said, "I work for TV now, Sister. My job, uh, if there's a breaking news story I have to, that is, I'm supposed to be available to cover it."

His tone of voice gave Giulia flashbacks to her years in the classroom. The forty-something tattooed biker dwindled into the schoolboy caught cheating.

"If you're here then you will film me next. Where is my veil? I can't be seen without my veil." She pointed a broad finger at the nurse. "Bring me my veil."

As Dorothy opened drawers, Ken Kanning moved between Giulia and the bed.

"Sister, I'm Ken Kanning, the voice of *The Scoop*. We're here tonight for—"

"Your teeth are false." Sister Agatha dismissed him with a gesture toward the opposite wall. "Go away. I want Clarence, not you."

Giulia pushed her face into her arm and almost choked turning laughter into a sneeze.

"Here we are." Dorothy worked a short modern veil over the invalid's loose wimple. "You're all covered now."

Pit Bull raised the camera into position and the red recording light appeared. "What do you want to say, Sister?"

She raised her index finger. "Remember to keep the principles I've taught you. Summer is a source of temptation. Your biggest temptation will be to slack off." The finger began to shake. "You didn't think I knew that...that slang..." Her voice shook now. "But I'm not too old...old..." The vowel elongated into a low moan.

Kanning and Pit Bull glanced at each other. Before they could make a decision, the moan turned back into words.

"I can't make you attend Mass when you're on vacation, but you know your duty to God and your family. You need the stability and inspiration more than ever. You...you need...you..."

This time when the moans returned her eyes closed and her head sank into the pillow. Pit Bull glanced at Kanning, who held up one hand in a decreasing five count. When his last finger closed into a fist, the cameraman's hand flicked the switch to "off."

"This is great copy," Kanning said. "We'll do you Sisters proud. For the moment, is there a bathroom I could use?"

Dorothy pushed herself off the wall. "I'll escort you."

Everyone filed out. When Kanning closed himself in the half bath between two of the bedrooms, Pit Bull maneuvered in front of Giulia.

"What's going on?"

Giulia gave nothing away. "Victor Eagle died in a break-in and arson attempt."

His expression was much ruder than his words. "You know what I mean."

"Mr. Bull, we are not working together."

"Yeah, yeah, you've said it before. Look, meet me for breakfast, okay?"

"You and your camera and your boss?"

"No. Me and you. Nobody else. The Pine Duff Diner on—"

"On the corner of Pine and Oak. I know it." She weighed the benefits of insight into *The Scoop* with her ability to fence while sleep deprived. "It's three fifteen now. I'll meet you there at seven."

Ken Kanning's charm hadn't flagged. Shepherded by Dorothy, he walked toward Giulia and Pit Bull, sympathy creating one transient wrinkle on his forehead.

"Bull, the Sister has graciously agreed to a brief interview."

The camera was up and running as soon as Kanning said the magic word. Eugenie wheeled herself into the shot. Kanning began with a heartwarming introduction and in the same sweet voice asked Dorothy, "Do you think this event tonight is related to the dreadful death of your fellow Sister?"

"Yes." Eugenie beckoned Pit Bull's lens down to her. "The connection is obvious to anyone with reasoning powers."

Dorothy temporized. "I think it would be wise to avoid speculation until the police have investigated further."

Giulia had reached her Daily Kanning Limit an hour ago. She headed downstairs where Frank and Nash were finishing with the Superior. Surprise filled Kathryn's face when she saw Giulia.

"Are those men still upstairs?" Her practiced authority asserted itself. "Help me get rid of them, please."

Giulia's fatigue abated. "With pleasure."

Years of getting booted into the street apparently gave Kanning a sixth sense of when he'd worn out his welcome. He wrapped up his double interview as soon as the combined forces of Giulia and the Superior reached the second floor.

The Scoop left as they'd entered, by the back door. Only then did Giulia remember Steve the Chihuahua.

"Your deceptive dog missed his chance to perform for the camera."

Olive said from the cellar doorway, "He's cowering behind the fridge. See his tail? Tonight was too many strangers and too much noise for his sensitive soul."

Bart coaxed the dog out with a Milk-Bone. "I wish I could hide when I want to."

Giulia sat next to her on the kitchen floor. "How are you holding up?"

A breathy laugh. "I sprayed a dead guy with CO_2. The only thing I want in the world right now is an obscene amount of Jack Daniels to keep me from dreaming. And being obedient to my vow of poverty, it's the one thing I can't have."

Thirty-Five

Giulia slapped her phone until the alarm stopped. Frank didn't even stir beside her. Her head fell back on her soft, welcoming pillow and she closed her eyes.

Five minutes later the snooze alarm startled her into sitting straight up. This time she shut down both alarm and snooze functions and did not lay down again.

When they'd finally returned home from the convent crime scene at four a.m. they'd been so exhausted they fell on the bed fully clothed. Anne's couch-shaking snores from the couch downstairs didn't keep them awake more than a minute.

Now Giulia stumbled to the bathroom unrested, wrinkled, and somehow feeling grimy. She left her clothes in a pile on the bathroom floor and brushed her teeth, took a four-minute shower, then brushed her teeth again.

No one stirred in the spare room when she padded from the bathroom back to her bedroom. Frank's only movement had been to sprawl across both sides of the bed. With minimal noise she pulled on a shirt and the loosest pair of pants she owned.

The Pine Duff Diner was only half full at seven a.m. on a Sunday. Pit Bull waved her over to a booth by a window facing the side parking lot. Giulia approved the choice. Passersby on the street-facing sidewalk wouldn't notice them.

"You're not late. I came early. Gonna need a lot of extra coffee to function today." He drained the mug in front of him and caught the waitress's eye.

"Good morning." Giulia slid into the padded vinyl seat across from him and picked up a menu.

"Got any juicy insider details you can share? Like did that nun with the braids off Eagle herself?"

She set down the menu. "Mr. Bull, if you requested this meeting to pry information from me, I'll leave now."

His hand reached out, but stopped before touching her. "Don't go. Sorry. Force of habit in the news business." He held up his menu. "Their home fries are a national treasure."

She accepted the change-of-subject peace offering. "So I've heard."

The waitress refilled Pit Bull's coffee. "A fine Sunday morning at the Pine Duff to you, Miss. This charmer would marry me if I slipped him our home fries recipe, but my mama always told me to keep the men guessing. So what can I get for you besides an order of home fries?"

Giulia wondered if Sidney knew she had a long-lost twin. The waitress was a little shorter and a little darker, but the level of perkiness was all Sidney. Giulia's morning improved.

"May I add coffee and one egg over easy?"

"Absolutely." She took both menus. "Your usual's already frying up, Tat-Man."

"You know the way to my heart, baby."

An old man turned on his stool at the counter. "You never flirt like that with me, Glenny."

"Jonesy, you're like a cat. You only sweet-talk me when you want freebies."

"You're too smart for me." He held out his mug. "Let's start with coffee."

"'Long as you pay for it."

When the waitress attended to her other customers, Giulia went on the attack. "How long before your boss shows up here for breakfast? Not that his arrival would have been planned, of course."

The cameraman shook his head. "We're not ambushing you. He doesn't know about this meeting."

Giulia reserved judgment. "Mr. Bull, what did you want to talk to me about?"

His nose wrinkled. "Call me Bull, would you?"

She drew back a fraction. "Perhaps I should say Mr. Finch?"

He grimaced. "I had my name legally changed when I graduated high school." His shoulder muscles bunched. "I was bullied something fierce in school. Sister Agatha taught me to defend myself."

Glenny approached, balancing three plates on her arms. "Here you go." Her left hand gripped the plastic handle of a round-bellied coffee pot. "Home fries and one over easy. If you ask for ketchup we'll have to show you the door." A wink softened the ultimatum. "Sunday Morning Special for you, Tat-Man." Before Pit Bull she set one plate with hash browns, sausages, and roasted tomatoes and a second with a stack of pancakes.

"Marry me."

"And leave paradise on earth?" She poured coffee into both mugs. "You need anything else, holler. Like those guys."

She jerked her head toward the rest of the diner. From three different tables came "Glenny, I'm dying from hunger." "Coffee, Glenny, coffee." "We're out of pancakes, Glenny."

Giulia grinned at her. "As long as they don't cheap out on the tip."

The waitress high-fived Giulia. "An extra good morning to a Sister in the Sorority of Arch Support."

"Not for a few years, but you never forget."

When she faced her breakfast, Pit Bull had already demolished two sausages and was sawing through pancakes so fluffy they should have been strapped to the plate lest they float away. Since he wasn't going to talk for a minute, she tasted the celebrated home fries. The stories didn't exaggerate. Even the coffee was almost good enough to be worth half her daily ration.

The circle of pancakes became a half moon before the cameraman slowed down. "My dad ditched us when I was born. My mom slammed her junker car into a city plow when I was seven." A mirthless smile. "Kids, don't drink and drive." He raised his coffee and downed half the scalding beverage in one gulp. "Tam and I got passed around foster homes for the next eleven years. I've been told some foster homes aren't practice for your time being tortured in Purgatory to expiate your sins. We weren't so lucky."

Giulia sliced her egg with her fork. If Pit Bull was making this up to win her to *The Scoop*'s side, he was working hard at it. He must know she could check up on his story using his real name.

Another quarter of the pancakes vanished. "Tam mixed vodka and Ecstasy at her senior prom and the loving couple pocketing money from the state for 'raising' me didn't bother to tell me about the first phone call from the ER. The gutless wonders she got foisted off on found a conscience and called me themselves. I got to the hospital in time to hold her hand while she died." He raised his voice. "Glenny. Coffee."

Like a rabbit from a magician's hat, the waitress materialized fresh coffee into his mug. "You ready for a refill, sister?"

It would be too much of a distraction from the purpose of this breakfast to explain why calling Giulia 'sister' was funny. "Thank you, no. I'm good."

He swallowed a tomato. "I've got to remember to eat these first. They're better hot. So you're thinking I'm giving you a sob story so you'll get all motherly on me or something. Yeah, I'm older than you, but you know what I mean."

She finished the egg. "The thought occurred to me."

"Ken thinks that way. Don't get mad. You're nothing like Ken, but you both have analytical minds." Another tomato. "I'm telling you this because of Sister Agatha. The people who got me when I was eleven finagled extra money to send me to Catholic school. You should've seen me then. I was half a foot shorter than most of the class, I weighed about fifty pounds, and I had thick, cheap hipster glasses before hipsters were a thing."

Giulia tried and failed to picture this tattooed six foot plus of solid muscle as the "before" half of one of those ads about bulking up to gain confidence. She used her energy on the home fries instead.

"Do they live up to the hype?" He pointed to her plate with his fork.

"They do." She turned in the booth to view the rest of the diner. "I can see why every seat in this place is filled now." She stabbed another forkful. "You were telling me about your first year in Catholic school. Did your sister pass when you were in Sister Agatha's homeroom?"

"No. Sorry. I'm telling things out of order. Tam was a year older than me. We were in different high schools because the families we bunked with lived across town from each other. You'd think the system would check to see if a brother and sister wanted to be together."

When Giulia didn't gush sympathy, he continued. "Sister Agatha's class was my first and only year in Catholic hell. The school was small enough for the nuns to know most of our names, but big enough to play host to multiple bullies. I got the jocks. Their refined sensibilities expressed their offense at my underdeveloped physique by beating the shit out of me once a week after gym class. They were just smart enough to keep the bruises to places the school uniform would cover."

Years of experience with talkative witnesses helped Giulia keep her mouth closed. She wasn't interested in Pit Bull's history. She was interested in augmenting her scant two hours' sleep. The word prompted a yawn, which she stifled.

He stacked his empty plates. "Back then Sister Agatha was one of the cool nuns. She played basketball. She brought sandwiches from the convent kitchen to supplement lunches for kids like me. She liked Prince and Duran Duran and U2. Kids with Walkmans would share their headphones with her before school." He swirled the remaining coffee in his mug. "I was one of the low-key problem kids. I kept quiet, but I slacked off on tests and homework. One day she kept me after school and read me the riot act. The day before had been one of the worst weekly after-gym beatings and I'd had enough. I told her exactly what I thought of her school, her God, and her opinions." A warped smile. "I remember blowing a great exit line by banging my leg against the corner of her desk, right where bully number one had kicked me with his hard leather wingtip shoe. I hit the floor and only shut up because I didn't want to blubber in front of a nun."

Glenny performed her rabbit and hat trick again. "Y'all finished? More coffee? Pie?"

Little Zlatan perked up. Giulia said with reluctance, "Pie?"

"Apple or strawberry? Baked last night so all the flavors are at peak blending."

"A slice of strawberry, please." She intended to pay for her own breakfast, so adding pie didn't trigger any guilt.

Pit Bull waited. The pie appeared in less than a minute. If Giulia harbored matchmaker tendencies, these two might be a job for the famous Dolly Levi. It was perceptive of Glenny to discern Giulia wasn't a romantic threat.

"I won't say our pie is better than our home fries because the boss would fire me, but it's a close second." She scooped whipped cream from a stainless steel bowl. "We serve the real thing here. No soybean and chemical concoctions at the Pine Duff. Enjoy."

Giulia scooped the first bite. Zlatan wriggled with happiness. Her attention dived inward. She'd felt Zlatan wriggle. Her hand reached for her phone to text Frank, but stopped. Not at this hour. He must still be asleep. Besides, she was working.

Pit Bull was saying something. She dragged herself back to the reason for her presence in this vinyl booth.

"...she kept telling me to take off my pants and I kept telling her she was a pervert. To shut her up I told her what my school days were really like." He tipped his mug upside down and stuck his tongue under it to catch the last drops of coffee. "She backed off and I dragged myself into my chair, the kind with a desk attached. I rubbed the giant bruise to get the throbbing to slow down. After a few minutes, I realized she still wasn't talking. When I looked up at her, she was writing something. She shoved it across her desk at me and told me to go home."

"I have experience with organized bullying. Let me guess. She didn't force you to go to the nurse and she didn't go after the bullies."

The wry face reappeared. "I forgot you used to be a teacher. Right on both counts. The note was for my foster assholes telling them she required my services for an after-school job." His expression became nostalgic. Some of the strain faded. "She taught me self-defense. She taught me how to throw a punch to the gut and chin and nose. And she did it all in secret so I wouldn't get branded as the nuns' pet."

"And get beat up even worse." Giulia set down her spoon. "If she meant so much to you, why did you lose contact with her?"

Thirty-Six

A new Pit Bull revealed himself: a shamefaced one.

"I did everything I could to forget my suckfest of a childhood. After sixth grade I got sent to a new foster home. They were too cheap to pay for Catholic school, which was fine with me. They dumped me back in the public school system. I got in trouble all the time for fighting, but the bullies learned pretty quick to find easier meat. I quit going to church. I quit everything except the gym and A-V class. Tam died when I was a junior and after graduation I shaved my head, changed my name, and never looked back."

"Were you worried Sister Agatha would track you down and lecture you?"

"Maybe. But I can help her now." He brightened. "I can pay her back."

Giulia savored the last bite of pie and whipped cream before answering. "What do you expect from me?"

"Jesus, a little sympathy?" He looked over at the air conditioner a second later. "Damn, did the temperature drop in here?"

Score one for still being able to frost an errant student without uttering a word.

He transferred his gaze to her face. Giulia reminded herself neither half of *The Scoop* lacked insight. Tact, maybe. Definitely.

"Sorry. Been working with Ken too long." He smiled. "Please, call me Bull. We've been fencing like the Scarlet Pimpernel and Chauvelin. I have nasty memories of arguments over meals. Truce, okay?"

"Again, no."

"Not even...Okay. Never mind. We're both professionals and we have the same goal here. We want to help these nuns."

Giulia inclined her head. "Do you really think the mugging and death of Sister Matilda is related to Eagle's death, or was your boss fishing for a melodramatic teaser promo?"

The cameraman didn't pause to think. "Ken shot a bow at a venture, but his instincts are good."

"And?"

"Ken will play this to the hilt. We have contacts in mainstream news. If Ken pokes them, they'll cough up anonymous source material for him." He signaled the waitress.

"What about Eagle's second in command?"

"Who?"

Glenny took their plates. "All set? How was the pie?"

"Worth every calorie."

She gave Giulia a thumbs-up. "A compliment all women understand. I'll bring the check."

Giulia continued their interrupted conversation. "Barbara Beech, Eagle's partner. I met her at their office. She's capable, intelligent, skilled, and respected in the business community. My guess is the business will be hers."

Pit Bull appeared to be taking mental notes. "No wife? No kids?"

"Not in the picture."

"She'll be running it. At least until the ex decides she wants a piece of the pie." He leaned across the table without getting too close. "I'm not Ken's puppy. Take down my cell number please."

She input it to his dictation and pretended not to see the relief on his face.

"If I find anything, I'll call you. If I find anything hot, we'll meet again. Okay?"

The check arrived. Giulia set her portion of the bill plus tip on it. He didn't argue.

"Okay," Giulia said.

Thirty-Seven

When Giulia came home, her sister-in-law was making chocolate chip pancakes. Her older nephew and her niece, still in pajamas, heated syrup and poured orange juice. The lack of noise surprised Giulia.

"Hey, Aunt Giulia." Cecilia waved a napkin at her. "Mom's making pancakes. Want some?"

"I was at a breakfast meeting, but thank you."

Anne beamed like the perfect housewife in an infomercial for the newest amazing griddle. "Giulia, I hope you don't mind. I knew these three would come downstairs as though their last decent meal happened a week ago."

"I'd planned to come home and do the same. Is Frank awake?"

"Would we be this quiet if he was?" Cecilia rolled her eyes. "I'm so repressed."

Pasquale snorted. "You're so funny I forgot to laugh."

Giulia cringed. "Grade school humor. How I've missed it."

The brilliance of Anne's smile increased. "I know, right? It's great to hear their jokes again."

Not being evil enough to explain her sarcasm, Giulia changed the subject. "Where's Carlo?"

Cecilia pointed out the back door. "Where else?"

Frank groped into the kitchen, plaid pajama pants on the bottom and a neon orange Police Benevolent Association basketball t-shirt on top. "Coffee?"

Giulia poured from the full carafe. He took the mug before she added sugar and milk.

"I need the hard stuff this morning." He pulled out a chair and buried his face in the steam.

Anne stacked the last four pancakes on a serving plate. "Breakfast's ready. Cecilia, call your brother in, please."

Since she wasn't eating, Giulia served. The kids did indeed eat like a starving horde and Frank kept up with them. Anne and Giulia cleaned up afterward and the kids packed.

"Thank you a million times for bringing them home with you." Anne flung her arms around Giulia, flapping the dishtowel against her neck.

"We're family." She set another plate in the dish rack. "Besides, we're also the founding members of the anti-Salvatore society."

Anne grimaced. "I talked to the doctors yesterday when I picked up the minivan keys. They have no idea when or if he'll wake up. One of the nurses gave me papers for when I file his disability claim." The angry face faded. "I'll need the money to pay the mortgage and feed us. He closed our joint bank accounts when I left, but Cecilia, the little spy, knows the new passwords so I don't have to try to explain our situation to another stranger."

"If Cecilia turns to the dark side, the world will be in trouble."

The spy bounded into the kitchen. "Let's go, let's go, let's go! I'm packed. Those two are being slugs. Want to leave them behind?"

"Are not and no way." Pasquale and Carlo dropped their bags on the floor. Carlo kept right on walking out to the garden.

Giulia called after him, "You can come visit her when your mom can drive you here."

"He can bike here," Cecilia said.

"If your mother's okay with it."

Cecilia headed outside to share the plot with her brother. Anne had her blissful smile on again. Pasquale looked at his mother like she was an unknown biological specimen. Carlo ran inside.

"Ma, can I bike here to visit Scarlett? Can I?"

Anne said without hesitation, "When your homework and chores are done."

Pasquale elbowed his siblings. "Ma, what's with the face?"

Anne broke down and wept on Giulia's shoulder. Giulia said to the kids, "She's happy she can be your mom again."

Pasquale made a rude noise. "She's always been our mom. She just did something stupid and Dad won't let her stop paying for it." He walked over to Frank and shook his hand, adult to adult. "Uncle Frank, I was going to be a cop when I grow up but now I'm going to be a lawyer because lawyers get to be judges. I'm going to make sure shit like Dad did to us doesn't happen to other families."

Frank answered adult to adult as well. Giulia passed napkins to Anne. The kids hauled their suitcases and sleeping bags to the foyer.

Anne threw open the front door, her smile belying her blotched face and puffy eyes. "Let's go home."

When the house was theirs again, Zlatan's wriggle was the first thing Giulia told Frank about the breakfast meeting. Frank swooped her up and deposited her on the couch. He spent the next fifteen minutes with his hand on her belly. He looked up at last with a ginormous pout on his face.

"I don't feel anything."

"Frank, he's only about eight inches long. Wait another month and I'll wake you up in the middle of the night and he can kick your hand as long as you like."

"It's a date. Now tell me how *The Scoop* tried to subvert you to their side."

Thirty-Eight

When Giulia entered the office Monday morning, Sidney and Zane were reading news stories from the local paper and all four network affiliate TV websites.

"This newspaper reporter must have had to make a deadline." Zane put on a Serious Newscaster Voice. "The cause of the fire is as yet unclear, as is the identity of the body." He broke character to laugh. "Listen to this comment: 'Is your journalism degree drawn in crayon by your kindergarten teacher?' Ouch."

Sidney jumped up and down in her chair. "Ooh! Ooh! Somebody got pictures of the body." She tapped keys. "It looks like Garfield's butt stuck in a cat door."

"I keep trying to find a picture from the inside, but nobody got lucky."

"Lucky is not the word I would use. I wish I could learn the art of unseeing things." Giulia went straight into her own office and booted her computer. With the same energy as her niece and nephews, Sidney and Zane ran in after her.

"You were there?"

"What really happened?"

"Who's the victim?"

"How did you avoid all the rubberneckers with cell phones?"

"Is Frank on this case too?"

"Is it one big double murder case?"

"I'll buy your next coffee if you'll tell us everything."

Giulia failed to keep a stoic face. She did manage a stern reply to Zane's last sentence. "Driscoll Investigations is not open to bribery." Then she softened it. "Besides, I hear there's new research out. Three cups a day instead of two. I'm trying not to get my hopes up."

Sidney opened the curtains and raised the window. "There's a beautiful breeze, which for a change doesn't smell of sausage from the pizza place. As you are refreshed by the morning air, take pity on your hard-working staff left out of your exciting weekend adventures with dead bodies."

Giulia's hands paused on her keyboard. "Sidney, motherhood is making you poetic."

"Dead bodies are poetic?" Zane grasped the edge of the desk. "Ms. D., log in please so you can tell us all the details."

Any time Zane cracked his MIT genius shell pleased Giulia. Also, Sidney waxing poetic deserved a reward. She logged in, scanned her emails, and saw nothing which couldn't wait.

"My phone rang at one in the morning."

Sidney groaned. "Did it wake the kids?"

"Spoken like a mother. Fortunately they sleep like rocks. I drove to the convent and was escorted to the cellar." She closed her eyes a moment.

Sidney bounced on the balls of her feet. "What was it like? Tell. Tell."

"Sidney, you are the queen of perky and sweet, and you're the one bugging me for gruesome details?"

Her assistant gave her a wide-eyed, innocent look. "All the best love stories have a villain. What's the point if the heroes don't have an obstacle to overcome?"

Zane reverted to human computer mode. "Gaston. Maleficent. Jafar. Darth Vader."

"Darth Vader?" Giulia ran through the plots of Star Wars IV, V, and VI.

"Zane watches Disney movies?" Sidney's expression switched to faux shock.

"My girlfriend likes them and she doesn't give me grief about my gaming weekends."

"Compromise can be beautiful," Giulia said.

"The true obstacle to Han Solo and Princess Leia getting together, if you're willing to discount their ingrained prejudices as the larger obstacle."

Giulia dragged the conversation back on track. "It was the most horrific sight I've ever seen and no, I'm not going to describe it."

"Boo," her staff said in unison.

"Guys, I watch horror movies without any effect, and the state of the body gave me nightmares."

Zane whistled.

"I will confirm three things: The body was Victor Eagle's, the visible evidence looked like he was trying to commit arson, and as of early this morning all of the nuns are suspects."

"Hold it." Sidney crossed her arms. "Old, sick nuns are suspects?"

"They're not all old and sick. Two of them have been continuously vocal in accusing Eagle Developers of underhanded practices."

Sidney's eyes tried to roll out of their sockets. "I don't care. Shooting off your mouth doesn't equal homicidal maniac."

"There's a revenge motive."

Sidney's eyes now tried to roll across the floor to Zane's feet. "Mr. Practicing Buddhist, one of those nuns is as likely to shoot, stab, or bludgeon someone as you are. Or I am. Or Giulia is."

Zane studied Sidney and Giulia in turn. "I can't argue with your reasoning."

Sidney spun on one heel and raised the window screen. Sticking her head out the open space, she shouted, "Attention, Cottonwood! Zane Hall admitted I was right! Someone call the newspaper!"

When she restored the screen and turned around, Zane gave her a sweet smile. "I'm being polite because we're in front of Ms. D., but payback looms in your future like an errant TARDIS."

Sidney's smile rivaled his in sweetness. "I've survived projectile vomiting and explosive diarrhea. Bring it."

"Ahem. We are in a work environment. As owner-operator of said environment, I officially did not hear this conversation."

They ranged themselves in front of her desk, the picture of repentant coworkers prepared to take on new duties.

"I am giddy with power," Giulia said. "Can you guys give me a hand? Zane, everything else you can dig up on Barbara Beech. And I mean *The Scoop* style of digging."

"Do I have time to run out and buy a can of hair spray to get into character?"

She allowed herself a smile. "A good cosplayer works from within."

"I am humbled."

"Sidney, can you apply your pre-nuptial mojo to Victor Eagle's personal life? I think Beech will take over the company, but perhaps an ex-wife or adult children are lurking."

"If Zane's Ken Kanning, does that mean I'm Pit Bull? I really don't want to shave my head."

"Since you can't grow a beard, my advice to you is the same as Zane's: Real cosplay comes from the heart."

A minute later the sound of dueling keyboards reached her ears.

Thirty-Nine

"Ms. D., a Sister Bartholomew is on line one and she's hyperventilating."

Giulia extricated herself from three different email strings involving current cases. "Bart? What's wrong?"

"They're tearing Crankenstein apart! They're taking out my clothes and my books and they're bagging up my painting supplies."

"Bart, slow down. Who's in your RV?"

"The police! They showed me a warrant and I knew I couldn't tell them no and Olive thinks I'm a suspect and Eugenie wants to know if I hid my baseball ba-a-t..." The last word ended on a sob.

"Bart, listen. I'm leaving now. I'll be over there in about fifteen minutes. Don't leave the house and don't interfere with the police."

Lurkers—the same or new ones or a mixture of both—massed on the convent sidewalk to watch the installment of the Police versus RV show. Giulia drove around the block to park the Nunmobile. Nash VanHorne met her as she cut through two rows of minuscule backyards.

"Morning, Giulia. The little nun said she called you."

"Morning, Nash. What's going on?"

"We're hunting for incendiaries. The fire was caused by—wait a sec, I have to get the names right." He tapped his phone screen. "Calcium hypochlorite and polyglycol." He turned his screen for her to read. "Also known as brake fluid and pool shock, among other things. Our chem guys gave us a list of possibles to look for. Two female officers are searching the nuns' rooms now." They neared the convent's back door. "Whatever happened to plain old gasoline and a match?"

"No one cares about tradition anymore." She smiled up at the tall detective. "Seriously, Nash, a convent of infirm and overworked nuns as murder suspects?"

"Look at it from an objective standpoint, Giulia. He was stuck head first inside their cellar window. We found the remains of an incendiary device. If he wedged himself tight enough, he was possibly helpless. Any one of those nuns except the one in the wheelchair could've come downstairs and—I'm reaching here—torched him with those chemicals or used a baseball bat to knock the plastic bottle out of his hands to keep it off the newspapers. We found melted remnants of a plastic bottle."

"I suppose so, being objective. But—"

"If we don't cover all the angles, no matter how far-fetched, our boss who you claim is such a teddy bear will turn into a rabid grizzly." He blocked her progress with one arm. "Reporter at two o'clock."

They cut hard right into the narrow aisle between two houses and peeked back around the corner of one like Charlie Chaplin and Jackie Coogan in *The Kid.*

"Clear," Giulia said.

Their trek across back lawns ended at the narrow convent driveway. The houses on either side squeezed so tight against Bart's RV, Giulia expected the brake lights to bulge. The police personnel dismantling it kept bumping into shake shingles on one side and peeling painted wood on the other. Faded green flecks clung to their clothes.

"How's it coming?" Nash said to the one labeling a bag containing a used bottle of turpentine.

"We're about ready to put it back together."

"Impressions?"

An annoyed face. "Waste of time. Baseball bat's clean. So is anything else weapon-like. This—" he held up the bagged turpentine— "isn't even worth testing, but we'll put it through the gamut."

"About what I expected." Nash turned to Giulia. "Your little nun has been staring at us through the window the whole time. See if you can calm her down, would you? I need to ask her some more questions."

The only good part of the morning was Steve the Chihuahua cutting his "adorable injured puppy" act short when he recognized

Giulia. He wouldn't even accept a pet before he turned his back on her and retreated to the kitchen. Bart's terrified face wiped away Giulia's lingering smile.

"Come sit with Aunt Giulia." She led Bart to the sofa. A spring stabbed her butt as a reward, so she squeezed onto the same sagging cushion as Bart.

Shudders coursed through Bart. "I was helping Dorothy for something to do, but I had to get away from Eugenie and Olive. Olive kept winking at me like we shared a secret and Eugenie cackled every time she looked at me. Then she wheeled herself into her room and told me she'd lend me her overnight bag for when the police hauled me off to jail."

Giulia grasped Bart's arms. "Look at me."

Bart raised Precious Moments eyes to Giulia's face.

"I don't use vulgar language, but what I think of Eugenie would shock my parish priest."

Bart snorted. Then she looked around with those big eyes as though Eugenie's wheelchair was sneaking up on them from the hall.

"Better now?" Giulia released Bart. "Detective VanHorne wants to talk to you again. Don't jump. You're not a frightened rabbit and he's a gentleman who volunteers with his girlfriend at the SPCA."

"Stay with me, please." Bart clutched Giulia's sleeve.

"If you need me, of course." She raised the window and called, "Nash, when you're ready."

"Come out here, would you?"

Bart hung behind Giulia until Giulia took two steps back and gave her a nudge between the shoulder blades.

Nash's crooked smile radiated charm when he chose. He chose now. "Sister Bartholomew, we're doing our best to put everything back where we found it. We're taking a few things with us, but we'll replace them when we're finished."

Bart's Precious Moments eyes returned. "Yes, sir."

"I don't bite, Sister. Now can you tell me again everything you recall about what woke you up early Saturday morning?"

"It was some kind of noise, but it didn't happen again after I was awake. I'm a light sleeper because I live in my RV." Anyone listening to Bart for the first time would think she was the worst kind of repressed nineteenth-century nun. "Then I heard a voice. The walls in there are thin enough to make paper airplanes out of. I was wide awake, but the voice came from downstairs and I couldn't tell if it was a man's or a woman's."

Nash kept his gaze on Bart. The last of the gawkers on the sidewalk drifted away. Lack of an immediate and sensational arrest, perhaps. No news cameras or reporters were in sight. Giulia did a sweep of the visible area and didn't see anyone—in other words, *The Scoop*—lurking around corners. Bart kept looking past the detective as her few possessions were reloaded into the RV.

"This isn't a great neighborhood, even now when most of the houses are empty. I'm the youngest one here, so I got the baseball bat and got ready to bust a kneecap." She swallowed. "I didn't hit him. I swear I didn't hit him. His head was in one piece. You saw his head, right?"

"We aren't prepared to release any details yet. What did you do next?"

Over her shoulder, Bart watched her supplies for the homeless reloaded into the RV. "I, um, sorry. I went through all the rooms on the first floor and when they were empty I opened the cellar door. I smelled smoke right away, so I dropped the bat and went for the fire extinguisher."

"Did you hear the voice again?"

"No...oh, could you ask them to be careful with my easel? It's rickety and I'm a lot better with car parts than wood."

Nash raised his voice. "Guys, the easel's fragile."

"Got it."

He continued after the easel survived its return trip into the RV. "So you only heard the voice from your room on the third floor?"

"Yes." Bart frowned up at him. "I didn't think of that until now. The cellar's walls are the only sturdy ones in the place. A voice from the cellar shouldn't carry up to my room."

"Not even a scream?"

Bart shivered. "I don't know."

Giulia shivered too, but she chose to blame it on heavy gray clouds which had rolled in. Nash looked up and got one of the first raindrops smack in one eye. He spluttered.

The front door opened and Sister Olive said, "Come inside before the Heavens open up."

"Busybody," Bart muttered.

Nash stopped them in the hall. "Just one more thing. When you brought the fire extinguisher down to the cellar, did you hear anything? Any voices, specifically?"

Bart closed her eyes. "I heard...flames crackling. Little crackles, like when a fire in a fireplace is just beginning to catch. I may have heard..." She opened her eyes. "For some reason I keep wanting to say I heard a really quiet voice laughing. I can't be sure anymore. I think my memory might be adding things because of what everyone else has been saying." She looked apologetic. "It's silly to think I heard someone laughing anyway."

Nash tried another smile. This time it called up an answering one in Bart. "Thanks for your help, Sister."

Bart leaned against the door after he left. "For the first time since I worked in Dad's gas station, I want a cigarette."

Giulia got in her face. "Bart, I want an honest answer: Have you been sneaking cigarettes while you're in this house?"

"Huh? I haven't smoked in years. I quit cold turkey in college when my best friend's mother got diagnosed with lung cancer and died six weeks after."

"All right." Giulia let it drop because Bart's honesty was obvious. "Would you call the teaching Sisters and ask them to come back here for an emergency lunch meeting?"

One item not on the lunch discussion: Her suspicions about the cigarette smoke. And the laughter.

Forty

Giulia sneaked into the backyard to call Frank, since there was zero privacy in the house. "Since Nash brought a crew to the convent, I gather you have autopsy results for Eagle?"

Frank shouted into the receiver, "Shut up or I'll tell the doc to skip you on her methadone rounds." He lowered his voice. "That wasn't for you."

"I gathered."

"Autopsy. Right." Several keyboard clicks. "As we all thought, Eagle died from massive burn trauma to the brain."

Giulia swallowed. "Can you give me details without causing me to lose my breakfast?"

Silence. "Maybe. Not this. Definitely not this. Okay. You know about the chemicals he used?"

"Yes."

"In essence, the chemicals burned at an extremely high temperature for an extended period of time. I'm abridging here...basically, the eyes lead to the brain, the brain is fragile, end of story."

Giulia revised the case she'd been building. "Eagle didn't strike me as the type to miscalculate an essential element of one of his plans."

"Everybody makes mistakes."

"He didn't strike me as an arsonist either." She caught Olive peering through the kitchen window and turned away. "If Eagle is behind the weeks of harassment here, there's a slim if stupid chance he tried the break-in from impatience."

"Hold on." Frank covered his mouthpiece and treated Giulia to a muffled three-way conversation. "Sorry. Go ahead. Assuming he's a serial harasser?"

"Yes. If that's the case, then he wouldn't have botched his chemistry experiment. He's too clever." She thought a moment. "This needs Zane. Thanks, honey."

After she hung up, she turned toward the convent. While still here, she also needed to unearth some history.

Forty-One

"Sister Dorothy, I need your help." Giulia was massaging Helena's left leg as the nurse massaged her right.

"Dorothy, please, and certainly. How may I help you?"

"What do you know of Sister Agatha's history?"

The nun smiled at her patient. "Helena, I forgot to tell you about how Agatha surprised us all." She described the moment of recognition and the epic Ken Kanning diss. The invalid nun laughed soundlessly.

Dorothy scooped two fingers of lanolin and passed the jar to Giulia. "Agatha entered later than most for her time. She attended college for two years first and was an amateur boxer."

"If only she could tell her story." Giulia concentrated on the patches of dry skin on Helena's ankles.

"I never knew her before the Alzheimer's reached its current stage. She taught middle school for fifty-six years. The doctors say she's become deaf to a certain range of sounds. The exact range of a few hundred preteens all talking at the top of their lungs in a cafeteria."

Giulia worked cream into Helena's heel. "I dodged a bullet."

Dorothy lowered her voice. "Kathryn's going deaf to the same register. She doesn't think we know."

Another soundless laugh from Helena.

"I won't tell if you won't," Giulia said to her.

Either Giulia was getting better at understanding, or the reply was too obvious to misinterpret: "We're bad."

Dorothy joined in the laughter. "We don't laugh enough in this house anymore. Agatha also taught self-defense before it was generally accepted. When she was moved in here a few weeks before her eightieth birthday, one of her classes sent her an old yearbook. They'd written some of their memories in it, which is how we learned anything about her other than the bare bones of her teaching career."

Eugenie wheeled herself in. "Our sleuth offers massages too? Where's the sign-up sheet?"

Helena said, "I have privileges."

At least it sounded like "privileges" to Giulia. She caught Helena's eye and the nun executed a slow-motion wink.

"Yeah, yeah, we know. I'll forgo a massage for inside information. Tell us about working with *The Scoop*."

Dorothy's hands stopped. Helena made an inquiring sound.

"Oh, yes, please," Dorothy said. "Mr. Kanning was such a gentleman when he interviewed me Saturday even though it was the middle of the night."

"Are you together on our case?" Eugenie crowded between Dorothy and Giulia.

Giulia bit the inside of her cheek hard. If she wanted continued cooperation from these fangirls she had to suck it up. "We only worked together on purpose once."

"The Doomsday Preppers," Dorothy said. "What an exciting episode. We carried the TV in here for the second part and had a watch party."

Eugenie fluttered. "We've never seen his cameraman before. If only Agatha could stay *compos mentis* for more than a minute we could learn all about how adorable he was as a child."

Before her real opinions slipped out despite her good intentions, Giulia changed the subject. "There's something I meant to ask you all. Have you ever smelled cigarette smoke in the house?"

Eugenie pounced. "Where did you smell it? When?"

"No," Dorothy said. "But I'm almost always on this floor, so if you smelled it anywhere else, you'll have to ask the others."

"Have you smelled it?" Giulia said to Eugenie.

"Twice in my room, but the window was open both times."

"It could have come in from outside."

Eugenie looked disappointed. "I suppose. At first I thought Olive or Kathryn were sneaking cigarettes when they thought no one was around."

Olive popped into the doorway exactly like a jack-in-the-box. "Who's talking about cigarettes? Did those policemen smoke in here? The whole house is a fire hazard."

Dorothy appeared to fall apart all at once. Her eyes sunk into dark circles and her spine shrank. New veins showed through her skin. "What if Eagle or one of his henchmen has been sneaking into our house the past two months? I mean before Saturday morning?"

Olive slammed a fist on the doorframe. "The convent used to be sacrosanct. We were never disturbed by unwanted intruders. People would ring our doorbell with prayer requests. They'd ask us to visit their sick relatives and were obsequious with their thanks. They brought their troubles to us and pleaded for advice. And now? Now we get harassed and invaded and robbed." Another fist slam.

Steve trotted in and Eugenie scooped him up. "At least you see people. We're stuck on the second floor all the time. Steve here is the only one who takes pity on us, don't you Steve?" The dog licked her face. "We couldn't afford a house with an elevator but at least the chapel is on this floor."

"You offer it up so well, Eugenie." Olive bared her teeth in a less than friendly smile.

"I never said I was Saint Francis. Do you really want to tally each other's sins in preparation for weekly confession, Sister?"

Giulia stood. "Is Bart still in her RV?"

"Last I saw, she was." Olive began a rant about officious police and Giulia escaped.

Forty-Two

"They're not always so catty. They've been on edge ever since Eagle bought out the neighborhood." Bart opened the attic door.

"Bart, that level of digging under the skin like a tick takes years to perfect." Giulia climbed the stairs in her new maternity pants and for the first time in a month didn't have to keep readjusting the material around her pregnant body. Their unexpected benefit: Freeing up her subconscious.

The attic still sported its thin layer of dust. Only Giulia and Olive's footprints from the other day disturbed the floor.

"What are you looking for up here?" Bart straightened one of the dust covers.

"Peace and quiet, for one thing. When you said you were surprised you heard a voice carry from the cellar to the third floor, are you sure the voice was all the way down in the cellar?"

"No, not really. You know what it's like when you first wake up. You wonder why you're awake and what time it is and maybe you should just roll over and go back to sleep." She unlatched the small octagonal window at the front of the house.

"What about the laughter?"

Her shoulders hunched. "I wish I hadn't said that to the detective. He'll think I'm bonkers."

"I won't think you're bonkers. Did you hear it?"

She turned a pitiable face to Giulia. "I was all about getting the fire extinguisher because this whole place should have a sign on it like they do for forests: Fire Danger Today is High."

"But?" when Bart didn't continue.

"But I wish my sister-in-law was here. The one who taught me how to smudge a room to cleanse it. She says she can sense things. I sure can't. I'm like a lump of wood."

Giulia tapped her foot. "Bart, you're dithering."

"Okay. Okay. I did think I heard someone laughing. But there was nobody in the cellar except the body and no way anyone could've gotten past me and out of the house. There." she yanked the window inward and showered herself with dust.

Giulia took out her phone and opened the EMF app. "WEEoooWEEoooWEEooo." She banged the home button to close it and turned off the phone. "Why did they make that sound so irritating?"

Bart came over to her. "Isn't that your ghost hunting noise?" She looked around the room, her braids flying.

"Yes." Giulia counted to ten and turned the phone on again. "It seems to be easily interfered with."

The stink of cigarette smoke reached her nostrils. She looked up, then around the room, then at Bart. Bart was staring at Giulia's phone. Giulia sniffed twice, wrinkling her nose. Bart remained oblivious.

"Is anyone outside?"

Bart ran to the window and back again. "Not a soul."

Giulia inhaled—no smoke this time—and opened the app. "WeeOooWeeOooWeeOoo."

One day soon one of Frank's Irish curses would slip out of her mouth.

She shut down the app. Her finger hovered over Jasper Fortin's phone number. The clairvoyant who ran the Tarot Shoppe across the street from DI with his aunt Rowan had told her she could call him anytime.

But Jasper and Rowan weren't running DI. She was.

Giulia pocketed her phone. "If you want to talk, I'm here to listen."

"Huh?" Bart said.

"If you need cigarettes, I don't carry them on me."

"What are you talking about?"

Dorothy's voice came from the bottom of the attic stairs. "Ms. Driscoll, please come down. The phone's for you."

Forty-Three

As soon as Bart and Giulia reached the first floor, Olive said into the phone, "Our representative is the person you want to speak to. One moment, please." She put her hand over the mouthpiece and whispered, "It's Eagle Developers. I don't know what to say to them and Kathryn's not here yet. Please?"

Giulia took the phone. "Driscoll Investigations speaking."

A beat. The voice on the other end said, "One moment, please." A click.

Giulia moved the mouthpiece away from her face and said to Bart, "'Purple Rain' as hold music." Bart made a gagging gesture.

Another click. "Ms. Beech would like to meet with the Sisters' representative regarding the sale of the house. What time would be convenient?"

If the developers thought this was a curve ball, they needed to up their research game. She checked the clock. Eleven thirty. "I'm available any time after four."

Without a pause, "Ms. Beech will expect you at four fifteen."

"Thank you." Giulia hung up.

If Olive were any closer to Giulia, she'd be breathing down her neck. "What's happening? What are you going to do? You'll have to clear it with Kathryn."

"Who has to check what with me?" Kathryn held the front door open for Diane as she finished locking their beater Subaru station wagon.

Before Giulia could explain, Olive launched into a wildly speculative narration of Giulia's phone call.

Kathryn held up a hand. "Stop, please. We've been fighting lunch traffic to make it here in time. Ms. Driscoll, what's happening?"

Giulia gathered everyone in the second-floor hall. Sister Agatha was either having a quiet day or napping. Giulia felt guilty for appreciating the silence.

"I'm meeting with the new head of Eagle Developers at quarter after four. I need to go in armed and ready. What options has the Order offered you for new housing?"

All the nuns looked at Kathryn.

"They will accommodate our second-floor residents into the Massachusetts Motherhouse. The rest of us are expected to find reasonably priced apartments on public transportation routes to our places of employment. Dorothy is to find a position at a hospice or as a home aide."

Silence followed her clipped words.

Giulia broke it. "What about the retired sisters and Bart?"

Kathryn's furious despair bled into her reply. "The retired Sisters are each expected to share an apartment with one working Sister."

Eugenie cackled. "Remember when steamy lesbian nun sex, AKA having a 'Particular Friend', was the worst sin any of us could commit, including murder? Now all that matters is living on the cheap."

Olive got in the last word. "Grab your ice skates because Hell has frozen over."

Kathryn finished, "Sister Bartholomew will also be accommodated at the Motherhouse."

Bart wailed. "They'll make me a glorified Novice. I'll end up with the laundry and the heavy cleaning. Aren't there about fifteen old nuns up there who still wear the traditional habit? I'll have to starch all their veils."

"It's That bad?" Giulia said.

She paced the hall. "There hasn't been a new Postulant in three years. They don't know how to handle nonconformity in that mausoleum."

Giulia dredged up an underground saying from her own Novice years. "They mold you and mold you and then they say, 'How moldy you are.'"

Olive snorted. "Sister Walburga said that to us when she taught us to starch veils."

Bart paced faster. "They want mold. They don't have to worry about mold. Mold doesn't make trouble."

To diffuse the growing atmosphere of hopelessness, Giulia brought out her research notes. "I have numbers. You'll need three apartments, assuming one of you is allowed to live solo. Average rent is eight hundred per month, plus utilities."

"I've checked Craigslist," Kathryn said. "Rent is as low as five and a quarter near Barberry Heights."

Olive's lungs expanded.

Giulia cut off what was sure to be an epic rant. "The worst, cheapest, 1950s throwback basement apartment I lived in after I jumped the wall would be better than living within twenty miles of that toxic landfill."

Olive used her exhale to cackle in Eugenie's style.

Dorothy temporized. "It has beautiful landscaping and there's no concrete proof it's toxic."

Olive gave her a pitying look. "Because local government is stonewalling the ecology lawsuit."

Eugenie said, "Jump the wall. Hee hee hee."

Kathryn threw the heaviest of wet blankets over the discussion. "We don't have a choice. The Order's legal counsel is pressuring us too."

Giulia opened her mouth to argue numbers but remembered in time the enormous load the Superior was carrying on her aging shoulders.

The doorbell rang. Kathryn closed her eyes. "Now what?"

Steve leaped off Eugenie's lap at the sound of the bell. Olive headed for the stairs. "If it's Eagle, I'll slam the door right in—" She stopped.

Eugenie wheeled herself to Helena's doorway. "He can't rise from Hell to bother us anymore." She followed her quip with a full-bodied laugh and rubbing together of hands.

"Sister, that's un-Christian." But Kathryn's rebuke barely deserved the name.

Giulia followed Olive downstairs. The delivery guy from the pizza place across the street from DI stood at the door with two large boxes.

Olive and Steve blocked the door. "We didn't order anything."

Giulia loomed over her. "I did." She carried the boxes into the kitchen, calling upstairs, "Lunch!"

Forty-Four

Dorothy came back downstairs empty-handed. "Eugenie said she'd feed the other two while we talk. She said she trusts us to make the correct decision for our future."

Olive brought a huge bowl of salad to the table. "No one can pile on the guilt like a Catholic."

Kathryn opened a bottle of wine. "We took the afternoon off and won't be driving."

"I'm not judging anyone." Giulia found a spatula. "Who wants sausage and peppers?"

"I do, please." Diane opened the miniature cupboard doors over the refrigerator. "How many wine glasses?"

"Five," Olive said.

"None for me, thank you." Giulia opened the second box. "Pepperoni?"

"I'll take one of each, please, and why aren't you drinking with us?" Olive's shift from helpful to belligerent bespoke years of practice as well. "Don't tell me it's because you're driving. You're young. You metabolize everything faster."

"I prefer water."

Olive pointed with her salad fork. "You're flouting the rules of hospitality. Diane, we still need five glasses."

Giulia set down the spatula with more force than required. "Another rule of hospitality is to make your guest feel welcome."

Silence. Two forks and one slice hovered between plates and mouths.

Olive jerked as though all the other Sisters had kicked her under the table. "I beg your pardon."

Giulia helped herself to sausage and peppers. "You have now witnessed what happens when you mess with the raging hormones of a pregnant woman."

The forks moved. "You're pregnant?" Dorothy said.

"Yes. I'm teetotaling for the duration."

"Whatever you do, don't name the baby Victor." Olive laughed at her own joke. No one else did.

Hormones were a good excuse for Giulia to shut down this conversation. She took a bite of pizza and said, "If you're all agreeable, this is the strategy I've worked out. I'll finalize a financial plan to show the Order. The plan will make it obvious keeping you together in a house is more cost-effective than splitting you up in multiple apartments. When I meet with Eagle Developers this afternoon, I'll make a counter offer to start negotiations. As of today, I'll take over this chore."

Relief emanated from Kathryn in palpable waves. "You will?"

Dorothy, the quiet one, took a page from Olive and got assertive for a moment. "Good. If you'll wait until I finish eating I'll dig up the latest messages they papered our windows with. You can give them back to them to recycle. Eagle claims to be committed to saving the environment."

Forty-Five

Giulia swung by the office before her appointment. "Guys, I have one for you."

Sidney held up one finger.

Zane said, "*The Scoop* has dedicated itself to a life of charity and self-sacrifice?"

If Giulia had been drinking anything, she would've done a spit take.

"Zane, stop being funny when I'm composing a sensitive email." Sidney pressed several keys, frowned at the screen, shook her head, and hit save. "I'll have to finish it later. Our newest prenuptial is about to implode. Her daddy ran a failed Ponzi scheme and they're a hundred grand in debt."

"If I had the energy, I'd insert a few apt biblical quotes." Giulia pulled out one of the chairs by the window. "All right. Zane, a test: What happens when you combine brake fluid and pool shock?"

Zane shut down. Because Giulia had seen it before, she neither panicked nor laughed. Sidney opened a drawer and took out a handmade GENIUS AT WORK sign taped to a disposable chopstick. Giulia shoved her arm over her mouth.

Zane rebooted. "A violent chemical reaction. Heat or explosion or both." His fingers were already on his keyboard. "YouTube can be useful." His voice was distant. "Here's one." A long pause. "Dear gods." Another pause. "I have to try this at home."

Sidney and Giulia laughed.

"I fear for your offspring," Giulia said.

"You and your current girlfriend are serious, right?" Sidney said. "Please have her visit us sooner rather than later."

"What?" Zane looked up from his screen. "I wasn't listening."

They laughed harder.

"Let's see these videos." Giulia came around behind Zane's desk.

Sidney joined her. "Me, too. I need to prepare myself if Jessamine turns out like Olivier's daredevil science experiment brothers."

Zane hit the replay button. Two excited young men poured brake fluid into an empty plastic water bottle, then poured granulated pool shock over the liquid, describing their measurements in eager voices. One screwed the cap onto the bottle, then both ran away fast enough to make the camera appear to be recording an earthquake. The camera settled a good fifty feet from the water bottle and breathless narration began.

"Fifteen seconds in and nothing happening yet."

"Remember, folks, don't try this at home. Go to an empty parking lot."

"Twenty-five seconds."

"Look—bubbles are forming."

"Thirty seconds."

"The whole bottle is filled with bubbles. Now it's expanding. Whoa—it's like a ball."

"Thirty-three—"

The bottle exploded with a POP. Flames and white smoke shot up and out from the melted wreckage.

Zane counted. "Thirty-eight. Thirty-nine. Forty. Forty-one. Eight seconds of serious fire after explosion." He hit the back arrow. "We need more data."

For the next several minutes, they watched video after video of the same chemicals exploding different sizes and shapes of plastic bottles, making tin cans leap in the air and scorching starburst patterns on asphalt. Zane opened a blank spreadsheet.

"Time to reaction varies from thirty-three seconds to one minute twelve seconds." He entered numbers into the cells faster than Giulia had ever seen him type. "Containers...plastic bottles, twelve and twenty ounces. Metal cans..." He glanced up at Giulia. How much does a standard coffee can hold these days? I grind my own."

"Twelve," Sidney said. "My parents use this coffee and chicory blend in the gift shop they buy in bulk from Amazon."

"Twelve." Zane entered the number. "Short cans of nuts, eight ounces. Pint cans of paint, sixteen ounces. Chemicals. Three tablespoons of calcium hypochlorite plus one-quarter cup of polyglycol, standard. I wonder where the proportions originated." He opened another window. "Brylcreem? Is that even sold anymore? I see it is. Ingredient list...Phenoxyethanol. Magnesium Sulfate. Methylisothiazolinone. Hmm. Brake fluid ingredient list...diethyleneglycol. Polyethyleneglycol. Triethyleneglycol. Butyls everywhere too. No wonder these daredevils switched to brake fluid. The reaction should be much more efficient than with hair goo. Duration of flames, eight to twenty-one seconds. Height of flames, approximately four to thirteen inches." More typing. "Observe. Nothing up my sleeves. Nothing in my snazzy top hat. Abracadabra." He clicked several choices at the top of the page. A multicolor bar graph appeared.

Giulia and Sidney golf-clapped. Zane hung his head. "My genius is unappreciated. My only option is to sell my house, move into a secure facility, and create a working time travel device to rewrite the past."

"Because nothing could possibly go wrong with that," Sidney said.

"'A Sound of Thunder,' Ray Bradbury," Giulia said. "The Butterfly Effect, 2004."

A theatrical sigh. "I knew you'd bring those up."

"I see you're learning dramatic effects from Sidney."

Sidney said with pride, "I needed to show him non-super-smart people have skills too."

Zane said, "Ms. D., why this particular chemical reaction?"

"A melted plastic bottle with residue from those chemicals was found in the convent cellar beneath Victor Eagle's body."

He whistled. "The head of one of the biggest companies in Cottonwood was trying his hand at arson?"

"The evidence is still inconclusive as of this morning."

"Someone busted into the convent?" Sidney whistled. "Don't they teach criminals in, like, Crime Kindergarten not to rob nuns? Nuns never have money anyway."

"Only the classy Crime Kindergartens teach manners."

Giulia said, "We don't know if there's a second suspect. Sister Bart says no one could have sneaked past her but she thinks she heard a laugh. If she did, we need the time of death to coordinate with the time

Bart heard the laugh."

"We're in serious Zane territory." Sidney returned to her desk. "You wanted to know what we've learned about Eagle's company?"

"Yes." Giulia sat in the window chair again. "I'm negotiating the house sale in two and a half hours. Can you give me the upper hand?"

Zane laughed his mad scientist laugh.

Sidney said, "The 'upper hand' sounds so much more professional than 'give me dirt.'"

"Words have power."

"Allow me to share my power." Zane opened a new window. "Barbara Beech is a textbook success story. MBA from Carnegie Mellon. In her first job she rose from Administrative Assistant to Department Manager in three years. A headhunter wooed her to a larger company where she started as an Assistant Vice President and within two years of the switch became the Executive Vice President. If that isn't enough, she's received multiple awards from the Women in Business Foundation. Why, you ask? Because she helps other women starting out in business."

Sidney took over. "Don't polish her halo yet. She and Eagle were an item while Eagle was still married to Wife Number Two and she was married to Husband Number One."

"Eagle and Beech made indiscreet social media posts?"

"Not on your life. Fortunately for us, Eagle's teenage kids had no such filter." She opened a document. "Their mother should've washed out their brains with soap. I won't repeat their nicknames for Beech, but here's the twist: They had a colorful list of names for Eagle too." She tsk'd at the screen.

"When I posed as a reporter to gain access to them, they all but told me the affair was long over and they were adult enough not to let it sabotage their business."

"Next you'll be buying the deed to the Brooklyn Bridge."

Giulia smiled. "My grandfather used to say that."

"Mine too. He had to explain it to me."

Tires squealed on the street below, followed by a CRASH, a second CRASH, horns blaring and the high tinkle of glass. They all crowded the window. One taxi's front end was embedded in the passenger side of a second taxi. The second taxi's hood was wrapped around a telephone pole. Six people had their phones out. Four were rushing to the taxis. Cursing voices from one of the taxis carried with ease to DI's second-floor window.

"I just learned a new curse word," Sidney said.

"One of my gaming buddies uses it when his avatar gets blown up." Zane craned his neck over Giulia's head. "The one closest to us has a passenger."

"Both cars are leaking gas." Giulia held up a hand. "I hear sirens."

"Here comes Jasper." Sidney said.

The tall, one-handed war hero dashed out of the Tarot Shoppe and leaped from doorway to curb in a single stride. He went straight to the rear passenger door Zane had pointed out and hooked his prosthetic hand around the handle. One tug. Nothing. He flexed his arms and pulled. The door opened with a metallic squeal. A pudgy body with a head in a baseball cap lolled out. Jasper cradled the head, supporting the neck. The ambulance and police arrived and Jasper relinquished the passenger to the EMTs.

When he regained the sidewalk he waved up at Giulia. She waved back. He made a "call me" gesture with his hand. Giulia gave him the "okay" sign.

"Because he's clairvoyant, did he know the accident was going to happen?" Sidney said.

"Come on," Zane said. "That's the same as saying all psychics should be able to predict the lottery numbers."

Forty-Six

For her second visit to Eagle Developers, Giulia went as herself: Tired, Pregnant Professional Who Doesn't Care If You Think All Women Should Wear Makeup. Before she left the office, she combed wet hands through her hair and let the early September humidity work its evil magic.

This time she wore a plain white shirt with her black maternity pants. She'd lengthened the strap on her messenger bag so it hit below her hip, drawing attention away from her face every time she moved. No fake glasses hung on her nose and no cotton wadding distorted her cheeks. Plus she didn't have to remember to flute up her voice.

She'd spent the drive schooling herself into calmness. They won't recognize her. She'd made herself up to look like a completely different person the first time. Her one superpower was the ability to fade into the wallpaper. They won't connect her one bit with the bubble gum-and-glitter freelancer.

"Good afternoon. I have a four fifteen appointment with Ms. Beech."

The receptionist didn't blink. "Ms. Beech is expecting you. One moment, please."

Barbara Beech came out of the CEO's office in unrelieved black. Gorgeous, expensive, designer black. Her impeccable makeup didn't conceal the circles under her eyes or the tension lines at the corners of her mouth.

"Good afternoon, Ms. Driscoll. Thank you for making time to meet today." Beech didn't give Giulia a "have I seen you before" look either. She said to the receptionist, "Hold my calls for the next half hour."

A splendid mahogany table dominated the long conference room Beech shut them into. The table's dominance was challenged by the fifty-five-inch screen mounted on the short wall. The table won. The chairs bowed before its polished splendor; the carpet prostrated itself beneath it.

Giulia wondered if she was more sleep-deprived than she realized. "Please accept my sympathy for the loss of Mr. Eagle."

Beech's mouth tightened and released. "Thank you. It's been a shock to all of us." She kneaded her watch band. The silence lengthened. Giulia had consoled too many grieving parents and children in her convent years to miss the signs of a strong person keeping a firm check on grief.

In a few more seconds Beech rolled the chair opposite the door away from the table and gestured to the chair in front of Giulia. "Please have a seat."

This put Giulia with her back to the door. Not a position she preferred, thanks to living with a police detective.

"I was interested to learn the Sisters have hired an advocate." Beech folded her hands on the polished surface. "I was even more interested their advocate is a private investigator. What exactly is your relationship with the Order of Sisters?"

Giulia's professional smile didn't reach her eyes. "As I indicated over the phone, I'm representing the Sisters in the negotiations for the sale of their convent."

Beech was no amateur at this game. She picked up a remote and an architect's drawing of trendy lofts, cafés, and green spaces appeared on the gigantic screen.

"Eagle Developers purchased the properties on the blocks including the nuns' residence for two reasons. First because we have a vision—if you'll pardon the cliché—to revive the area. In a statelier time it was a neighborhood of elegant homes. Those times will never return, but we can make it an attractive destination again."

With each click she changed the view of the proposed redevelopment. Children playing. A band in the middle of an outdoor café with happy people at bistro tables. Loft apartments with brick and distressed shutters on the outside. Cream walls and pastel furniture arranged tastefully on hardwood floors for the inside.

"Eagle can create this from this." With the second "this" the screen changed to the worst houses in the convent's neighborhood. Photographed on a cloudy day, their broken windows became empty eye sockets and gaping mouths. Their dead front lawns with trash and scraps of newspaper could've doubled as the "after" photo from a fire or explosion.

"Most of the houses were in foreclosure and as of this morning all the remaining owners have agreed to our fair market buyout offers. The convent is three months in arrears on the mortgage. The Massachusetts home office of the Order of Sisters has no objection to our offer."

Giulia anted up. "Few things are as simple as they appear on the surface. One issue you may not be aware of is the pressure the home office is putting on the Sisters here." She conveyed ruefulness. "Nice people wouldn't bad mouth a group of nuns, but this is business. They're trying to force the ambulatory Sisters into low-rent apartments and are grudgingly allowing the bedridden Sisters into the central infirmary."

The new CEO of Eagle Developers ran her thumb along the edge of the remote. Up and down. Up and down. Her eyes were aimed in Giulia's direction, but they weren't looking outward.

The thumb stopped moving. "I see." More clicks. A new set of drawings filled the screen. "Old houses are dangerous and inefficient. They put people at risk for black mold, fire hazards, and vermin. Yet their outward charm is undeniable. For this project we're trying something new. We want to retain the best of the façades to upsell the new builds behind them."

Giulia played a neutral card. "An interesting choice." She opened her phone. "Based on tax assessments and recent sales numbers for the block—" she typed in a number— "here is our counter offer."

Beech was too experienced to flinch. She typed into her own phone and faced the screen at Giulia. "The nuns' house is worthless to anyone except our company."

Giulia hadn't fenced with a master since her exit interview from the convent. It was stimulating. "Except to the Sisters who take care of the homeless in the neighborhood. I don't know if you're aware of the nuns' concept of Mission?"

Polite snark. One of the many services DI offered.

Giulia continued. "The Order is not wealthy. One of the costs factored in is moving three invalids to an accessible home." She typed in a new number and showed it to Beech. "This figure is closer to the cost of finding a reasonably priced house in a neighborhood not named Barberry Heights."

Beech wrinkled her button nose, her only cute feature. "Horrible place. Victor put in a bid for the project without telling me. I discovered it in our system as part of my research for a presentation I was creating. I informed him I would resign if we were awarded the contract. Fortunately we lost, a phrase you won't ever hear out of my mouth again." A brief smile.

"Cancer rates are on the rise in people living within a one-mile radius of the landfill." Giulia didn't need to trust the smile to respond to it.

The wrinkled nose became full anger. "Eagle Developers has evolved over time, as a robust organization should. You will never see us involved with Barberry or any similar project." She aimed the remote and the screen winked out. "We'll be in touch with you soon."

Forty-Seven

Giulia's phone rang as she was unlocking the Nunmobile. Little Zlatan's insistence on SUPPER NOW distracted her so much she accepted the call without checking Caller ID first.

An authoritarian female voice said, "Stop whatever you're doing and listen to me."

Relieved it wasn't the nuns calling in a panic over a new disaster, Giulia slid into the driver's seat and closed the door. "Yes, ma'am."

Rowan Froelig, the owner of the Tarot Shoppe across the street from DI, huffed at her. "Don't call me ma'am. It makes me feel old. And don't think you can deceive me with polite silence. I'll get Jasper to find out what you're really thinking, which may or may not be 'Rowan, you are old,' which I know. My knees remind me every morning."

Thinking, Hold your horses, Zlatan, Giulia fitted her back against the lumbar support in the seat. "I was referring to our teacher-student relationship, which has no connection to our relative ages."

"Can't argue with you there, which reminds me to remind you that you're due for another practice session in Tarot reading and general clairvoyance techniques. Practice is the key to success in the spirit biz."

"Yes, ma'am."

"I should whack your knuckles with a ruler. Didn't you see Jasper give you the 'Call us' signal this afternoon?"

"I've been in meetings."

"You're an entrepreneur. You should be able to bail out of meetings." The tak-tak-tak of a pencil hitting the desk with force punctuated her declaration. "Have you stopped? Are you prepared?"

"I am sitting in my car by myself while He Who Deprives Me Of Coffee clamors for supper."

"Tell him his mother's busy. Now listen. My sunrise Tarot card reading could've doubled as a series of TV commercials. New people everywhere, new meetings, new encounters. It was like my cards signed a contract with one of those dating websites. I even cleansed the deck and set the cards in a different layout to make sure I wasn't misinterpreting."

Outside the Nunmobile's closed windows, rush hour traffic inched, literally, toward peak. The cacophony of multiple honking horns seeped into the car. Giulia turned up the phone's volume.

"Rowan, I've met enough people in the past week to field both sides of a basketball game." Brakes screeched. "There's about to be a car accident."

"Stop anticipating me." The pencil scratched on paper now. It conjured up an immediate and complete picture of Rowan sitting at the small table she used for readings. No doubt she was dressed in one of her flowing, layered outfits in different shades of purple, a tall mug of herbal tea at her elbow. "We told you you had gifts. How else would you know the cards also forecast accidents?"

A chill prickled Giulia's neck. "I didn't know and I think you're assuming more than actually exists."

"I never assume and don't say that awful sentence with the letters. Oh, right, you don't swear. Good. I hate clichés. Half my customers expect clichés. You'll marry a tall, dark, handsome man. You'll be rich. You'll be famous. Those types think I dress for effect. They're lucky I happen to dress the way I do. Old, fat women aren't exactly on Tommy Hilfiger's design radar."

CRASH. Screech. CRASH. CRASH.

Giulia jerked around in her seat.

"What was that?"

"As predicted—don't say it—an SUV rear-ended a delivery van which rear-ended a hatchback." Giulia opened her window halfway. "Nobody seems to be hurt. They're out of their cars." Dueling shouts reached her ears with too much clarity. "When I was a teacher, the language these people are using would've had me reaching for a bar of soap I kept in my desk."

"Your son will be the best-behaved child in the state. I hope no one in those vehicles is packing."

"Not so far. You know, this is the second accident I've witnessed today."

"Hold on a minute. I need to read again with you on the phone."

Giulia rolled the window back up to better hear Rowan. A distant siren crept closer. The SUV driver punched the van driver in the mouth. Two teeth went flying. The van driver pulled out a handgun and fired. The SUV driver fell backward against his crumpled hood. Blood blossomed on his pale blue shirt. The hatchback driver screamed.

A police car braked in the middle of a lane. The officer jumped out, gun aimed at the van driver. The SUV driver writhed and screamed. The van driver drew on the officer, who shot him in the knee. The van driver collapsed, his falsetto screams rivaling the SUV driver's. The officer holstered his own gun, picked up the van driver's gun, and turned him onto his face, cuffing him and reading him his rights at the same time.

"I didn't even have time to get my Glock out of the glove compartment." Giulia spoke more to herself than to Rowan.

"As well you shouldn't," Rowan said. "I heard the shots. Road rage. You don't need to confirm it. You have a baby to protect. Are the cops there yet?"

"The second gunshot was a legal one. Shooter disabled and cuffed. Victim alive and possibly calculating the money he'll win in the inevitable lawsuit."

"Good. Dismiss it from your mind. We have other concerns to discuss. Accidents, for one."

"Coincidence, Rowan."

"There are no coincidences." More pencil scratchings. "You can record and talk at the same time on your phone. Do it."

Part of Giulia wanted to laugh at Rowan's apparent eccentricities. Then she remembered the little ghost she saw a month ago in the cellar of the Dahlia mansion and the urge to laugh vanished. She put the phone on speaker and began recording. "Ready, Obi-Wan."

Rowan chortled. "Brown isn't my color and I never wear cloaks. They make me look like a circus tent. First, we backtrack to the 'all meetings all the time' reading. Every layout brought a stranger into your life. We know it isn't the baby, because he's no stranger to any of us." The cards snapped against the table. "The stranger does something or has a personality trait which irritates you. I can't guarantee it stops at irritating, but I didn't get an immediate sense of danger."

"Your cards have a connection to *The Scoop*."

"Those two are hemorrhoids on the butt of Cottonwood. Don't distract me. Immediate doesn't mean nonexistent. You have to watch yourself. Don't trust anyone."

"I distrust most strangers on sight. Hazard of the profession."

"You're not paying attention. Did I say 'most?' No. I said 'all.'"

Giulia paused the recording. "To wrap up the road rage incident, ambulances have taken the injured away. Tow trucks are adding to the chaos by continual honking as they try to fit into spaces not designed for their girth. I will be taking an alternate route home..."

Rowan pounced into Giulia's pause. "What are you thinking?"

"One second." Giulia created a mental bullet list. "First tell me about the reading you did after the accident here."

Papers being shuffled. "It wasn't as pervasive as this morning's. Keep an eye out for malfunctions."

"For what?"

"Not what you expected? Me neither. I thought the cards would focus on obvious accidents. Cars, falling down stairs, you know. But things breaking or breaking down is what came through." Scribbles. "Make sure your phone is charged. Is your AAA membership paid up?"

This time Giulia did smile. "Yes, mom."

"Everyone needs a mother and I know yours is dead and she gave you trouble when you kicked the habit. Take it where you find it. Now tell me what you were thinking earlier."

If she couldn't tell a psychic, who could she tell? "My current clients live in an old, run-down house. They're dirt-poor nuns, which is important. Three times when I've been in the house I've smelled cigarette smoke. Some of the nuns claim to have smelled it too."

"A ghost!"

Giulia rubbed her temple. "Rowan, do you have to sound so happy?"

"Are you kidding?" I haven't seen a ghost in twenty-three years. I haven't talked to one in thirty. My first ex-husband was haunted by his mother. You won't be surprised to learn I was the first in a long line of ex-wives." The pencil was back in action. "You think you've met helicopter moms? The woman hovered at the end of the bed whenever we had sex."

Laughter spurted from Giulia's mouth. "I wouldn't have been able to keep a straight face."

"I know, right? Thing is, the doofus couldn't see her. The man was as sensitive as a cinder block. Whenever we fought about Mommy's haunting, she'd lurk at his shoulder and pet his hair. With her other hand she alternated waving goodbye at me and flipping me off."

"Stop making me laugh. I'll get the hiccups." Giulia forced herself to breathe slower and deeper.

"Back to the point. You haven't seen your cigarette ghost yet?"

Reality doused Giulia in ice water. "No, but this morning when I smelled smoke again—"

"You invited it to manifest? Good. You've taken the correct first step and I know you were the epitome of politeness."

"What if there really is a ghost? Strange things have been happening at the convent. Dangerous things."

Sshh. Sshh. Sshh. Pieces of thin cardboard shuffled against each other on Rowan's end. "Hush. I'm redoing the cards. You're my unofficial whetstone. You keep me sharp."

"I'm pleased to be of use, although the image isn't one I'd apply to myself."

"You're too close to your own skills. That's why you have me and Jasper. My mentor showed me my skills when I was a pudgy outcast teenager. Until then I thought I was merely a goth before goth became cool."

Zlatan made his wants felt again. Giulia tried to concentrate on Rowan.

"All right. I'm still not seeing anything urgent, but stranger danger hasn't abated."

"Stranger danger?"

A beat. "Did I say that? Blame my grandkids. They visited this weekend and talked nonstop about school. Are you still recording?"

With a pang of guilt, Giulia pressed the buttons again. "I am now."

"Good thing you have mental tricks to remember important information. What are your plans for the rest of today?"

"First, supper."

"Wrong. Go to a mini-mart for sugar, carbs, and protein. Trail mix or a couple of granola bars. No booze. Right, you're pregnant and booze-free. Good. Eat and go to the room in your convent where you sensed the ghost. If it's not there, try every room in the house where it may have manifested. Do not be afraid of it. You're a tower of spiritual strength and your little guy is a turbo booster. Make the ghost work with you." Crumpling paper filled the speaker like static. "And watch out for accidents."

Forty-Eight

When Sister Dorothy opened the convent door, Steve the scenery-chewing Chihuahua once again turned his back on Giulia.

"I'm no longer worthy."

"He's a diva. Come in, please. Monday is soup kitchen night. Everyone else is out working."

"Not a problem. I'd like to check over a few areas of the house."

"Have at it. You're a refreshing change from police and firefighters and dead bodies." She shivered much like Steve. "May I offer you a hamburger and some fries?"

"Thank you, no. I've eaten already." She'd mollified Zlatan with fruit and nut granola.

She climbed straight to the attic. All three invalids were in their rooms. After closing the attic door, she opened her EMF app. Silence. Certain it was malfunctioning the opposite way, she powered down her phone and powered it up again. Still silence.

Rather than waste time exploring the nooks and crannies of the attic, Giulia descended to the third floor. Sister Agatha's low moans could be heard in the stairwell and Steve was barking his head off in the kitchen. As she stood listening in the center of the spare bedroom not a single car drove down the street to break the silence. Neither Agatha's voice nor Steve's yapping reached her through the closed door.

No laughter, either. She opened the app. Not a blip.

For this she skipped dinner? She should be home grilling the shark steaks she'd bought on sale while Frank watered the vegetables and teased Scarlett the chameleon.

She couldn't even stomp downstairs in frustration to the chapel

NUN AFTER THE OTHER   163

on the second floor because only a complete scumbag would disturb the chronically ill. Instead, she walked in the sedate manner dinned into her from her days as a nun.

The chapel adjusted her attitude. The eight-by-nine-foot space must have started out life as a child's bedroom. A black floor lamp with a frosted glass shade was hooked into the room's main light switch. At some point the ubiquitous forest green rug had been inflicted on it. Its pale green walls were the only ones in the house besides Helena's without chipped paint. Antiquated Venetian blinds hung in the windows. A cast bronze crucifix hung on the north wall. Below it, a closed Bible lay on a wooden bookstand, supported by a mission-style coffee table. A matching floor lamp stood next to it. A semicircle of five wooden chairs in the same style faced the Bible and crucifix. Extra space had been left near the door, no doubt to accommodate Eugenie's wheelchair.

Giulia flashed back to the tiny chapel on the Novices' floor in the Motherhouse. Once it had been the only refuge for overworked, harassed young nuns. The same bubble of peace enclosed this little room. She opened the EMF app out of duty, but was not surprised at its silence.

Down to the first floor. Steve was now the only noisemaker in the house. Sister Agatha was silent and no one was watching TV. An ideal setting for a ghost hunter. Since she'd gotten herself into this, she'd better see it through. She left the cellar door ajar, remembering too many horror movies in which characters met with nasty ends in old cellars. *Night of the Living Dead. The House by the Cemetery. The Blair Witch Project. The Evil Dead.*

She pulled the light cords and typed "Borrow classic Disney movies from Sidney" into her Notes app. She'd need at least a week of perky animated sweetness after this case. Then she glanced at the window where Victor Eagle had been dangling. The stack of newspapers was no longer there and the wall was as clean as old whitewash could get.

Hesitation would make it worse. She opened the EMF app and it ululated loud enough to make the phone vibrate.

"What an irritating noise."

Forty-Nine

Giulia experienced another biblical cliché first hand when her knees turned to water. Ezekiel, maybe. She should look it up. As those thoughts scattered through her mind, she noted again how the brain distracts itself with trivialities in moments of panic.

"Turn it off. It's almost as annoying as that moaning nun upstairs."

Giulia turned off the app. Between her and the furnace stood—do ghosts stand on anything?—a misty woman. The furnace was visible through the woman's clothes, if Giulia stared hard enough.

Ghosts wore clothes. This ghost wore a skirt that swept the floor. Its waist was corseted to a circumference which must have cinched its diaphragm and both lungs. If ghosts needed to breathe. A blouse dripping with lace and a hat festooned with peonies and a huge, drooping ostrich feather completed its ensemble. She squinted at the outfit. Looking at the ghost was like looking at a monochrome mannequin through dense fog. The skirt and blouse might have been blue or gray. The lace was pale, its color too similar to the overall ghost mist. The hat might have been the same shade as the blouse—fog is the new black?—with dark and light flowers. The ostrich feather appeared dyed.

She raised her phone to take a picture.

"You're new at this, aren't you?"

Without replying, Giulia snapped a burst in natural light and a handful of single shots with her night vision app.

"You were a Gibson Girl."

"And a Suffragette. And I designed this house. Sit down before you fall down. Women these days have no stamina." She raised a cigarette to her lips, inhaled, and blew a smoke ring.

At least Giulia would've sworn the ghost inhaled and exhaled.

"Would you mind not blowing smoke in my face?"

"I despise croakers." She vanished.

Giulia backed to the laundry folding table. When it was supporting her butt, she gave herself permission to react. Her knees gave out. Her hands shook so hard she lost her grip on her phone and had to dive for it before it hit the floor.

One minute and forty-four seconds later by her phone clock her fingers stopped trembling enough to open the Contacts folder.

Frank answered on the first ring. "Hey, babe. I was just about to call you. We're bringing in a snitch and we have to deal with him tonight. I'll be way late. What's for supper?"

"I don't know." Her voice must have sounded even stranger to him than to her because she heard his desk chair screech against the floor in the detectives' office.

"What's wrong?"

"There's a ghost."

"A what?"

"A ghost. In the convent. It smokes. I mean, she smokes."

"Back up. The convent where Eagle got torched?"

His voice was helping her calm down. "Yes. I tried to take pictures, but I don't know if any of them came out."

"Babe, wait. I remember you telling me about that thing you saw with your camera at the Dahlia house. You weren't sure if it really happened, though."

Every raging pregnancy hormone and missed cup of coffee arose in Giulia. "Francis Xavier Driscoll, I'll thank you to remember you are not the only professional in the family."

"Honey, I'm only saying—"

"I understand quite well what you're saying. I'll see you when I get home." She stabbed the End button hard enough to make her finger joints ache. Her instant outrage subsided.

"A real woman in this house at last."

Used to not showing surprise when a client or suspect tried to startle her, Giulia did not jump. She looked up from the phone. The dead Gibson Girl stood—appeared to stand—in front of her.

"I am sick to death of withered virgins." A fresh cigarette in her hand lit itself. "Ghosts with jokes. Too bad a comedy club didn't buy my house."

Giulia pressed Record on the voice memo function in case her call with Rowan hadn't filled it up. "What's your name?"

"Florence Gosnall. Go ahead, type it in. You'll find me."

Her thumbs refused to obey her. Google took her best guess at the jumble of letters she gave it. Giulia made a show of comparing the "Florence" thumbnails on the Image tab with her personal apparition.

"Yes, I died young. Why do you think I look this good now?"

"I didn't know there were rules. Is there a—"

"If you say 'Handbook for the Recently Deceased,' I'll haunt that bedridden crone upstairs until she remembers how to scream like she means it." Several puffs on the new cigarette.

Giulia bit her lips. "I like *Beetlejuice.*"

"You won't after you kick off."

"Ms. Gosnall—"

"Oh, please. I'm haunting you. We're allowed to call each other by our first names."

Giulia hadn't watched horror movies for years without assimilating their key points. She'd already violated one: Don't go in the basement. As for the one where true names have power, she was out of luck. Most of the nuns spoke to her as "Ms. Driscoll," but Bart called her "Giulia."

She'd have to have an emergency session with Rowan and Jasper. For now, she smiled at the ghost and said, "Thank you, Florence. I do have a question. Were you down here during the break-in and the fire?"

Ticktackticktack-bump on the stairs did make Giulia jump. The ghost snickered. Steve came into view. Giulia kicked herself. The dog trotted up to the ghost, who bent over and scratched its ears.

"I was allergic to dogs and cats when I was alive." Florence raised her eyes to Giulia. "You want to know more about that butterball who got stuck in the window?" She gave the dog a pat on the rear. "Scoot. I'm in the middle of a haunting." Steve scooted behind the furnace. Florence stood upright. "Wouldn't you rather know how I can do this?" A new cigarette appeared between her fingers.

"I would, but I'm working on a case."

"A female detective. I suppose a man is your boss?"

"No. I own the business."

"You make me happy. I knew women would move beyond working for Pinkerton's."

"If you're tied to the house," Giulia did not bring up plot points from *Beetlejuice*, "you should know I'm here to negotiate a deal between the nuns and the developer. Every house on the street will be demolished."

A string of incongruous profanity spewed from the translucent mouth. Upstairs, the front door opened and Steve scrambled upstairs, barking and panting. The Gibson Girl vanished.

Giulia followed Steve. A haggard Sister Kathryn stopped an argument with Sister Olive when she saw Giulia.

"Now what?"

An irritated human pleased Giulia to an unexpected degree. "I was double-checking certain things. Do you have a few minutes?"

She recapped her meeting with Barbara Beech as all the ambulatory nuns crowded together in the hallway. Cautious hope replaced Kathryn's irritation.

"Do you think they'll go for it?" Dorothy said.

"I gave her a higher figure than necessary on purpose. Even my second offer was more than I expect my final one will be." While Giulia spoke, she surreptitiously sniffed for cigarette smoke. The only smells her nose identified were old wood and ripe dog.

"Steve!" Olive picked the Chihuahua up by the scruff of the neck. "What did you roll in?"

Fifty

A midnight blue Honda CRV drove down the street below the speed limit as Giulia walked to the Nunmobile. She palmed her phone and walked faster. The SUV followed her. Half a block. A quarter. Ten steps and she would reach her passenger door. Key in hand, she ran for it.

The CRV honked and a hand waved out its window.

"Giulia, it's me."

She recognized Pit Bull's voice and stopped with the key in the lock. The CRV's detailing of a tattooed pit bull dog holding a TV camera should've clued her in. If she hadn't been a wee bit off-kilter from her conversation with the convent ghost.

"Do you have time to talk?"

"Yes. Follow me to my office." She led the way, passing two food trucks and her favorite hot dog place. She'd have to remember to keep granola bars in the glove compartment with the Glock. All the fashion-forward pregnant PIs were doing it.

She giggled, heard its keyed-up sound, and forced herself to stop. Her hands started to shake again and she gripped the steering wheel tighter. Talk to Pit Bull now. React later.

Ten miles from the office they got stuck behind a four-car pileup. The side streets were too far away to try to back up and police had stopped traffic in both directions to give access to fire engines, ambulances, and tow trucks. The wait added half an hour to what should've been a fifteen-minute drive at this time of night.

Accidents, Giulia thought. Rowan said to watch out for accidents.

They parked in the building's empty lot at quarter after eight.

Giulia opened the back door. "No one is in the building at this hour."

As they climbed the stairs something skinny and dark ran down and shoved them into the wall on either side. Pit Bull reached out one long arm and grabbed the something by its hoodie.

The kid inside the black hoodie and jeans choked and struggled. Pit Bull cuffed the back of the kid's head. Giulia continued upstairs and Pit Bull followed, dragging the still-squirming kid, who emitted a jangling sound at each tread.

Fresh scratches marred the doorknob plate on DI's door. She should've been furious, but a human thief was familiar territory. She doubted the kid could make cigarettes materialize at will. She took pictures before she unlocked the door and relocked them all inside. Pit Bull turned one of the window chairs around and dropped the kid into it. Giulia approached and Pit Bull clamped the kid's arms to the arms of the chair. The kid was two-thirds Pit Bull's size and half his weight, and Giulia estimated Pit Bull at six foot two and one eighty or ninety. She reached into the kid's hoodie pocket and pulled out three professional lock picks.

"Who hired you?"

The kid said nothing.

She repeated the question.

Pit Bull loomed over the kid. The kid side-eyed the cameraman's impressive muscles. Pit Bull flexed. A whimper escaped the kid before he cut it off.

Giulia took out her phone. "Being married to a police detective has its privileges." She angled the screen toward the kid and pressed '9'. The kid bleated. She pressed '1'.

"Don't!" The kid looked up at Pit Bull and shrank into the seat.

She hovered her finger over the '1' button. The kid tried and failed to turn his butt cheeks into feet and walk himself out of the chair.

"I just got out of juvie. I can't go back inside." He started to tremble.

Pit Bull released one arm and picked up a lock pick. "We caught you breaking in with professional tools." He held the pick an inch from the kid's face.

"I got no job. I gotta get food for ma."

"What are you, twelve?"

"Twelve and a half, and don't talk to me about school and shit."

Giulia pinched the bridge of her nose, glad she was no longer teaching. "Why us? We aren't retail."

The kid muttered, paused, and shrugged.

Giulia's first thought was Eagle, except Eagle was not directing minor criminals from beyond the grave.

She hoped.

She said to Pit Bull, "Kanning?"

The cameraman considered.

Non-violent Giulia Driscoll, advocate of peace, said, "I'll break his microphone over his hair-sprayed head the next time we meet."

A crafty expression replaced the fear on the kid's face. "Will you cut me a deal if I spill?"

Giulia fired up Sidney's computer and logged in as herself. "Give me your name."

"James...Driscoll."

She didn't dignify the lie with an answer. Her fingers poised over the keys, she waited. Pit Bull worked magic and made himself appear larger. The kid swallowed and said, "Jimmy Haynes with a 'Y.'"

Giulia emailed Frank: Will explain later. Please look up record of James Haynes. Email here ASAP.

Pit Bull said, "No. He wouldn't shoot himself in the foot."

"All right." She knew he meant Ken Kanning, but since he depended on Kanning for his job, the assertion carried less weight than he might have thought. If not Kanning, what about Beech? Closing Eagle's last deal would cement her position as leader.

Frank's reply pinged. Giulia read it out loud. "Probation at age eleven for shoplifting. Three months at age twelve for breaking and entering." She looked over the monitor at James Haynes with a "Y." "Did you steal the lock picks?"

"Who'd steal something that small? They were part of the deal."

Giulia pounced. "Deal with who?"

The kid shuddered hard enough to rattle the chair. "I'm screwed. I'm so screwed."

"Language," Giulia said.

Pit Bull picked up the kid by his scrawny biceps. "Kid, if you shit yourself on her floor, she'll make you clean it with your tongue."

The kid's hands clamped over his butt cheeks.

Pit Bull raised him so they looked eye to eye. "Tell her who hired you or I'll make sure you spit shine her floor."

The kid turned large, deep, soulful eyes on Giulia. Giulia crossed her arms and waited. The kid's feet twitched. Pit Bull affected a bored expression, as though he could hold this position for days. The kid licked cracked lips. "Keep me out of juvie and I'll tell you who's paying me."

Giulia nodded to Pit Bull, who plopped the kid into the chair again. When Giulia had a Word doc open, she said, "Go."

The kid talked fast, always keeping an eye on Pit Bull. "This guy I knew in juvie met me at this place I hang out. He said I could earn a hundred bucks easy. Told me to be at a certain place at a certain time to meet a guy."

Pit Bull clenched his fists, flexed his biceps, and made his neck veins stand out as the kid talked. Every time the kid saw muscle movement, he spoke faster.

"I ain't stupid. I need the money. I met the guy, he gave me the picks and paid me half up front. Told me to grab anything that looked like it'd have private info. Laptops, papers, stuff like that."

Giulia typed. "When are you meeting your contact?"

"Tonight, duh. He wants the stuff."

"When?"

"Nine."

Giulia thought. The kid's legs wouldn't stay still. Pit Bull inspected his fingernails. The kid couldn't seem to take his eyes away from Pit Bull's hands. Giulia wondered if he expected Wolverine's claws to spring from the knuckles.

Giulia called Frank.

"Babe, what the hell's going on?"

"I caught the kid with the record trying to break into the office."

"What? I'll send a car to bring the little shit in."

"No. Wait. I won't press charges if he leads us to the guy who paid him."

The kid started to get out of the chair. Pit Bull convinced him it would be wise to stay put.

Giulia interrupted Frank's argument. "Bigger fish."

Frank started to argue again and stopped. "What's the rest of it?"

"Pit Bull says Kanning isn't behind this. I think I know who is. I have to be sure. If you meet us at the rendezvous, you land the fish."

"If the fish turns out to be Kanning, I'll shove his microphone down his throat and take him on a tour of the state before bringing him in to get it removed."

"You're so sweet when you're Neanderthal. We're leaving now."

"Nash and I will wrap up in five more minutes and meet you there."

Fifty-One

Pit Bull kept a hand on the kid's shoulder all the way downstairs into the parking lot.

"You wanted to talk to me," Giulia said to Pit Bull. "I'll call you when this mess is finished and we'll meet. An hour, tops. Okay?"

"Yeah, fine. Thanks." He pushed the kid into the Nunmobile's passenger seat and stuck his head in after. "Remember: You touch her, you touch anything in the car, you do anything to screw up, and I promise you will clean her floor with your tongue. *Capisce*?"

The kid tried to disappear into the upholstery. "Got it." His voice cracked.

"Buckle in."

It took the kid three tries.

"Sit on your hands."

He obeyed.

Pit Bull stood and said to Giulia across the top of the car, "Got me on speed dial?" He winked.

"Right here." She opened her phone to his entry in Contacts, moving it across her window so the kid would see it.

She buckled herself in, not glancing at her passenger sitting on his hands lest she giggle. Even though no part of tonight's adventure was funny.

The kid regained his voice at the second stop sign. "Look, lady, I'm not shooting up or anything. I'm clean, you get it? I'm doing this for my mom."

"Your mother might appreciate a son who finishes school so he can get a legitimate job."

"Jesus Chr—"

"Stop. You will not curse in my car."

Giulia's tone of voice stopped him but the command appeared to baffle him. He opened his mouth half a block later. "My dad got my mom hooked. He beat the sh—uh, he beat me and Mom whenever he got a skinful and then he OD'd, but Mom's got shi—dammit—sorry, uh, Mom can't pick guys who ain't bad for her. Her next two hookups used and beat us too. Fun life, huh? Mom tries to stick with methadone but she doesn't always do good at it and the only places she can get work are dollar stores and stuff."

"Am I now supposed to open my heart and wallet to you?" Giulia learned long ago to distrust sob stories.

"F—" The kid coughed, muttered, and cleared his throat. "I'm marking time 'til I hit puberty. Then I'll bulk up like your bodyguard and I'll beat Mom's latest hookup like he beats us and I'll kick him out and I'll take care of Mom. But I gotta get money somehow." His body jerked with the effort to keep his hands under his butt. "It's your fault I got caught anyway. You weren't supposed to be there."

"Take responsibility for your own actions." Giulia turned left onto the public library's street and parked in front of the first house on the street.

Frank and Nash exited their car when she opened her door. Giulia came around and opened the passenger door.

"Out."

He slunk out. Giulia handed him a manila folder she'd stuffed with printouts not needing to be shredded.

"Okay, Haynes," Frank said, "get over there. You won't see us, but we'll be breathing down your neck."

The kid walked to the library's parking lot. Giulia, Frank, and Nash sequestered themselves in the stand of birches around back by the dumpster, the assigned meeting place. The irony was palpable.

The kid shuffled from one foot to the other for a minute and a half. At the start of minute two, another vision in black approached the dumpster. The vision said nothing until it reached the kid.

"You better have good stuff or we're keeping the rest of the cash." It spoke in a hoarse baritone.

Frank and Nash crept toward the other side of the dumpster. The kid reached under his hoodie and produced the folder. The vision grabbed it and flipped it open.

Frank and Nash flanked the vision. He cursed and tried to dodge.

Frank shoved him against the side of the dumpster and read him his rights as Nash cuffed him.

The kid made a break for it. Giulia cut across the corner of the parking lot and tripped him. Nash hustled the vision into their car. Frank hauled the kid up by one arm.

"You lying bitch!" The kid tried to elongate his legs to kick Giulia. "We had a deal! You double-crossed me!"

Frank clamped his hand on the kid's cheeks. "Shut it. Now listen carefully. I am taking you to the station—I said, shut it—where you will help us deal with the Rhodes scholar in our car. Then, if you watch your mouth, you get to go home."

The kid stopped aiming long-distance violence at Giulia. "No shit?"

"Language," Giulia said.

Frank turned his head away. When he turned back, his expression betrayed nothing.

"Do you know the other one?" Giulia said.

"Nash thinks he remembers him from his time in the Narcotics division. He's calling his old partner to meet us downtown."

"Speaking of meetings, Pit Bull wants to talk," Giulia said. "I don't know when I'll be home."

Her husband grimaced down at the kid's head. "Me neither."

Fifty-Two

An hour later in one of Cottonwood's late-night diners, Giulia ate a ham sandwich and tomato soup. Pit Bull wolfed down a cheeseburger and fries.

"What did you want to talk about?" Despite her hollow stomach, Giulia kept to ladylike bites to appease Zlatan.

Pit Bull finished chewing. "I figured out how we can work together."

A magnetic voice said at Giulia's shoulder, "If you did, I'll recommend you for a merit raise."

Ken Kanning snagged a chair from a nearby table and parked himself at the end of their booth. Giulia refrained from wondering out loud if a force existed in the known universe capable of disarranging his hair.

Kanning filched three fries and dragged them through the blob of ketchup on his cameraman's plate. "Bull, we're in this together."

Giulia set down her soup spoon. "Did you LoJack his car?"

"Didn't need to."

"Ken, are you stalking me?"

Kanning shook his coif at his cameraman. "My investigative skills seldom fail me. I found you at the second restaurant I tried."

Pit Bull gave a short laugh and returned to his burger. "I'm in a rut."

Giulia stirred her soup. "Be honest with me. Are you here because of your partner or because you have your teeth in a juicy story?"

Kanning's eyes slid to Pit Bull's "Both. Okay? Honest answer."

Pit Bull laughed. "You need to change up your routine."

The Smile appeared. "Consistency is my middle name. You always know what you're getting with me."

The waitress came over with a paper placemat and napkin. "What can I get you, hon?"

"Coffee to start. Is it too late for blueberry pancakes?"

"Breakfast any time of day or night is our motto. Be right back."

"We're going to use the nuns as our springboard into national syndication," he said to Pit Bull.

The waitress returned on the heels of his last word with a full glass pot and a heavy white mug. "Hi-test okay?"

"Anything else doesn't deserve to be called coffee." He flashed The Smile.

The pot handle slipped. She caught it and set the coffee pot on the table without a splash. "You're Ken Kanning."

The Smile gleamed. "Let me shake the hand of a Scooper."

"Oh my God." She stared at her hand after he released it. "Arnie! We got a celebrity in our diner!"

The cook stuck his head through the pickup window. "Yeah? Who?"

"*The Scoop.*"

"You kidding me?"

"Come out here and see."

By this time the three couples at booths and two singles at the counter had stopped paying attention to their food. The cook came through the swinging doors next to the pickup window, untying his apron. "Ken Kanning," he said in an awed voice.

As though his awe was a signal, the other eleven people crowded Giulia's booth. Kanning signed napkins, posed for selfies, and told humorous anecdotes from stories he'd gone after.

Pit Bull and Giulia finished their food in peace.

"We can take over digging dirt on Eagle's outfit," he said in a low voice. "We have TV archives and legal contacts from that mess they got into with the Attorney General last year."

Giulia said in the same tone of voice, "I appreciate your offer, but we've already uncovered the company's history."

"We can take on the other employees. That Lolita bimbo who kept herself glued to Eagle's heels every time he was on TV."

"We have it covered, thank you."

His muttered "Tight ass" wasn't quiet enough. Giulia finished her grilled cheese before her phone vibrated.

Frank's text read: Thug used to be a runner for one of the minor dealers. He's not talking. We're holding him for the standard 72 hours.

Giulia texted back: Maybe Jasper will read his mind for me.

Pit Bull watched her fingers. While Giulia doubted it was possible to key capture texting, his attempt brought her to her senses. *The Scoop* was a distraction. Her priorities were already set. Number one, re-house the nuns. Number two, prove or disprove the Eagle harassment and turn it to the nuns' advantage. Number three, pump the ghost for information.

Her life sounded like a paranormal sitcom.

In ones and twos, *The Scoop*'s fans returned to their seats.

Pit Bull was not DI's client. His guilt was not Giulia's problem.

She snapped shut her phone case. *The Scoop* stared at her.

"Gentlemen, I need to cut this meeting short."

Kanning said, "Wait—"

Pit Bull said, "I thought—"

She said to Pit Bull, "I appreciate your help tonight with our little criminal. If we find a way for you to help with the Sisters, we'll loop you in." She placed the price of her meal plus tip on the table.

"What criminal? What happened? Bull, did you get film?"

Giulia scooted out of the booth.

Fifty-Three

Her phone rang as she walked in the door.

"Honey, it's Aida. Your brother is giving indications of waking up."

Giulia moved the phone away from her face not to let the nurse hear her yawn like a hibernating bear. "Thanks for letting me know."

"Can you come down?"

Her shoulders sagged. Her ankles were swelling. Zlatan was informing her a sandwich and single cup of soup was not enough nourishment for a growing boy. Her bed upstairs was singing a siren song to the rest of her body.

"I'll be there in twenty minutes." She hung up and called her sister-in-law.

"Anne? It's Giulia. Were you asleep? No? Good. The hospital called. Salvatore might wake up any minute. I'm going down there."

Anne stifled a yawn. "Why inflict more Salvatore on yourself?"

"I need the time off of my inevitable sentence in Purgatory."

Another yawn. "According to my loving husband, I'm going straight to the pits of Hell, which means tonight I'm going straight to bed."

"Your kids are more important."

"Exactly. Good luck."

She taped a note for Frank to the inner garage door and hit the road again. At this hour she had her choice of spots in the Emergency Room section of the hospital parking lot.

Aida was waiting for her when the sliding doors opened. Ice cream sundaes decorated her scrubs. "Honey, you look like you need to sleep for a week."

The "s" word triggered another yawn from Giulia. "Is he awake?"

"His EEG is spiking in all the right places. The doctor estimates thirty minutes or less." She hooked her arm into Giulia's. "You want some coffee?"

"I'm rationed."

The nurse whacked her forehead with the heel of her hand. "I forgot. How's the second trimester?"

Giulia patted her stomach. "The same as the first, except for this one rearranging my internal organs."

"My three each picked an organ to sit on. First one hated my stomach, second my lungs." They walked under a PA speaker and she waited for the page to finish. "My youngest liked to kick my kidneys."

"You're making me reconsider more pregnancies."

Aida laughed. "Once you hold your first in your arms, you'll want more." She stopped outside a closed door. "Ready?"

"As I'll ever be."

Sneakers flapped on the Linoleum. A breathless voice said, "Wait."

Giulia and Aida turned their heads. Anne Falcone skidded to a halt. "Is he awake?"

"Anne? I thought you weren't putting yourself through any more of him."

"I couldn't let my Fellow Salvatore Sufferer go it alone. The busybody who lives across the street was happy to house sit in exchange for all the details when I get back."

Aida cleared her throat. "Miss, are you a relative of the patient?"

"I'm his wife. Are you his night nurse? You weren't here last week when I came to pick up the car keys."

"Aida, this is my sister-in-law, Anne. Anne, this is Aida, the best nurse in Cottonwood."

"Don't make me blush, honey. You ladies ready?"

"No," they said together. Giulia recovered first. "Let's get it over with."

The overhead fluorescents glared off the gray walls and speckled floor of the small room. The machines surrounding Salvatore beeped and hummed.

Anne whispered, "He's dreaming. His eyes are moving back and forth beneath his closed eyelids."

Aida said in her usual voice, "He's made some sounds, too. Eye movement and brain activity have been increasing all day." She picked up the clipboard hanging at the end of the bed and made notes. "Go ahead and talk to him. Your voice may be the trigger he needs."

Anne gave Giulia a wry smile. "My semi-weekly chastising is overdue. I'm sure his sense of duty will come to his aid." She raised her voice. "Salvatore, it's time to wake up. Anne and Giulia are here. You must have something to say to us."

A young woman in basic green scrubs entered the room and discussed the chart and readouts with Aida.

"Mrs. Falcone?" When Anne raised her hand, the woman continued. "I'm Doctor Stryker. We're pleased and encouraged by your husband's progress. While each coma patient is different, in this case we—"

Giulia said, "Salvatore, do you recognize us?"

Everyone looked toward the head of the bed. Salvatore's eyes were open, but unfocused.

Anne said, "Salvatore, it's me."

The brown eyes closed. For a moment Giulia thought nothing else would happen, but they reopened and by degrees lost their blurry aspect. Her brother's lips separated with difficulty. Aida poured water from a plastic pitcher into a Styrofoam cup and added a bendy straw. She held the straw to his lips and he blinked again and sipped.

His eyebrows met over the bridge of his nose. "Where are my children?"

"Home in bed. Mrs. Esposito is sitting with them."

"She is an idler, a gossip and a busybody." His eyes switched their focus to Giulia, but his eyelids fluttered and closed before he said anything else.

Giulia said to Anne, "First Timothy, right?"

"Chapter five, verse twelve, I think. No, thirteen." She gave her husband a hard smile. "He trotted out First Timothy and Second Corinthians at the beginning of every work week. He thought it would keep me in line."

The doctor dictated and Aida wrote more notes. When Aida re-hung the clipboard, the doctor said to Anne and Giulia, "Please don't be discouraged. I've seen this before. I can't make any promises, but keep your phones on. He's asleep now, but his number are dropping back into coma range already. See?" She flipped to a printout of an EEG screencap and held it up to the actual machine. "However, because of this episode there's a good chance he'll wake up again by the end of the week. If that happens and he follows the progression I've seen with these cases, he'll stay awake for longer and longer periods each time."

Anne and Giulia walked to the parking lot together.

"Well, the silence was good while it lasted." Anne yawned. "I'd better put my alarm volume to the maximum or I'll never get them out of bed in time for the school bus."

"I'm going to use my executive privilege and sleep an extra hour." Giulia yawned too. "What are you going to do if he makes a rapid recovery and gets discharged?"

"I'm trying not to think about it. I'm enjoying each day as it comes."

Giulia unlocked the Nunmobile. "I've torched my 'Get out of Purgatory Free' card by thinking the kids would be better off without him."

Fifty-Four

Frank, already in bed, pulled the sheet over Giulia. "Welcome home."

"I love this bed. At this moment, I love it more than..." She yawned.

"As long as you don't say 'more than your hardworking husband' I agree."

"You don't have a pillow top, but somehow I still prefer you."

He snugged her against him. "Where do you want to start?"

"Salvatore came out of his coma for about a minute and didn't yell at either me or Anne. We should play the lottery while my luck is in."

"Babe, I'd be happier if your brother moved to Assisi and became a hermit under a vow of silence."

"He'd have to leave me alone, then. I like the idea."

"Forget him. I want to hear about the ghost."

Giulia described her "Ghost and Mrs. Muir with added cigarettes" experience.

"A what?"

"A Gibson Girl. The idealized woman from the turn of the last century. Big bouffant hair, giant picture hats, waists corseted to unbelievable circumferences."

"Uh...it may ring a vague bell."

She rubbed his cheek with the top of her head. "You're sweet."

"True, and right now I'm trying not to tick you off again." He pulled her closer. "You really think...wait, bad choice of words. You really saw a ghost."

"I saw and talked with a ghost." She extricated herself. "I tried to take pictures." She stretched her arm to its limit to reach her phone on the nightstand. "Maybe I have proof."

He sat up. She opened her photos and they examined each photo in the regular burst. "Furnace. Furnace. Furnace. Oh, come on. Furnace. Furnace." She switched to the night vision camera folder. Her breath hitched.

"*An bhfuil tú ag mágadh fúm?*"

"Was that G-rated?" Giulia asked out of habit.

"I could teach it to Zlatan. It's 'Are you kidding me?'"

All her attention was on her screen. Light green furnace, lighter green walls, a thin rectangle of blinding green from the streetlight outlined the window curtain. And between the camera and the furnace, the barest suggestion of an hourglass-shaped haze.

She swiped to the next photo. Nothing. The third. Nothing. She swiped back to the first. The haze was still there.

"She told me the camera wouldn't work. She didn't know about night vision." Giulia touched Frank's arm. "You see it too, yes?"

"No one—" he cleared his throat— "mouth's dry. Can't imagine why. No one will believe this picture. It's not clear enough."

She enlarged the photo, but it lost detail instead of becoming sharper. "Rats."

Frank kissed her. "*Muirnín*, one of the things I love about you is your naturally G-rated language."

"Mm. I'll show this to Rowan tomorrow." She closed the phone. "Don't I sound calm? I'm only pretending."

"You're doing it well." He put his hands over hers. "I apologize."

She reversed her hands and squeezed his. "Accepted."

"And I thought your only secret skill was working magic in the kitchen."

"A smart woman always maintains an air of mystery." She became serious. "I'm worried Zlatan is going to become a paranormal junkie on top of being an adrenaline junkie."

"We'll make his childhood a memorable one."

"Frank..."

"Just don't bring any of them home. I don't want an audience while sleeping with my wife."

Some of the tension sloughed off her. "Let me tell you about Rowan's first mother-in-law."

Fifty-Five

Giulia slept as late as she dared Tuesday morning, which was nowhere near as late as she wanted. She made three phone calls from home, packed her demon-busting equipment in her messenger bag just in case, inhaled half a peanut butter sandwich, and arrived at the office at ten after ten.

Sidney said without looking up from her keyboard, "Continual tardiness is not the habit of a successful entrepreneur."

"If clients would stop calling me out of the house at all hours, I would have no reason to be tardy." She didn't have to see Zane's face to know he was staring at Sidney in trepidation. "Zane, it's called banter. You will have noticed we indulge in it on occasion."

"...Okay, Ms. D."

"Good. Now, two things." Giulia waited for them to stop typing. "First, lunch is on me."

"I have no plans, especially when the boss is buying lunch." Sidney looked over at Zane.

"Yes. Same here." He waited a beat. "Why?"

"Rowan and Jasper are also coming for lunch. I need to consult them. The second thing is someone tried to break in last night."

"What?" they said in perfect synchronization.

"The operative word is 'tried.' Pit Bull wanted to meet and we came here around seven thirty. An inexpert twelve-year-old was attacking our door with lock picks." She opened the door. "Did neither of you notice the scratches on the back plate?"

"No." Zane came around and crouched in front of the doorknob. Sidney hovered behind him.

"And you work at a detective agency."

"We abase ourselves in spirit before you." Sidney straightened. "Not in fact, because I lifted one of the baby alpacas last night and threw out my back."

"Chiropractor?"

"I have an appointment at five fifteen. Why would somebody want to break in? I mean, they could steal our computers, but it's obvious we're not a retail store."

Zane twisted himself into an unnatural angle to see Giulia. "We need to up our encryption."

"Agreed."

"I'll comparison shop if you want, but I can write a program tailored for us."

"I'd much rather have your handiwork than something mass produced."

Zane's seldom-seen grin appeared. "Give me a week." Then it disappeared. "Will that be too long? Do we need physical security?"

"We're getting it. I'm having a security system installed today."

"The break-in can't be Eagle," Sidney said. "He's dead."

"Funny you should mention Eagle." Giulia waited for Zane to stand and close the door. "After some encouragement, last night's thief agreed to lead us to the middleman who hired him. Frank and Nash met us and took charge of both criminals. Nash recognized the middleman. We're all waiting for him to give up the name of who's really responsible.".

Sidney's email ping sounded. "Which you think is?"

Zane said from his desk, "Logic would dictate the new head of Eagle Developers."

"It would." Giulia headed to her own office. "But I don't rely on logic alone."

For the next hour the tapping of three keyboards was almost the only sound in the two offices. The phone rang twice, both times handled by Zane. He put it through to Giulia the third time. "It's Mr. D. on one."

She picked up. "He caved?"

"He caved. You're not going to like it."

"Not *The Scoop*?"

"No, not that bizarre. Besides, they like you now."

"I can't imagine what heinous sin I committed to be punished on such a regular basis."

"The answer to your next question is Eagle."

Giulia didn't reply.

"Are you still there?"

"Yes. But Eagle's dead." She tapped a pen on the nearest legal pad, her go-to method to help herself think. "Did he talk to Eagle face to face?"

"Claims he got his orders from the top dog. His words."

"When?"

"He didn't say."

The dots progressed to concentric circles. "The question is, how reliable is any statement out of the middleman's mouth?"

"Hold on a second." Muffled conversation, then Frank's voice came clear again. "Gotta run. I'll talk to you tonight."

"Thanks." She hung up and said to the silent phone, "The question also is, were Eagle and Beech of one mind in all aspects of the business?"

She wouldn't have pegged Beech as a saboteur. Not so much from her first interview where she and Eagle were playing out a well-rehearsed script, but from the second. Beech gave all the indications of a practical business owner. Plus, she'd won mentoring awards. Plus, she'd seen the business through a state investigation. Plus...

The clock in her icon tray read 11:40. She wrote *Beech or a Cadre of Addicts?* on the legal pad and propped it against her monitor. A bullet point list would have to wait. She locked her monitor and came into the main office.

"Food should be here in five minutes. Sidney, do we still have plates and napkins?"

Sidney held up one finger, typed for a few seconds, and saved. "I should lock my screen."

"I did because we have people coming in. Zane, you too."

"Already locked. It pleases me how readily we've adapted to the new paradigm."

Sidney came out of the combination bathroom and storage closet with paper plates, napkins, and plastic utensils. "We need a checkered tablecloth."

A knock at the door. Zane opened it on a white-haired older man carrying two paper bags by handles of dubious strength.

"Delivery from The Smokehouse."

Zane took the bags. "Come on in."

The old man shook his head. "Prepaid, tip included. Thanks and enjoy your food."

Rowan and Jasper stepped aside for him to exit. Rowan floated in wearing layers of lilac chiffon accented with daffodil, with ribbons of both colors in her long black and violet braids. Jasper's concession to late summer consisted of a dark blue t-shirt instead of black tucked into his jeans.

"Giulia, you have our undivided attention for two hours. You look radiant." She engulfed Giulia in a hug, her Bingo Lady arms flapping against Giulia's biceps before she clasped them around Sidney. "Sidney, sweetie, I am so jealous of your flawless skin." A minute later Zane disappeared within the chiffon-covered arms. "Zane, I want you to moonlight for us. I'll clear it with Giulia."

Giulia was unpacking an assortment of sandwiches from the first bag. "Rowan, you don't have to clear anything with me. Everyone's free time is their own."

"Jasper knew you'd say that. The Shoppe needs a database and who better to create it?" She kept one arm around Zane and began rattling off a list of wants. Zane managed to snag paper and pen from his desk while still being hugged.

Jasper held up a small box with a cellophane window from the second bag. "Are these chocolate chip snickerdoodles?"

"They are. There should also be six raspberry-filled honey cakes. The first two belong to Sidney."

Sidney dived into the bag and clutched the pink box to her chest. "You are the best."

"Rowan, Zane, chow time." Giulia stood at the table like Vanna White showcasing a new puzzle on Wheel of Fortune. "I ordered mini versions of everything so feel free to try something new. Roast beef, turkey club, vegetarian, and chicken salad. To accompany the repast we have Coke, Sprite, and water. You already know about dessert. Dig in, please, and I promise to entertain you during lunch."

Fifty-Six

Giulia didn't keep her promise until she devoured one each of the roast beef and turkey mini subs. To avoid an attack of the hiccups, she kept to water. What she really wanted was a snickerdoodle, but a good hostess feeds her guests first.

"It's time for the entertainment portion of our afternoon to begin." Giulia held tight to her bottle of water. "Rowan and Jasper, one of our current clients is a small convent in an area bought out by Eagle Developers."

Jasper raised an eyebrow, but said nothing.

"I met Eagle once," Rowan said. "I got suckered into setting up a booth at one of those Psychic Fairs. His daughter was about fifteen and dragged him around the entire fair until she saw my Tarot cards. She decided they were the 'right' ones and made him pay for my time." She finished her Sprite. "I prostituted my art and gave her a happy-happy-joy-joy reading."

"You never do that," Jasper said.

"She was the last time. I had to get Eagle away from me. The man wasn't evil, but he was unprincipled and slimy. Don't snicker, Jasper, slime is as visible as ectoplasm and you know I can see it."

"Yes, Aunt Rowan."

"Humility would sound sincerer if it wasn't spoken through a mouth full of chocolate chip snickerdoodle."

Jasper plucked one of her beribboned braids with his prosthetic hand. She huffed. "Go on, Giulia."

"You may not have heard about Eagle's death."

Rowan sat up straight, all her chiffon layers fluttering. "What?"

"He was found stuck in one of the convent's basement windows. A pile of newspapers below him was burning next to remnants of a homemade incendiary device."

"What kind of device?" Jasper the explosives expert said.

"We have videos." Zane took out his phone and played one of the YouTube clips.

"Idiot," Jasper said. "Only a fool would play around with imprecise combustibles." He looked up from the phone at Giulia. "It exploded sooner than he planned, or was more powerful. Or both."

"Our best guess is sooner."

He continued to stare. "I won't ask you to describe how he looked when you found him."

She made a face. "Thanks. All that was backstory. More than once when I was in the convent I smelled cigarette smoke. The nuns deny a secret cigarette habit and are too poor to afford cigarettes anyway."

"Open windows?" Sidney said.

"Do nuns lie?" Zane said.

"Possibly to the first and I won't say absolutely not to the second. The ancillary occurrences were my handy-dandy EMF meter losing its electronic mind."

Rowan belly-laughed. "One of those gizmos like on the ghost hunting shows? Really?" She held out her hand. "Let me see. You need to come in for another lesson. I won't have a student of mine using shortcuts."

Giulia opened the app and placed her phone in Rowan's hand. Still chuckling, Rowan aimed it at everyone in the room in turn. "We can all sleep well tonight because this thing says we're not haunted." She returned to phone to Giulia. "How could I forget? You invited communication. What happened?"

Jasper said after Giulia pocketed her phone, "It's okay. You have the resources to handle it."

Giulia wrinkled her nose at Jasper. "Why do you sound like my personal spiritual advisor who knows exactly what I need to hear?"

He pointed to his forehead. "Clairvoyant. Comes with the territory."

"Wait." Sidney leaned backward in her chair.

"No," Zane leaned forward. "Go on."

Giulia drank, capped the bottle, and gripped it until the thin plastic buckled. "I followed your advice and searched the house. When I reached the cellar the EMF meter screeched like crazy."

"And?" Rowan said.

"The ghost appeared." There. She'd said it in front of four witnesses.

Sidney jumped out of her chair and walked to the window. Jasper made a movement toward her, but kept his seat. Zane's eyes widened until the whites around the pale blue irises showed.

Rowan radiated triumph. "I knew you could do it. What was it like? What did it say?"

With a glance at Sidney's stiff back, Giulia said, "It—she—has a foul mouth."

Jasper laughed.

"She was a Gibson Girl." Giulia dug out her phone again and opened a search window. "Like this." She showed Jasper and Zane. "It's funny. I'm the least fashionable person you'll meet and this is the second case this summer involving high fashion."

"The universe is giving you a hint." Rowan waved the phone away. "I know about Gibson Girls. What did she say?"

"She didn't like the noise from the EMF meter. She doesn't like nuns. She designed the house herself."

"Progressive for the time," Rowan said. "Jasper's right. It's funny for your first ghost to have a potty mouth." She studied Giulia. "You're going to poke a hole in your water bottle if you keep squeezing it like that. Did she threaten you?"

A tight head shake. "She was sarcastic and full of herself. She wanted to scare me."

Jasper said in his calm voice, "The simple fact of her existence threw you off balance."

Giulia gripped the water bottle between her knees and clutched her head in her hands. "I'm completely freaked out. If I look like I'm handling this as though it's another detail in an ongoing hunt for clues, I'm a better actress than Scarlett Johansson."

Rowan admired a fresh snickerdoodle. "You should've seen my face the first time my ex's mother's ghost popped into my life. My ex thought I was going to hurl. He said I turned green and gray and then green again." The memory appeared not to affect her enjoyment of the cookie.

Giulia gave a short laugh. "I don't know how I stayed upright. The bones in my legs melted. At least that's what it felt like."

"I wish I could have seen her." Rowan's voice filled with nostalgia.

Giulia sat up. "I have a picture."

Sidney turned away from the window. "You have what?"

"On my phone. Come into my office and I'll upload it." She unlocked her monitor and plugged the phone into her tower. "When I got over the shock, my first thought was to take a picture. The ghost made a snarky comment, but I tried anyway. Then I thought to try my night vision camera, because why not?" She clicked through all the regular-light pictures. "Here we have several glamour shots of the cellar." Her voice wobbled on the lame joke.

Zane pointed. "Is that the window where Eagle tried to break in?"

"Yes." Giulia heard the tightness in her own voice.

"She manifested between where you were standing and the furnace?" Rowan invaded the last safe millimeter of Giulia's personal space by planting her round chin on Giulia's left shoulder.

"Yes. The ghost posed in one spot and gave me a 'you're such a newbie' look." Giulia took a breath and tried to make her voice even and calm. "After I took these I remembered the night vision camera." She clicked to the first green picture.

"*Pühad jumalad.*" Zane's deep voice lost all timbre.

Giulia gave him her Sister Mary Regina Coelis glare.

He held up both hands. "It's not swearing, Ms. D. It's just 'holy gods' in Estonian."

Sidney spoke for the first time in a while. "I thought you said your uncles taught you how to swear and nothing else."

"They did. My oldest aunt taught me polite words. Ms. D., can you enlarge it?"

"Wait," Rowan said. "I see a human shape with a big, blobby head. Jasper?"

"I get nothing from a photograph."

Giulia clicked so the picture filled the screen, then enlarged it with the mist at the center. "Frank and I tried this on my phone last night. Enlarging the mist makes it cloudier instead of clearer. It shouldn't. I don't know why."

"Go back to normal." Rowan pushed her nose up to the screen. "No detail at all." She drew away. "Now I see it again." She punched

Giulia's shoulder in a ladylike manner. "Contact with evidence. You have the gift, young lady."

"I think I'd rather be promotion manager for *The Scoop*."

Sidney sat with a thump in Giulia's client chair. "At least you're still you."

Fifty-Seven

"Hello? Anyone here?"

Zane dashed into the main office. "Welcome to Driscoll Investigations. How can we help you?"

"We're here to install your new security system."

Giulia came into the office, hand out. "I'm Giulia Driscoll. I'm so pleased we could step into a cancellation."

The thirty-something man stepped aside and the forty-something man behind him wheeled in a dolly stacked with boxes of tools, cameras, and cables.

Giulia poked her head around her office doorway. "Guys, the other important happening of the day is we're installing a security system. Our privacy is not our own for the next hour or so."

Jasper put a hand over his heart. "I am willing to make the sacrifice for the greater good."

Giulia laughed. The ghost-related knots in her neck loosened. "Let me clear my screen." She closed the photo viewer and unhooked her phone.

Out in the main office, the security installers were measuring walls and checking for studs. "Ma'am, our work order says you want motion sensing after hours and a DVR linked to your network. Cabled or wireless?"

"Zane?" Giulia said.

"Cabled. Better picture quality."

Thirty-something said, "For a space this size, wireless is fine. The cameras won't be far from the receiver."

Zane shook his head. "That's not the issue. Wireless isn't up to the standards we require."

Thirty-something made a note on the work order. "Okay by us. You only have the one door? What about a fire escape?"

Giulia walked the two offices and the bathroom with him, discussing optimal camera placement. His partner unpacked a drill and various hardware. Sidney cleaned up the remains of lunch. Zane and Rowan fixed an appointment to discuss her new database. Jasper snagged the last snickerdoodle.

Forty-something measured everything a second time with a laser measure. Thirty-something opened one of the camera boxes. Rowan hovered near both the installers and the honey cake box. Giulia offered to make tea.

Jasper chose chamomile, Rowan peppermint, Sidney green plus jasmine. Zane passed. Giulia decided she'd had enough stress for one day without adding herbal tea to the list.

When everyone was seated in her office, Giulia began. "The going theory is a mugger or junkie killed an old nun last week. Frank and I found her body when we were out on a date. This brought us into the case of the haunted convent."

"Nancy Drew," Sidney said. "We're in a Nancy Drew mystery."

"I loved those books when I was a budding goth," Rowan said. "They're proof opposites attract. Little miss blonde rich girl and me."

"Auntie, you're sidetracking the story."

Rowan made a zipper motion across her lips.

"The mugger theory isn't proven," Giulia continued, "because neither fingerprints nor DNA evidence were found on her body, but I'm convinced the scream Frank and I heard was caused by more than a sudden heart attack." She waited for her audience to pay attention to her and not their tea. "I don't see the convent ghost as a suspect at the moment."

"She might not be able to leave the house," Rowan said. "You said she designed it. Depending on the manner of her death and the strength of her attachment, she might believe she's trapped there."

"Which brings me to my next idea. What if she's responsible for the rest of the vandalism?" Giulia explained the harassment the convent was experiencing. "She said more than once she doesn't like the nuns."

Rowan sipped tea with a meditative expression. "If she can

manifest cigarettes, it's possible, but I don't like the feel of a ghost as sole agent."

"Neither do I," Giulia said. "Too much has been happening via outside agents." She summarized the convent's two earlier break-ins, labeling the dead rats in the cellar as a possible third.

"She could be helping the harassers along." Jasper raised a finger for each item he listed. "Phone calls with hang ups in the middle of the night. Noises in the back and at the windows to augment the jump scares." He closed his hand. "I can't quite see how she could get access to X-rated magazines."

"Or tape them to the outside of the windows," Rowan said.

Giulia collected the empty Styrofoam cups and tossed them in the trash. "All right. We can't rule out the junkie population and we can't rule out Eagle. At least his ghost isn't hanging around the convent. What advice do you have for me to try and convince the current ghost to help?"

Rowan and Jasper shared a glance. "Because she's the type to give attitude, you might have to trick her into helping."

"Great."

Zane said, "Offer to have *The Scoop* tell her story."

Giulia picked up her desk phone. "Zane, I will call your girlfriend right now and tell her you've become a Brony."

Sidney laughed and laughed. She bent over and clutched her stomach and kept laughing. Giulia sagged with relief. She'd been worried Sidney was mentally composing her resignation letter.

Jasper looked around at the various facial expressions: Zane's horror, Giulia's recovered sternness, Rowan's amusement, Sidney's guffaws. "What am I missing?"

His aunt answered. "It's a cartoon show about anthropomorphic, multi-colored ponies who have adventures and learn life lessons. My granddaughters love it."

Jasper didn't appear enlightened.

"It's also gained a large adult male following. There's even a convention. They cosplay."

Sidney wiped her eyes. "Anyone have a tissue?"

Giulia opened her lower desk drawer and handed her the square tissue box she kept there.

Jasper said in a measured voice, "Zane, you may want to retract your suggestion about *The Scoop*."

"I do. I do. I take it back. No, I'll invent a working time machine and take us back to the minute before I said it."

The handset returned to the cradle. Giulia relaxed her stern face. Zane inhaled for such a long time she wondered where he'd found the breath to gabble his last four sentences.

Rowan stepped into the breach. "Back to the original question. You might have the best luck playing to her love of the house. Tell her any continued attempts to scare the nuns away will accelerate Eagle's efforts. Did you tell her they want to tear the place down?"

"Yes. She cursed enough to deserve her mouth being washed out with soap. Then she vanished."

"Good. You've planted the seed of fear in her."

"A ghost can be afraid? Serious question."

"Yes. Remember my ex-mother-in-law? She put on a show of anger but fear gave her a green and black outline, all swirling together. I knew she was afraid I'd replace her as her son's favorite person." Rowan shook her head. "He died eleven years ago after two more failed marriages. I hope he and his mother are happy together."

The forty-something knocked on the doorframe. "Ma'am, we're all set out here. We're ready for you to download our software to your computer and phone."

Rowan squinted at him. "Young man, you need a spiritual cleanse."

Fifty-Eight

Rowan took the technician by the arm and read his aura in detail, adding explanations and advice. His partner sidled around them and took over walking Giulia through the downloads.

"Remember," Rowan ripped a phone message slip from Zane's desk and sat in Zane's client chair to write, "orange signifies underlying stress. You need to identify the stressors in your life, because orange is bleeding into your good, solid red of practicality. You also have a beautiful emerald green foundation. You should consider volunteering for one of those animal rescue places. And get a physical. Your turquoise is all wonky."

She thrust the paper into his shirt pocket. His face had the look of someone's new boyfriend being introduced to a houseful of kooky relatives at Thanksgiving dinner.

The minute Giulia signed the invoice, Rowan blocked the other technician's exit. "Stand still, please. I need to focus."

His face took on the same trapped expression.

Giulia locked her screen and left Rowan in possession of her doorway. Jasper, Zane, and Sidney were sitting around the window table. She joined them.

"What a beautiful shade of royal blue." Rowan's hands spread in front of the technician's torso. "And the hot pink. All my husbands' auras had that same shade of hot pink. It's a good thing my current husband has it too." She cackled.

Giulia put her head on the table and held her breath.

Sidney leaned over. "Do you want me to pinch you or anything?"

Giulia whispered, "Give me a second." She raised her head but the look in Jasper's eyes made her bite her lips and stare out the window at the pizza place sign.

"She loves taking people by surprise," Jasper whispered. "Her readings are correct, but those poor guys are so off-balance their reactions are muddying their auras the longer she talks."

Rowan tucked a note in the second technician's pocket. "Don't forget to cut back on salt."

He spoke for the first time since she buttonholed him. "You can see that in my aura?"

She shut him up with a look. "No, I can see your fingers are retaining water."

After the security team left, Rowan dragged Zane's client chair to the table.

Sidney said in a small voice, "Did the ghost die of lung cancer?"

Everyone stared.

"Well, cigarettes are poison."

"That's an interesting question," Zane said. "When were cigarettes with all the additives first marketed?"

Jasper's phone alarm went off. "Rowan, you have a two fifteen past life regression and I'm meeting a buyer for our excess healing crystal inventory."

"You are the best nephew and business partner." Rowan squeezed Zane and Sidney and hugged Giulia with much less force. "In two months all we'll be able to do is bump bellies. Thank you for lunch and don't forget to tell us what happens the next time you talk to your ghost."

The downstairs door skreeked closed a minute later. Giulia let out a long breath. "Some days Rowan has too much energy for me to process. Are there any honey cakes left?"

Sidney opened the box on her desk. "One. Want to split it?"

"Yes, please. I have a long afternoon ahead of me."

She started with the easy search. James Bosnack invented a cigarette machine in 1881, well within Florence's timeframe. Florence could have purchased pre-made cigarettes or rolled her own. Women smoked in public in the 1900s in Greenwich village, shocking the neighbors. Florence seemed the type to walk down Cottonwood's main street smoking and showing off her ostrich feathers and extreme corset dresses.

Giulia flipped over the "Beech or addicts?" placeholder page on her legal pad.

Florence Gosnall
• Ask her about cigarettes. This should please her.

Then Giulia took a leap of faith. She typed the ghost's name in quotes into the search window.

And there she was.

Giulia released her mouse and sat back. "Guys, she was real."

Like magic, Sidney and Zane were at her shoulders, reading her screen.

"She's buried in the First Church of Cottonwood's cemetery."

Sidney read the listing. "Florence Bertha Gosnall, born January fifteenth, 1887, died July second, 1912."

Zane said, "The other gravestones have extra lines. 'Beloved wife.' 'Beloved husband.' Colonel US Cavalry.' Hers has nothing."

Sidney said, "Men were intimidated by confident women a hundred years ago too."

"Possibly." Giulia hit the back button. "There doesn't seem to be much else...Wait. She said she designed the house." She typed several search strings with no luck. "Women didn't get hired by architecture firms back then."

"Try a title search," Zane said. "When I bought my house I found out the previous owner had gone bankrupt and the house had been foreclosed. I paid extra for two separate inspections in case it had hidden damage from being empty too long."

"I should've thought of that. Our Cape Cod only had one owner before us, so we didn't have any issues." Giulia typed. "Bingo. First owner, F.B. Gosnall. Six bedrooms, two bathrooms. Not anymore. Some of the bedrooms have been cut in half. She may be annoyed about that too." Giulia rubbed her hands over her face. "I'm still much too calm about this."

"Ms. D., I think it's cool. Maybe you'll end up like Whoopi Goldberg in *Ghost*, where once she hears Patrick Swayze's voice, ghosts stampede her psychic business to make their contact their relatives."

"Zane, if you make Sidney resign I'll take to drinking hard liquor, which is bad for the baby."

Sidney commandeered the client chair. "Full disclosure time. When I saw that freaky green picture on your monitor I was this close to running out the door and never coming back." She held her thumb and index finger a millimeter apart. "But Jessamine needs a college fund and we need health insurance. So I guess I'm staying."

Giulia exhaled. "You have no idea how relieved I am."

"Besides, someone has to supply your garden with alpaca poop fertilizer."

Zane shuddered. "I don't want scatological details on what makes my vegetables big and tasty, thank you."

"Wuss."

Giulia made shooing motions. "I have to organize my information."

She added to the ghost's list:

- Ask her about designing the house.
- Was she married? Note: This might make her angry. If she gets angry enough to disappear, she may stop giving me information.
- Ask her if she smoked in public. She may enjoy telling shocking stories.
- Play up to her clothes.

Giulia pulled up all the Gibson Girl information she could find, but Florence wasn't anywhere. Perhaps she failed the audition. Better revise.

- Play up to her clothes. Did she ever model for Gibson? Reveal frumpy maternity pants and express a wish for her figure (not really a lie).

At which point Giulia ran out of ideas. She'd have to sneak in questions about Eagle's arson attempt in between girl talk. She wrote across the bottom of the page:

She's not "my" ghost.

Fifty-Nine

The "Beech or a Cadre of Addicts" page would no longer work. Her bullet point system rebelled at the concept of two major suspects per page. She tossed it and started fresh.

Barbara Beech
- How intimate was the Beech-Eagle connection?
- The professional connection, not as ex-lovers.
- Does Beech own Eagle Developers now?

She checked for probate information and made a face at the answer on the screen.

- Probate takes six months minimum.
- Any way to find out before probate if she owns Eagle Devs. now?

Her Google-fu was strong today. The first hit on Beech's full name brought up dogster.com in the main window and a studio portrait of Beech and three Pomeranians on her member profile page. A little searching within the Community page on the dogster site brought up a Pomeranian-specific discussion board.

- What is she like outside the office? Beech is besotted over her Pomeranians.

More searching.

- Divorced. No kids.

- She sky dives.
- Thus she's comfortable with risks.
- Thus she's Eagle's logical successor.
- Enough to have hired the thug who subcontracted the break-in to the twelve-year-old?
- Or does she have a faithful assistant who asks no questions?
- Or is a faithful assistant in on everything?
- Would the faithful assistant be mulling blackmail?

Too many sensitive questions and too few ways to get answers.

The phone rang, and the second line rang a few seconds later. Zane buzzed her. "Ms. D., it's Eagle's office on two."

She rubbed her face again and pressed the button. "Did you ever read *Through the Looking-Glass, and What Alice Found There*?"

"Uh, a million years ago in grade school, I think."

"A poem from the book is called 'The Walrus and the Carpenter.' When the title characters trick a school of oysters into coming on land the poem reads, 'And thick and fast they came at last, and more and more and more.'"

"Okay..."

"My life is imitating this poem. I'll take the call." She waited for the line two light to blink. "Giulia Driscoll speaking."

"Please hold for Ms. Beech." A click.

At the same time Zane's arm reached over to close her door to block out Sidney on line one.

"Ms. Driscoll, I'm glad I caught you in." Beech's voice was smooth and professional. "Here is our current buyout offer." She named a figure a few thousand less than Giulia's last counter offer. "Please convey this to your client. I hope to hear from you very soon."

Giulia walked into the main room and waited for the typing to stop. "Let me share today's business lesson. Barbara Beech called with a counter offer. She ended the call with 'I hope to hear from you very soon.' Not 'soon' and not merely 'hope to hear from you.'"

Sidney said, "A demand camouflaged in polite words?"

"Exactly. I wish I'd recorded the call. Her voice was a sledgehammer wrapped in bunny fur."

Zane choked. "I need to design that as a weapon for my next

gaming weekend."

"It's all yours. Too bad I can't call the convent. The Superior is still teaching school."

"They'll take the offer?" Zane said.

"I'll convince them. The offer is two thousand above the amount I was willing to settle for. It will give them a few choices for new housing and still cover the extra moving expenses for the invalid Sisters. At least one thing is going right today."

Sidney said, "I bet your ghost won't like it."

"We're working for the nuns, not for a rude ghost." Giulia replayed her words in her head. "A statement I never dreamed would come out of my mouth. And she's not my ghost."

The phone rang.

"Unless it's the Pope himself offering to put us on retainer, I'm not here."

Sidney snorted. Zane held out his phone. "It's Mr. D."

"Okay, two exceptions." She took it. "Yes, dear?"

"We got confirmation. The chemicals in brake fluid and pool shock were embedded in Eagle's face and hands. The hands pretty much clinch it. He was trying a little homemade arson."

"Great."

"Not the news you wanted?"

"Yes and no. Thanks for letting me know. I'll see you tonight."

She relayed the information to Sidney and Zane. "This means...wait...maybe..." She turned on her heel and spread her bullet lists over her desk. "The smart PI never assumes she knows who did it."

Sixty

Giulia tore off another page from the legal pad.

<u>Victor Eagle</u>
- Yes, he's dead.
- Was he Machiavellian enough to have orchestrated the harassment campaign on his own? (Corollary to Beech's page: If not solo, was/is Beech in league with him?)

In league. She opened the folder of all their compiled research. Another new page.

<u>Addicts, Singular or Plural</u>
- We have to find out if the muggings are related to Matilda's death.
- And the convent harassment (thin, but possible).
- And if Eagle's company is involved.
- In muggings? Makes zero sense.
- Even with the thug plus James Haynes with a Y.
- Only the possibility of a mugger + Matilda makes it worth a thought.

She reread her stream of consciousness outline. It made even less sense written out. She pushed the page to the outer edge of her overcrowded desk and ripped another one from the pad.

<u>Arson Attempt</u>
- Florence makes lit cigarettes appear.

- Therefore she controls fire.
- Can she manipulate physical objects? There may be brake fluid in the cellar (check next time in house), but how would she get hold of pool shock?
- Was Eagle really trying to burn down the house?
- For what possible reason, besides saving money on demolition?

Another page.

<u>Sister Matilda</u>
- What about Florence?
- Is Florence tied to the house or can she follow the residents outside?
- What reason would she have to scare Sister Matilda to death?
- Not liking nuns isn't reason enough.
- Corollary number one: I need to know more about ghosts.
- Corollary number two: Despite Olive and Eugenie's vendetta against Eagle, the logical conclusion is most of the crimes are plain old illegal acts committed by the usual suspects.

Giulia knew better than to let her ideas about Florence slip through the legitimate investigation cracks. She called Rowan and explained the ghost's dark possibilities. "She may not only be annoying. If she can leave the house, she may be homicidal."

Rowan was delighted all over again. "Fascinating. Jasper!" A pause. "Giulia's ghost may be shoving people into the next life before their time."

Giulia bit her tongue so she wouldn't snap "She's not my ghost" at Rowan.

A brief conversation on the other end and Rowan returned. "We're in agreement. Don't let yourself get thrown off-kilter because this is your first ghost. Remember what I said earlier about your inner strength combined with your little guy's? Use it."

All Giulia's frustration hit boiling point. "How? Is there an instruction manual? Does Barnes & Noble stock it?"

"See? Even when you're stressed you balance it out with humor.

Here, Jasper wants to talk to you."

"Giulia, if you force her to admit to an actual crime, she may change quickly from a charming antique ghost into something evil and otherworldly."

"Jasper, do you have any idea how many horror movies I've watched in my life?"

Now Jasper sounded amused. "*Ringu? Ju-On?*"

"All of them, plus their better imitators. Don't forget *Kairo.*"

"I see." He became serious. "I won't tease anymore, because this is reality and not cinema. What's your schedule later this afternoon?"

"I'm free..." She considered the best time to visit the convent about the new offer. "I'm free from now until seven-ish."

"How about five o'clock here?"

"Yes. What should I bring?"

"Something to take notes with. I'm going to throw a lot of information at you."

The phone rang again the instant she hung up. Only budgetary concerns kept Giulia from heaving it out the window.

Sixty-One

"Ms. D., it's the hospital."

Thanks to years of discipline, Giulia did not indulge in one of Frank's extreme Irish curses.

"Giulia Driscoll speaking."

"Ms. Driscoll, your brother is awake again and demanding to see you."

Speaking of soap operas, Giulia wasn't going to explain her family to a nurse she didn't know. "Thank you for keeping me updated, but I'm in the middle of a workday."

Muffled voices on the other end, and then Aida took the phone.

"Honey, I know, but his vital signs are spiking and his EEG is fluctuating. We're worried about a brain bleed. Please come."

Giulia's forehead hit her desk.

"Please."

"All right."

"Hurry, honey."

Sidney's voice from a short distance away: "Is everything okay?"

Giulia raised her head. Sidney and Zane stood in her doorway, faces puckered with worry.

"My brother's awake and yelling for me. The nurses begged me to come." She pushed herself away from her desk. "No good deed goes unpunished. He'll damn me to Hell and tell me again what a vile creature I am for leaving the convent. If he's in top form, he'll bring out his favorite line: I spit on the cross every time I darken the door of a church."

"Whoa." Zane thought for a moment. "I have a few friends who could curse him. Want me to call in a favor?"

Giulia's laugh was bare of humor. "Thank you, no. He makes plenty of misery for himself on his own. Also, I can't afford to lose you because of a karma payback."

"Good point."

Sidney elbowed him. "Your ego is appalling."

"What? We're busy."

Giulia shut down her computer. "We are indeed. I'm heading to the hospital and then to the convent. Can you both squeeze in another search on Eagle's ex-wife and kids? Don't spend more than half an hour, tops. I want to know if they've been vocal about the business. Do they feel the money belongs to them, what about back child support, that kind of thing." She handed Sidney the bullet list. "If one or more of them has an eye on the business, everyone's stuck until probate."

Sidney took the paper. "I'm still trying to wrap my head around the whole 'ghosts are real' thing."

"Try being haunted by one." Frustration ripped through Giulia one instant and then vanished. "I'm sorry. This case is getting to me."

"Plus baby hormones." Sidney gave Giulia a one-arm squeeze.

"Plus baby hormones."

Giulia walked down the hall to Salvatore's room concentrating on the noise from all sides: Rolling carts, endless PA announcements, nurses on phones, doctors dictating notes. Sooner than she wanted, she reached his closed door. She didn't hear any shouts from inside cutting through the surrounding din.

Maybe Salvatore had slipped back into his coma and this trip would be a waste of time. Wasting time didn't usually please her. She opened the door.

The number of people in the room exceeded its maximum occupancy limit. Aida, two doctors, and another nurse stood on both sides of the bed. Anne and all three kids squeezed against the walls.

Aida beckoned Giulia inside. The door swung shut behind her. The air in the room grew warm and stuffy with so many people breathing in it. The other nurse wrote on the clipboard from the end of the bed. The doctors spoke in low voices as they glanced at the beeping monitors in the room.

Cecilia, nearest the door, pulled Giulia next to her. "The nurse called Mom and she said we should come too." Cecilia's whisper was anything but. "Dad was awake before we got here. She said maybe next time Dad wakes up he'll be the way he used to be. She said brain injury does that sometimes. Wouldn't it be awesome if Dad was normal again like he was when I was little?"

The patient's eyelids fluttered. The doctors stopped talking. Anne stretched her arms across her children in the same protective gesture parents use when a car makes a sudden stop. Giulia stepped to the end of the bed to deflect her brother's wrath from his children.

Salvatore's eyes opened. His eyebrows met over the bridge of his nose. He raised a hand against the glare of the overhead light.

"Mr. Falcone?" the doctor on the left said.

Salvatore pointed at Giulia. "Demon!"

Sixty-Two

The medical staff took a step backward in unison. Giulia clenched her teeth.

"You brought the demon! You are an abomination!" Salvatore's finger trembled. "In the hotel—I saw it in the wires—the wires..." His voice faded. His hand dropped.

The nurse clipped a pulse monitor on the now-quiescent index finger. Aida checked his EEG readout. The doctors each took a different machine.

"So much for getting our old dad back." Tears lurked in Cecilia's voice.

"The children must be kept uncorrupted." The pulse meter's white cord waggled like a loose garden hose as he shifted his admonishing finger to Anne. "She has given herself to evil. Demons will possess the children! I can see them now! They surround the Jezebel!" The cord whapped against one of the doctors. "Throw them from the window and let dogs devour them—"

Cecilia inched closer to Anne and Salvatore's bloodshot eyes seemed to see her for the first time. "You are all Jezebels at heart!" The pulse monitor unlatched. It sailed over the bed and landed at Cecilia's feet. "The dogs of the Lord will devour your flesh! Only then can you be purified! The window...they must be devoured..."

His heart monitor flatlined. Aida began CPR. The other nurse ran into the hall and wheeled in the crash cart so quickly everything on it rattled.

Anne and Giulia herded the kids into the corner. The room was too small for them to leave without impeding the resuscitation efforts.

The defibrillator whined on an upward note until it held steady.

"Charged."

Salvatore's body jumped. The line remained flat.

The upward whine repeated.

"Charged."

This time after Salvatore's jump the EEG resumed its regular beeping. The medical staff moved with efficiency and within five minutes Aida and both doctors escorted Giulia, Anne, and the kids into a consultation room.

Giulia pulled three chairs together and seated Anne in the middle one. Cecilia was crying and wiping her eyes with her hands. Carlo leaned over the back of Anne's low chair and clutched her neck. Pasquale's bravado had deserted him. He clung to his mother's hand with enough force to make both their knuckles bloodless. Giulia ran into the general waiting room and carried in a fourth chair.

Aida mouthed at her, "A chair for you?"

Giulia waved it off and pointed to the rug. "I'll stand," she mouthed back. She plucked several tissues from a box on the desk and handed two each to Anne and the kids.

Aida brought in a fifth chair anyway. "Sit." Her strong hands squeezed Giulia's shoulders.

The doctors turned on a micro-recorder and spoke in low voices with each other while the family got settled. Then the one who'd successfully used the defibrillator turned the recorder toward Anne.

"Mrs. Falcone, we apologize for causing you and your family distress."

"Please don't worry about it." Anne made a motion as though to clasp her hands in her lap, but Cecilia and Pasquale were still gripping them. "Your first concern was to save my husband."

"Mr. Falcone's coma state has returned."

"Good," Pasquale muttered.

"May I ask a few questions in relation to his, ah, outbursts?"

"If you have to." She shook herself. "I'm sorry. Certainly. What do you need to know?"

The doctors glanced at each other. "Has he been abusive in the past?"

"Giulia?" Anne said.

The doctors shifted their attention to her.

"My brother has taken religion to extremes for many years." Giulia chose her words with care. "I used to be a nun but left the convent a few years ago. Salvatore excoriated me to my face and made so many phone calls to verbally abuse me I had to change my number."

"He says awful things about Aunt Giulia during Bible study," Cecilia said.

"He says awful things about women no matter what." Pasquale patted his mother's hand.

The doctors's faces revealed nothing.

Anne said, "My husband changed everything about our household last year. He no longer permitted us to have contact with anyone not of the Catholic faith. He removed all reading materials from the house not related to Catholicism."

"He threw out Mom's makeup and made her quit the gym and took away our cell phones," Pasquale said.

Carlo spoke for the first time. "He goes on and on during Bible study about how we're terrible sinners and makes us do penance, like extra chores or say the Rosary on our knees in the kitchen because there's no rug in there."

The second doctor said, "The Rosary?"

Giulia took up the narration again. "It's a Catholic meditation using beads to count more than fifty repetitions of its main prayer plus repetitions of other prayers. It takes—"

"It takes twenty-three minutes," Cecilia said. "We can't rush it because Dad times us. If he says we've really been sinful he makes the boys roll up their pants and me move my skirt so we kneel on bare knees. See?" She pulled up her school uniform and stuck out her leg. Rough, red calluses disfigured both knees.

Both doctors nodded.

"Thank you," the first one said. "Ms. Driscoll, if you could take the children we'd like to speak with Mrs. Falcone a moment."

Giulia and Aida took them to the main waiting room.

Pasquale dropped into a hard plastic chair and kicked the legs. "I've got homework."

"What a waste," Cecilia said. "Like I haven't heard the Jezebel bullshit before."

"Language," Giulia said.

"Come on, Aunt Giulia."

"I didn't say you were wrong."

Cecilia's surprise morphed into a brilliant smile. "You're the coolest aunt ever."

"Then make your cool aunt happy and stop swearing."

Anne joined them. "Let's go. I'll tell you in the parking lot."

The minivan was closest to the doors. Anne gathered them into a circle by the back bumper. "The doctors said their report will indicate in their professional opinion the behavior Salvatore's exhibiting since the head injury renders him a danger to minors—that's you three." She spoke faster, repressing excitement. "Then they turned off the recorder and said if Salvatore ever gets out of the hospital and comes near us, they'll give us ammunition for a restraining order."

Carlo was the first to reply. "Dad won't come back?"

Pasquale said slowly, "Dad won't be allowed to come back?"

"Holy sh—" Cecilia clamped her lips together. "We'll be a normal family again."

Giulia said, "Anne, don't cry. I don't have any more tissues."

Anne pushed her hands against her eyes. "Besides, I have to drive home."

Pasquale winked. "Yeah, mom, we have homework. A good mother wouldn't impede our education."

Cecilia gave him an incredulous look. "Impede?"

"Learned it in school today."

Sixty-Three

Giulia called Barbara Beech from the Nunmobile. "We were required to shuffle a few appointments this afternoon. I won't be speaking with the Sisters until after six. Did you wish to wait until tomorrow for the answer?"

"No. Everyone involved would like this settled, don't you agree? Here's my cell number. Call me anytime this evening. I'll bring the paperwork with me. If you're amenable, we can meet this evening to sign off."

Giulia hung up but didn't put away her phone. Enough wondering. There was no more time to waste. She stuffed tissues into both nostrils and dialed Eagle Developers.

Neither Giulia Driscoll the PI nor Maria Falcone the hopeful freelancer answered the receptionist's "Eagle Developers. How may I direct your call?" This Giulia hacked into the receiver. "Sorry. Germs aren't contagious over the phone so you're okay. Who's in charge there?"

The receptionist paused a brief second. "I beg your pardon?"

"Charge, chicklet. The one with the power. Who's running the show now that your boss offed himself?"

"Ma'am, I really don't—"

"Oh yes, you do. Strike a blow for women everywhere and tell me someone with the right plumbing signs your checks now."

"Ms. Beech, of course. If you'll state your business, I'll see if she can—"

"Atta girl. I knew you could do it. You tell Ms. Beech to keep fighting the good fight. Remember what the Iron Lady said: 'If you want something said, ask a man; if you want something done, ask a woman.'"

Giulia hung up and yanked the tissues out of her nose. She inhaled two huge lungfuls of air, then she laughed, and laughed. She had no concrete idea who she'd imitated for that bizarre call. The attitude was the Silk Tie Killer's. The execrable diction belonged to the wives in DI's last divorce cases. And where did she get the idea of stuffing her nose to fake a head cold?

Maybe she did possess acting skills.

Sixty-Four

Giulia parked in the post-five p.m. empty lot behind DI's building and started to run across the street to the Tarot Shoppe. She thought better of it after five strides and settled for a rapid walk.

Jasper looked up from an old-fashioned ledger when the bells over the door tinkled Giulia's entrance. "You said you were running ten minutes late and here you are at ten minutes after five. I'm impressed."

She sat in the nearest chair to catch her breath. "I didn't break any speed limits, either."

He went into a room behind the counter and returned with a paper cup of water. Giulia gulped it. "Thank you."

"I won't imitate my aunt and give you an unplanned aura analysis, but were you not pregnant I'd recommend an inch of Tullamore Dew."

"Were I not pregnant, I'd drink it neat." She inspected her empty water cup. "Family."

Jasper closed his ledger. "One day I'll tell you about my cousin."

"Radical Bible thumper who feels compelled to tell you you'll roast in Hell?"

"Scientologist."

Giulia winced.

He came around the counter and pulled down the window shades. "I'd almost rather deal with a high-ranking devotee of Anton LaVey." Then he turned the hanging sign on the door to "Closed" and sat kitty-corner to her. "I'm at your disposal."

Giulia held up her iPad. "I'm ready to take notes."

"First rule of engagement: All ghosts are unstable. For their first appearance they may try to unsettle you, like your ghost and her cigarettes."

"She's not my ghost."

"Actually she is."

Giulia's bubble of satisfaction in denying ownership burst. "What do you mean?"

"You issued an invitation to talk. She accepted." He held up his hand. "Don't worry. I'm not saying she's going to follow you home."

"I prefer to leave my work at the office when possible."

"A good policy. What I'm saying is you've both signed a contract. Until the issues are resolved, you're connected."

Giulia put her hands over her mouth and hyperventilated through them like they were a brown paper bag.

Jasper broke protocol and put his hands over hers, the silicon-covered one on the outside. "It's not like *The Fog*. Remember that movie?"

"Jamie Lee Curtis, Hal Holbrook, 1980." The overlapping hands muffled her voice.

"Right. I don't imagine you've murdered and stolen gold and melted it down into a giant cross."

"Not that I remember."

"You've confirmed my opinion of you. Do my hands smell like liverwurst? I had a late lunch."

Giulia's rapid breathing hitched in a laugh. "I smell the faintest whiff of metal."

"Much better than metal plus pig livers mixed with allspice." He removed his hands. "Better?"

She sat up. "Embarrassing over-reaction finished."

He had the gift of a smile that diffused warmth. "Rowan played down her reaction when she told you the story of seeing her first mother-in-law's ghost. She's told me the uncensored version. When it appeared at the foot of the bed on their wedding night she threw him off her so hard he broke his tailbone on the floor."

Giulia snorted.

"It gets better. The ghost told Rowan her hair was stringy and her belly was flabby and to go take care of her precious boy or she'd be sorry. Rowan told her where to stuff it, all while the precious boy was whining in pain on the floor."

"Not an auspicious start to a marriage. The worst thing I did was forget my shoes and walk down the aisle in my stockings."

"And no ghosts?"

"Definitely no ghosts." Giulia retrieved her iPad. "All right. I've entered into a temporary contract with a one-hundred-year-old ghost. She indulges in an excess of snark and she may only be shamming harmless. In reality, she could snap and become the Incredible Chain Smoking Hulk at any moment."

"Concise and correct. There's always a chance a ghost will do a one-eighty and turn into a sugary version of Shirley Temple singing 'On the Good Ship Lollipop,' but not in our experience."

"You wouldn't have a pamphlet with a step by step list, by any chance?"

"If only." He spread his hands. "But despair not. While all ghosts are different, the rules of the game still apply. It's a matter of finding the effective rules for each ghost."

"I'll have to hurry the process of elimination. Events are speeding up."

"I'll be as succinct as possible. I know we already discussed rule number one, but I think the order should be rearranged. Here's new rule number one: Ghosts lie."

"If I can't trust the dead, who can I trust?" Giulia typed while she spoke.

"No one but yourself. If Rowan were to die and haunt this shop, I wouldn't interact with her as though she were my talented and funny aunt. I'd use every atom of skill I possess to probe her words and actions for the hidden sorrow or anger tying her here."

Always a fast typist, Giulia finished recording his words almost as soon as he spoke. "Number two?"

"Words have power."

"The contract you said I bound myself to." She looked up from her tablet. "The Scooby-Doo show should've had a series of episodes covering these when I was growing up. Childhood is supposed to give us a solid foundation for life's requirements."

"We carry on as best we can. Ghosts have infinite time on their hands in which to consider the meanings of words. They like to mess with the living. Sometimes they merely trick us into harmless promises, like making sure the TV is always tuned to NASCAR."

"Or irritating everyone in the vicinity with cigarette smoke."

Jasper made a hacking sound. "I quit cold turkey two years, one month, and seventeen days ago. Even a whiff of cigs makes me want to hurl."

"She tried to deflect my questions by teasing me with how she's able to smoke. I doubt her smoke contains actual nicotine, but it sure smells authentic."

"She wouldn't like dealing with me. But you're a different story. You have an excess of compassion. Assume she's already scheming how to play on your sympathy and latch tighter to you. Protect yourself."

With a stiffened chin: "I will become Giulia the hard-hearted."

"Rule number three, the one I mentioned earlier: All ghosts are unstable. She's already tried to unsettle you. This may limit itself to harmless pranks, or it may turn dark in a heartbeat. Never let your guard down." He paused. "May I suggest typing that in large, bold, capital letters? Preferably in red."

Giulia opened the formatting tab and complied.

"You'll be pleased to know rule number four is also the last: Believe."

She put a dozen ways of saying "Are you kidding?" into her expression.

He laughed. "I once heard you were a naïve pushover."

"I once was."

"It's a good thing you aren't any longer. Lest you dismiss the way Rowan keeps insisting you have spiritual power and your little guy adds to it, I assure you she's right. We all have a core of power. Yours is much easier to access than most people's because of your background."

"Serious question: How?"

"You're going to complain again about the lack of an instruction manual, because the answer is 'it's different for everyone.'"

"Jasper..."

"Honest. Rowan accesses her power core by envisioning the Fool card. It's hers because she embraces its deepest meanings: Risk, spontaneity, and unlimited potential. I envision water, because of its strength and serenity." He waited for her to stop typing. "It helps if I don't have to pee at the time."

She chuckled. "These sessions always seem to involve homework."

"Homework helps cement new ideas in the mind."

"Spoken like a true teacher. To implement rule number four I need to discover the trigger for my spiritual strength." She looked up from the keyboard. "It would be a big help if my trigger is a crucifix or something equally familiar and Catholic."

"It may be. When you discover it you'll have no doubts. Use it to resist the ghost. Your strength will reveal holes in its anger or games or pity party."

"I need a month to process everything that's happened in the past two days." She saved and closed. "You are so kind to put in overtime for me. I'll get out of your hair now and let you get some supper." Her stomach growled. "I'll do the same."

He unlocked the door, but stopped before opening it. "I almost forgot the most important rule."

She reached for her tablet. "What?"

"You have to make the ghost sneeze."

"Sneeze? How?"

"With a ghost pepper."

Jasper released the door handle and bent double with his hands on his knees. His laugh was hoarse and deep and contagious. Giulia tried to keep a disapproving face on, but couldn't maintain it. She opened the door and let herself out, laughing.

Still under the shop's purple awning, her phone rang.

"For once I'd be glad if it was a telemarketer." She pressed the screen. "Hello?"

"Giulia, you have to come here right now!"

She sighed. "Bart, what's wrong?"

"We found Eugenie in the cellar next to a broken gas pipe."

"Is she okay? Wait. How did Eugenie get into the cellar?"

"We don't know, we don't know. The cellar was full of gas. Emergency people are swarming the house. Please come. Please. Right now."

Sixty-Five

Giulia parked across the street from the convent because a fire truck, an ambulance, a police car, and a Pennsylvania Gas & Electric truck crowded the other curb. Onlookers had once again materialized despite the lack of actual neighbors.

Firefighters in full gear including oxygen masks clomped in and out of the front door. A middle-aged man stood next to the driver's seat of the PG&E truck. His beer belly strained the bottom buttons of his uniform as he rested one foot on the running board and spoke into an oversized phone. One police officer kept an eye on the rubberneckers.

Giulia walked two houses past the convent and slipped into the narrow space between them. All the patches of backyard grass were empty. She crossed them and dialed Bart.

"Let me in please. I'm on the back stoop."

Bart cracked open the kitchen door and pulled Giulia inside. Steve the Chihuahua trotted into the kitchen, saw Giulia, and huffed his way onto his braided rug.

"Steve, I apologize for not being a new audience."

"Forget him. Come into the living room. We need someone to explain what's happening to us." Bart tugged Giulia toward the front of the house. All the windows were wide open.

"Bart, I don't smell gas now, but why aren't you all on the front lawn until you get the all clear?"

"They started to herd us outside until Dorothy turned into the Wicked Witch of the West." She choked back a giggle. "The firefighters hauled their testing gizmos into Agatha and Helen's rooms. She'd already opened every window on the second floor. They said parts per million was negligible, 'but as a precaution'... and that's when Dorothy redefined the wrath of God."

Giulia swallowed her own giggle. "But down here?"

A voice from the cellar shouted, "Hot zone decrease."

Another voice answered, "Outside clear."

A firefighter in the front door blocked the early evening light. Giulia and Bart scooted into the living room doorway to give him room. He held a black and yellow instrument in one hand. Small lights in a glass globe blinked green as he aimed it into each room before heading down to the cellar.

Bart said over the footfalls and distant shouting, "Eugenie looked so bad they said they couldn't afford to waste time transporting her anywhere. We opened every window and door and are waiting for permission to set up fans."

Eugenie lay on a blanket on the flattened green rug in the front room, a floral throw pillow under her head. A tube attached to a portable oxygen cylinder connected to a clear mask covering her nose and mouth. A blood pressure cuff circled one bicep. The EMT on her right side monitored the oxygen flow. The EMT on her left checked her heart. Dorothy paced the narrow end of the room like a power walker. Kathryn, Olive, and Diane hovered in the corner. Bart and Giulia joined them.

"Giulia will fix everything," Bart said.

"Bart, please."

"You will. Kathryn, tell her what happened."

The EMTs read numbers out loud to each other.

"I came home late from school and Steve was barking his head off at the cellar door. He does that sometimes. I told him to hush and went into the kitchen to make a cup of tea." She pulled at her short graying hair. "I never thought anything about it. I turned on the burner—"

"You lit the gas?" Giulia said.

"I didn't know. I didn't know." Her hands clenched harder.

Diane reached up and disengaged them. "You're beating yourself up over nothing. Why would any of us think anything other than Steve was imagining rats in the cellar again?"

"But we did find rats," Olive said.

"Not now, please." Kathryn's voice thinned.

Giulia intervened. "What happened next?"

"I poured Steve's kibble into his bowl because he always shuts up for food. When he kept barking, I turned off the burner and opened the cellar door." She waved a hand in front of her nose. "I still smell it. The stairwell reeked of natural gas. Steve jumped down two steps, but I grabbed him and threw him into the hall. Then I put my arm over my nose and ran downstairs and found Eugenie on the floor next to the gas meter. The oldest pipe had broken away from the wall and gas was spouting from it with such force it whistled."

"Penelec should've replaced those pipes years ago," Diane murmured. "Rust is the only thing keeping them together."

"How did the pipe come loose from the wall?" Giulia kept one eye on the group on the rug. The left-hand EMT raised Eugenie's eyelids and shone a light into them.

"I wish I knew," Kathryn said.

Olive said, "I wish I knew how wheelchair-bound Eugenie got down to the cellar." She called over to Dorothy, "How long has she been able to walk?"

The nurse joined them. "I have no idea. When she was assigned to me her records said her advanced diabetes resulted in neuropathy which caused her to slip on an icy sidewalk. She's never moved her legs on her own as long as I've taken care of her."

"What a sneaky piece of work she is." Olive's voice conveyed admiration rather than annoyance.

On the floor, the patient gasped and began to cough. The EMTs raised her to a sitting position and eased the oxygen mask away. Not soon enough, because on the next cough Eugenie projectile vomited into the mask and onto her white blouse, one EMT's hands, the blanket, and the rug.

Diane ran into the kitchen and brought back a roll of paper towels and three wet cloths. Olive walked upstairs and returned with a clean shirt. Kathryn made her own trip into the kitchen and returned with a cup of water. Eugenie stopped puking and groaned.

The non-splattered EMT took a wet cloth from Diane's outstretched hand. "Thanks." He wiped Eugenie's face and shirt. The other EMT wiped vomit out of the oxygen mask with a new wet cloth, then flipped the cloth over to clean herself.

A firefighter passed the doorway. The female EMT called after him. "Joe, can you bring us a new oxygen pack?"

He gave her a thumbs-up and kept walking. She unbuttoned Eugenie's filthy blouse and worked it off her arms. Olive passed her the clean shirt. The replacement oxygen mask and tubing arrived. Kathryn handed the water to the EMT, who held the cup to Eugenie's lips and helped her sip.

A breeze blew through the open windows, wafting the stench toward the nuns. Bart stepped into the hall to gag. Steve the Chihuahua ambled into the room and made a beeline for the puddles of vomit. Diane scooped him up and held him despite loud protests.

The EMTs checked Eugenie's lungs, blood pressure, and eyes.

"I feel terrible." The wheelchair-bound nun's voice quavered.

A white-haired, wrinkled man in a Pennsylvania Gas & Electric uniform entered the room. He looked at the group by the wall with a questioning expression.

The Superior stepped forward. "I'm Sister Kathryn."

"Are you in charge? We replaced the old pipes and attached the new ones to the wall. You should get your cellar checked out. The drywall's starting to rot." He handed Kathryn a work order. "About the leak. The hot zones have dissipated, so you're okay to use cell phones and other electronics again. Keep the windows open all night."

"Open windows on the ground floor aren't a wise decision in this neighborhood."

He looked around. "Oh. Yeah. Well, keep these ones open as long as you can, and don't close the second- and third-floor ones for twenty-four hours. If you'll follow me downstairs I'll show you the new fixtures."

Kathryn beckoned to Bart and the three headed to the cellar.

The EMTs poked and measured and inspected a passive Eugenie. Giulia approached the group on the floor. "Sister Eugenie, what happened in the cellar?"

Her face sagged like a bloodhound's into jowls and plump wrinkles. "I'll only talk to my confessor."

"I beg your pardon?"

The old nun shivered at Giulia's Sister Mary Regina Coelis voice. But instead of explaining, she started to cry and repeated, "I need confession. I need confession."

Before Giulia had a chance to try another tactic, Eugenie fainted into the arms of both EMTs.

A few years ago, Giulia would've tripped all over herself to help. But despite the gas and vomiting Giulia took into account Eugenie's love of manipulation. She said to the EMT closest to her, "Is she faking it?"

The EMT might have spent a few years in Catholic school by the shock on her face. Her partner perhaps had not, since he checked the nun's pulse and eye reactions.

"She's unconscious."

Dorothy said, "I don't hear Agatha."

Giulia listened. The invalid nun's moans and groans had run as an undercurrent through the hubbub created as the fire and power crews responded to the emergency. Now she heard only cleanup noises and muted conversations from the rubberneckers on the sidewalk.

Dorothy and Giulia ran upstairs. Because all the doors and windows were open, they saw Sister Agatha's head turn toward the stairs as they reached the landing. Her eyes were open and aware. Her mouth was closed.

They came straight into her room. Dorothy said, "Sister Agatha, can we help you? Do you need anything?"

"Bring Clarence here."

"Clarence?"

A trembling finger pointed at Giulia. "You. Bring Clarence."

"Sister Agatha," Dorothy's voice was soothing, "the house is busy right now. Maybe if we—"

"Bring Clarence. Bring Clarence. Bring Clarence." The voice ratcheted up and up with each repetition. "Bring Clarence. Bring Clarence."

Dorothy looked helplessly at Giulia. "Do you know who she means?"

Giulia nodded and raised her voice over the invalid's bawls. "I'll call him."

She took refuge in Eugenie's empty room. "Pit Bull, it's Giulia Driscoll. Sister Agatha is having a lucid episode and is screaming for you."

"Look, Giulia—sorry, I meant Ms. Driscoll—I'm in the middle of edits for tomorrow's show."

If there were any buttons Giulia knew how to push, those buttons belonged to Catholic school survivors.

"Your desire to help was ephemeral, then."

"It's not that. It's just, my job requires odd hours."

"I see."

"Ms. Driscoll, I'd like to help, I really would, but we're under deadline."

She walked back to Sister Agatha's room. The instant the old nun saw her, she resumed her demand at the high decibel she'd left off at. Giulia put her phone on speaker.

"Bring Clarence. Bring Clarence. Bring Clarence."

Pit Bull's voice couldn't compete with Agatha's. "Son of a—" He cleared his throat in a burst of static. "I'll be there in fifteen minutes."

Sixty-Six

Giulia left it to Sister Dorothy to calm her patient while she climbed to the attic. The small round windows at the front and back of the house were open. The air smelled only of dust.

"Florence."

And cigarette smoke.

"You came back. You have more spine than I expected." The Gibson Girl floated a good eighteen inches off the floor.

"Please stand closer to the floor. I'll get a crick in my neck."

"I don't stand, I waft. I'm the sylph of the afterlife."

Giulia didn't have time for posturing. "Did you try to kill Sister Eugenie?"

The ghost sank to the floor so fast Giulia's ears added a thump when it "landed."

"What kind of monster do you think I am?"

"You're dodging the question."

Florence rolled her misty eyes. "No, I did not try to kill that old besom. It isn't my fault her fat fingers couldn't properly manipulate something as simple as a rusty pipe."

"How did you carry her downstairs?"

Florence's laugh was as unpleasant as her habit of blowing cigarette smoke in Giulia's face. "You have one thing in common with these useless virgins. You're too trusting."

Giulia chewed the inside of her lip. "She could walk but chose to live in a wheelchair?"

"Close. She likes secrets and she likes being waited on. If her voice didn't grate on my undead ears like nails on a blackboard, I'd almost admire her gumption. Today for some reason known only to her greedy little brain, she bestirred herself enough to bump down the stairs on her ample behind while clutching the railings for dear life." Another snide laugh. "Nice of her to give me a little entertainment. When she reached the cellar floor she was so pleased with herself she managed to lurch across the room like a toddler taking its first steps."

"A human being's brush with death is not your personal command performance. Emergency personnel are downstairs trying to clear the poison from Eugenie's lungs."

"I saw. Whoo, did her puke stink."

"Vomiting is the issue, not the accompanying stench. She caused a dangerous gas leak."

"Oh, stop preaching. She'll be fine. She's a lot healthier than she pretends."

Giulia's phone rang. "Yes, Pit Bull?"

"I'm outside. The place is barricaded by cops. Can you escort me in?"

"Go around to the back door please, like you did last time. I'll meet you."

Florence clapped, the omnipresent cigarette disappearing while she did so. "The tattooed cameraman is here? He's worth looking at, let me tell you." She vanished.

The sound Giulia made could best be described as "Aaarrgh." She avoided the exiting firefighters and police officers on her way to the kitchen. Steve apparently considered her one of the household by this time, because she heard his nails tick-tack-tick-tack on the floor behind her.

She opened the door on Ken Kanning.

Steve saved her from tarnishing her "never caught off guard" reputation by limping into his "injured puppy" act. He squeezed between Giulia's ankles, one paw raised. When he lifted his head all the way up to Kanning's six-foot height, his brown eyes somehow became bigger. His whimper should've earned him a nomination for Best Supporting Actor. Eugenie was a lock for Best Actor.

Kanning's show business moxie was no match for Scenery-Chewing Steve. The face of *The Scoop* squatted on the doorsill and relinquished his carefully crafted image.

"Oh, you poor puppy. What happened to your paw? You want

some skritches? On your ears? Yes, you do." He rubbed the dog's bat ears until Steve's eyes closed in ecstasy. "Who's a good boy? You're a good boy, yes you are."

Pit Bull had stepped to one side and turned on the camera.

Giulia cleared her throat. "Mr. Kanning, please come in."

Without a shred of embarrassment, Kanning got to his feet. "It's good to see you again, Ms. Driscoll."

He stepped over the threshold. Steve shook himself all over and trotted over to his blanket on his four healthy legs.

Kanning's jaw dropped. On him the look was a good one, revealing capped teeth and showcasing the dimple in his chin. "Why, you shivery little weasel."

Pit Bull crossed the threshold, camera down. "Ms. Driscoll, what's with the fire truck and ambulance and police?"

Kanning snapped back into *The Scoop* mode so fast Giulia feared for his neck alignment. "Bull."

The camera was up and recording again. Kanning donned his "serious news" face.

"It's an average Tuesday night in Cottonwood. Families are finishing the evening meal. Children are playing fetch with their dogs." His eyes glanced down to Steve chewing a rawhide bone. The camera followed him. "Yet pandemonium is happening behind the doors of one charming old house on a quiet residential street." His serious face switched off. "Okay, Ms. Driscoll, your turn."

Giulia indicated the camera with her eyes, glancing up at Pit Bull, then over to his shoulder. He lowered the camera and she said to him, "Are you two joined at the hip?"

Sixty-Seven

Pit Bull shrugged. "We were together in the studio when you called."

Giulia frosted him. "I repeat my question."

Kanning invaded her personal space once more. "We're all in this one together. You, me, Bull. *The Scoop* will prevent Eagle's surviving henchmen from giving these nuns a raw deal."

"Mr. Kanning, I assure you if Driscoll Investigations ever again has need of *The Scoop*, we will not resort to subterfuge as a means of contact."

Kanning showed all his perfect teeth. "Don't call us; we'll call you, is that it? Well, you called Bull."

"Indeed. I contacted Mr. Bull."

"*The Scoop* is a well-oiled machine, Ms. Driscoll. You know this from experience." He placed a hand on Pit Bull's shoulder. "When you talk to Bull, you talk to both of us."

Pit Bull maneuvered his head a quarter turn away from Kanning's line of sight. With the right side of his face only, he made extravagant grimaces at Giulia.

She didn't need Jasper's clairvoyant skills to interpret Pit Bull's message: "I don't tell him everything. Believe me."

"Mr. Kanning, I disagree with your interpretation of my phone call tonight. However, as you have attached yourself to your cameraman, you may be of use to us." She said to Pit Bull, "If you'll follow me upstairs I'll take you to Sister Agatha."

"What's up with her?"

"We aren't sure. With all the commotion in the house you'd think she'd be worse. But at one of those odd moments of silence, we realized she'd stopped moaning."

"The twenty-minute lull," Kanning said from the end of the line. "You know, the phenomenon that in crowded rooms, everyone will stop talking at twenty past the hour. I still want to do an April Fool's Day show on it."

Dorothy came out of Helena's room as Giulia reached the second floor. "She slipped back for a few minutes, but now she's calling for Clarence again." She pointed at Pit Bull. "You're Clarence. I remember now. I'll be in her room with you in a minute. Sister Helena needs meds."

Giulia knocked on Agatha's open door. "We brought Clarence to visit you."

The pale eyes moved from their focus on the sky through the open window. The head with its scraggly gray hair turned a second later, as though the eyes pulled it along. The mouth opened as though to begin wailing again.

"Clarence."

The cameraman entered the room, equipment low at his side. "I'm here, Sister."

"Repeat the prayer I taught you."

He set the camera on the floor. "Which prayer, Sister?"

The nun attempted to raise herself on one elbow. Giulia ducked in front of Pit Bull and sat at the head of the bed. She put one arm behind the invalid and with an effort half-raised her so she leaned against Giulia's side.

"The prayer for the souls in Purgatory. Say it now." A ghost of bygone authority echoed in the last three words.

Pit Bull's expression was one Giulia had seen many times from the orchestra pit at the Cottonwood Community Theater: The actor who'd forgotten his lines. A moment later his mouth opened and the old-fashioned rote prayer came out.

"Eternal Father, I offer Thee the Most Precious Blood of Thy Divine Son, Jesus, in union with the masses said throughout the world today, for all the holy souls in Purgatory, for sinners everywhere, for sinners...uh...in the universal church, those in my own home and within my family." After a beat he added, "Amen."

A film of flop-sweat formed on the crown of his shaved head. Giulia had seen actors' memory come to the rescue almost as many times.

Instead of approving her former pupil, Agatha pushed against Giulia to gain another inch of verticality. "You have been neglecting your duties. I taught you to pray St. Gertrude's prayer every single day. How many days did you choose laziness over releasing souls from Purgatory?" Her finger aimed at his heart.

Pit Bull's head blossomed cranberry. "Well, Sister, you see..." But the nun had fallen onto Giulia, her eyes closed again.

"Bull, where the hell's your spine?" Ken Kanning's voice held surprise and disdain. "I've never seen you cave in front of authority."

"Shut up, Ken," Pit Bull's hissing retort spoke more of kids on a midnight kitchen expedition trying not to wake up Mom than of anger.

Giulia was considering whether to lay her burden onto the pillow when Dorothy said from the doorway, "How is she?"

"I am talking to Clarence." The voice was clear. "Responsible." The eyes opened and found Pit Bull. "You are responsible."

He looked over her head at Giulia. When she mouthed, "No idea," he met the nun's unclouded gaze. "Responsible for what, Sister?"

"You were a bright student. You see what's happening in this house." Her lower lip cracked and a bead of blood formed in its center.

Dorothy left and returned with a cup of water and a tissue. She dabbed at the blood and held the water to Agatha's dry lips.

"He was punished. She is in torment. He is in torment. Through their fault, through their fault, through their most grievous fault."

Giulia said, "What did he do? What did she do?"

Agatha was silent so long Giulia started to ease her flat onto the bed, sure she'd missed an opportunity in the short lucid interval.

"All must pray!"

Giulia started. Agatha's eyes swiveled up to reproach her. Giulia resettled the nun in a more comfortable position.

Pit Bull knelt by the bed. "Pray for what? Pray for who?"

Giulia added, "Why did she do it?" without being certain who "she" was, but if Pit Bull could make the clearheaded spell last a few minutes longer she might get an edge on the ghost.

Agatha began mumbling. Giulia and Pit Bull leaned over her. Giulia caught the second sentence of the Purgatory prayer Agatha had made Pit Bull recite. She looked up at Dorothy and shook her head.

Dorothy made a resigned gesture. "She'll go into default mode now."

This time Giulia succeeded in laying the old nun flat on her bed. Dorothy straightened the covers. Pit Bull picked up his camera. Ken Kanning tested teaser lines for one of *The Scoop*'s promotion clips. "Not even women of the cloth...No. In a world where nothing is sacred...Maybe. Bull, let's try a few by the stairs."

Quiet versions of Agatha's usual groans punctuated Kanning's "build up the excitement" voice.

"Mr. Clarence." Dorothy called after him.

Pit Bull returned to the doorway.

"She's not following her usual pattern. I think she's going to open her eyes again. Would you mind staying here for a little while longer?"

This time his boss urged him on. "Go on. Get it over with so we can get back to work."

Setting down the camera once more, Pit Bull walked the two steps to the bedside and stood looking down at the wreck of his sixth-grade teacher. From her place at the head of the bed, Giulia watched impatience, guilt, sorrow, and frustration chase themselves across his face.

"Wake up, you old biddy," he muttered. "You used to be a fighter. Stop trashing my only good childhood memory."

The moans kept their expected pace for another minute by Giulia's phone clock. At its expiration, they stopped like someone pressed her Off button. Giulia snapped a photo.

"Clarence, yes." Her voice was hoarse but intelligible. "Barbara, yes. Jane, no. Jennifer, no. Bruce, no." One eye peeled itself open. "You two are the only ones left. The task falls to you."

"What task? Stop talking in riddles."

Her hand darted out from under the covers and aimed a slap at Pit Bull. "Respect, young man." The abrupt gesture sapped the last of her energy. Her head fell back on the pillow and her mouth opened. Instead of a moan, she began to snore.

"Jesus Christ." Pit Bull stalked out of the room, picking up his camera on the way. "Come on, Ken."

Giulia said to Dorothy, "Has she ever mentioned any of those names before?"

"No. This is the most she's spoken since last Christmas. They could be former students."

"Associations from seeing Pit Bull again. Thank you." Giulia strode into the hall.

The Scoop blocked the stairs. Kanning straddled the third step. Pit Bull balanced on the newel and angled the camera down at him.

"We can do a lot with this shot, Ken. The light's good and creepy."

Sixty-Eight

On the main floor, Giulia tried the front parlor first. The EMTs were gone. Eugenie had been moved to the couch on a clean blanket with two more blankets covering her. Her snores rivaled Agatha's.

Kathryn sat at the kitchen table drinking from a mug. As Giulia approached the table, the back door closed on Olive and Steve.

Giulia pulled out the chair next to the Superior. "I expected Eugenie to be headed to the hospital."

Kathryn pinched the bridge of her nose. "She refused. I started to order her to go, but the medical personnel got skittish. I'm not a relation and she doesn't have a health care proxy. Then she surprised us all again by sitting up. She apologized for vomiting and recited her name, address, and the list of her meds with their correct dosages. Then she demanded something to drink. The medical tech put her through more tests with her giving them attitude throughout. Finally they said they couldn't force her to come with them and advised plain water and clear broth for twenty-four hours." She sipped from her mug. "And she still refuses to tell anyone but her Confessor why she went into the cellar. So here we are. One big happy family."

Giulia indicated the mug. "The long-delayed tea?"

"I'd add brandy, but not while we have guests." She made a move toward the stove. "Can I make you a cup?"

"Thank you, no. You need to stay off your feet for ten minutes. I want to talk about the buyout."

Kathryn dropped her forehead onto her hand. "I never want to hear about Eagle Developers again."

"I'm your fairy godmother." Giulia opened her phone. "The new head of Eagle called me with their latest offer. It's two thousand more than the minimum I was willing to settle for. The money is enough to move everyone into a house in a decent part of town. There may even be a few dollars to spare to stock the wine shelves." She typed the figure into her calculator function in case Kathryn required a visual to push her from hesitation to decision.

"That much? Really?"

"Really. I strongly advise you to take it."

Kathryn sipped her tea while her gaze stayed on the phone screen. Giulia gave her time. The kitchen clock ticked. A series of excited yips came closer and closer. The Chihuahua squeezed through the door as soon as Olive opened it a crack.

"Go to your blanket." Olive stamped her foot and pointed. "Now."

Tail between his short legs, Steve slunk to his bed by the refrigerator.

Kathryn said in a weary voice, "What did he do?"

"He imitated the goofy dog in *Up.*" Olive rubbed her right shoulder.

"Squirrel!" Giulia murmured.

Kathryn snickered.

"Go ahead and laugh. The little rat didn't try to dislocate your shoulder." Olive glared at Steve, who covered his eyes with his paws.

"Dorothy can fix you," Kathryn said. "*The Scoop* is on the second floor," she added.

"They are? Both of them?" Olive produced a burst of speed and disappeared up the stairs.

"Squirrel!" Giulia murmured again.

Kathryn set down her mug and laughed into her sleeve. Her face when she raised it became ten years younger. "I agree. We'll take the offer."

"I'd like to have Eagle invade your house tonight to make it official. She's eager and we all want to get this over with, correct?"

"Correct. I can sleep when I'm dead."

Giulia opened her phone. "Ms. Beech, it's Giulia Driscoll. Are you still willing to confirm sale tonight?...Good. We'll see you in a few minutes." She hung up and grinned at Kathryn. "She just happens to be running an errand within a mile of here."

"Good. I think I'll hover around Ken Kanning while I wait."

Kathryn's face sloughed off another five years when she said it.

When Kathryn was safely upstairs, Giulia called Sidney from the cellar. "It's me, and yes, clock this as overtime. What did you unearth about Barbara Beech?"

"Olivier," Sidney said to her husband on the other end, "I'm on a quick work call." A pause. "Olivier and Jessamine are watching Sesame Street. He says he'll use the time to teach her how to psychoanalyze Cookie Monster."

"That child will be scarred for life."

"Or she'll earn her Ph.D. in psychology before she turns twenty-one. Let me put you on speaker while I log in." The sound acquired another dimension with Sidney's keyboard clicks. "Got it. Did you know she sky dives?"

"Yes, and that she's the Pomeranian version of a Crazy Cat Lady."

"Ooh, I missed that."

Giulia put Sidney on speaker at low volume and opened the dogster site. "Here's a sample discussion post from the new CEO of Eagle Developers, and it is not couched in standard business language: 'Mr. Fluffy Pants survived a scare today. He ate a spider!!!' Three exclamation points after spider."

"No judging here. I'm not a fan of multi-legged creatures."

"Now I know what to dress as for Halloween. To continue, 'I had to MacGyver it out of his mouth. Good thing I had a spare poop bag in my pocket. Neither of us was bitten, but when I use this in a story it will add drama. Stay tuned.'"

"Mr. Fluffy Pants? Really?"

Giulia wasn't listening. "A story." She scrolled down. "Several more comments amounting to requests to write faster."

"She needs a punctuation refresher."

"No, wait. I'm going to join this site right now. Keep talking, please." She blew through the registration process, using the dummy email she reserved for undercover work.

"Beech went to Catholic school up to eighth grade."

"Franciscan? Please say yes."

"Yes. Saint Anthony of Padua elementary. The school was one of a cluster on the south side before the area demographics changed and they were closed one after the other starting fifteen years ago. But that's not the good part."

"It might be, but keep going."

"Tease. Ms. Beech has always used her maiden name in business, for which we should thank her. She made the news in a minor way when she was in eighth grade. Her homeroom nun teacher got suspicious of the excuse notes her parents kept sending instead of showing up at parent-teacher conferences."

"Please don't tell me she murdered her parents and kept their bodies in lifelike poses around the house."

"Ew. Olivier watched *Psycho* the other night too. No, thank God. Her homeroom nun and her parish priest showed up at her house unannounced one Saturday morning. It was a huge old house falling apart at the seams. Here's the icky part. Her father had walked out on them when Beech was in sixth grade and her mother was—to be polite—working as an escort. Out of the house."

"Ew."

"I know, right? Beech tried to keep them out and her mother came into the kitchen wearing not much and walloped her. Then Mommy's man of the night came in, cursing everyone for waking him up and walloped Mommy and Beech. At this point the parish priest chose not to allow the women to turn the other cheek and assisted the thug into unconsciousness with a left hook."

"MacGyver again," Giulia muttered, reading threads.

"Giulia, speak up."

"Sorry, I'm trying to find a link. By the way, excellent sleuthing on Beech's childhood. Tomorrow or Thursday please show me the rabbit trail you followed."

"Will do. It was like one of those Family Circus cartoons where the little kid takes a dotted line path all over the neighborhood. To continue, the nun called the cops and Child Protective Services. The cops hauled Mommy and her paying customer away and CPS started Beech's five-year foster home odyssey."

Silence.

"Are you still there?"

"Yes."

"Picture me waiting patiently for you to say, 'Got it.'"

"Got it," Giulia echoed. "Wait, what?"

Sidney was laughing. "Go ahead. Tell me the connection."

"Two connections. One, she writes overwrought stories about Pomeranians with the skills and intelligence of Gromit. One of them rescues MacGyver."

"Please bookmark this and read it to us tomorrow."

"I will, but after we've all finished our coffee. That's not the important part. In a thread about therapy dogs, she refuses to join another Pom owner on a trip to a retired nuns' nursing home. She gets quite emphatic...oh, look. She says she'll never name one of her dogs Agatha. It's apparently a long-running joke, because two people in the thread made snarky comments about penguins."

Sidney said, "I believe the word is 'bingo.'"

"It is indeed. I will now spring a trap on Eagle Developers' new CEO. You are a treasure. Go rescue Jessamine before Olivier starts in on Oscar the Grouch."

"I'm already there."

"I'll see you tomorrow. The time of my arrival in the office will be a surprise to us all."

Sixty-Nine

Only Barbara Beech's silver Lexus sedan disturbed the quiet of the empty street. The emergency vehicles were long gone and the rubberneckers had dispersed in search of new thrills. Giulia rose from the front stoop and met Beech on the sidewalk. They shook hands.

"Thank you for coming."

"The workday doesn't stop at five p.m." Beech's business suit illustrated her words.

"Indeed." Giulia preceded her inside. Both of them waved away a snootful of cigarette smoke. Beech's manicured eyebrows rose, but she didn't comment.

Steve came to the rescue. Giulia stood back while the Chihuahua provided the entertainment. Unlike Ken Kanning, Beech resisted Steve's piteous charm. Perhaps her affections were reserved for Pomeranians.

Giulia looked around for the ghost, but the smoke appeared to be her only manifestation for the moment.

Kathryn came down the hall to meet them. "Steve, go to your blanket."

The little dog obeyed, and Beech reacted to his sudden access of health.

"He puts on a wounded act for visitors? Smart dog."

"He thinks he is." Kathryn and Beech shook hands. "I'm Sister Kathryn, Superior of this convent. Please excuse our kitchen, but it has the only practicable table."

Beech sat on one side, Giulia and Kathryn on the other. Beech opened her briefcase and summarized the three-page document as she passed it over. Giulia and Kathryn read it together.

"This is quite clear," Kathryn said.

"Eagle Developers was one of the first adopters of plain language contracts." She winked—a stiff attempt at camaraderie. "The practice also saves us excess legal fees."

"We understand frugality." Kathryn made a face. "I forgot to bring in a pen."

Beech whipped one out of the briefcase. "Please use mine."

The Superior initialed the first two pages and signed and dated the third. As she repeated the initials and signature on the second copy, Beech did the same for the first. In another minute the transaction was complete.

More handshakes.

"Sister, the money will deposit into the convent's account within a week. Our project for these two blocks is in final planning stage, but we all know how quickly local government moves."

Polite chuckles.

"Contractors are responding to our call for bids, and after we choose, we'll need to negotiate purchase of materials. Permits have been applied for. We were surprised not to see ambulatory skeletons staffing the permit office. All of which is to say you have a good month or two to find new living quarters."

Olive poked her head into the kitchen. "I beg your pardon, Sister Kathryn. Sister Eugenie is awake and asking for you."

Kathryn stood. "Please excuse me. One of our Sisters is ill."

When they were alone, Giulia sprang part one of her trap. "Ms. Beech, I understand you went to a Catholic school staffed by this Community of Sisters."

The slightest of shivers rustled Beech's linen suit. "Those were not happy years. Oh, I don't blame the nuns, but I certainly haven't attended any school reunions." She began repacking her briefcase. "To tell you the truth, I wondered if I'd recognize anyone here. It's hard to be sure who is who since they've been allowed to resume their normal names."

What a lovely opening for Haunted Convent Trap Part Two. Giulia brought up the photo of Agatha she'd taken earlier. "By any chance do you recognize her?"

Beech glanced, then stared. "Every rule has an exception. She's older in this picture, but she was Sister Agatha back in my day. She did a lot for the class outcasts." She took refuge in an awkward laugh. "I wasn't always a well-dressed, confident business professional."

Giulia smiled. "None of us were. Sister Agatha lives here and is dangerously ill. Would you mind paying her a short visit?"

If ever a human resembled a trapped animal, Beech was that human. She gathered herself together in a moment and attempted a light laugh. It failed.

"I didn't know closing tonight's deal would end with me facing an old phobia." She snapped shut the locks on her briefcase. "The nuns used to quote the Bible to us impressionable pre-teens. It's been a long time, but I believe the appropriate quote in this instance is something about when we visit the sick and feed the hungry and such, we're tallying up good deed points in heaven." She pushed back her chair. "I can spare time for a brief visit."

Giulia preceded her up the stairs, texting Frank as she climbed: Meet me at nuns' house?

An immediate reply: Not even going to ask what I discovered?

Giulia: In the middle of something.

Frank: Are you about to show me up?

Giulia: Maaaaybe.

Frank: 30 minutes.

Giulia kept climbing, leading Beech closer to the trap. If "Clarence" in Agatha's rant was Pit Bull and Agatha had also taught Beech in middle school, then the odds the "Barbara" from the same rant was the new CEO of Eagle Developers were looking pretty good.

Agatha's browbeating had startled Pit Bull into more honesty than Giulia had ever seen in either half of *The Scoop*. If Agatha were to tyrannize nun-hating Beech, she might just get Beech to cough up damning information on why Victor Eagle ditched his henchmen and tried to torch the convent himself.

Seventy

Another cloud of invisible cigarette smoke assaulted their nostrils as they reached the landing.

Beech said in Giulia's ear, "Nuns sure have changed since I was in school. Back in the day we'd get detention for a week if we got caught smoking. The nuns didn't give study hall detention either. We had to scrub the classroom floors and vacuum the hall carpets."

Giulia tallied the times the nuns had smelled Florence's cigarettes plus the times she only had smelled them, plus tonight's two instances. The nuns had never seen or heard Florence. Only Steve had. Without letting herself get distracted by the school of thought which held that animals were inherently more sensitive than humans to the Other Side, Giulia came to a logical conclusion: Florence chose when and to whom she manifested her tricks.

"Excuse us, please." Kathryn said from behind them.

They stepped aside. Kathryn and Olive toiled sideways up the stairs, Eugenie slung between them, complaining all the way.

"My head is killing me. Olive, quit bouncing me. I'm going to throw up again if you don't hurry. Oh, my head. Where's Dorothy? I need a dozen aspirin."

Dorothy ran toward them with the wheelchair. She parked it behind Eugenie and the other two lowered the passive nun into it.

"That sucked." Eugenie's shirt rucked into her armpits as she landed. She squirmed and tugged the cloth into a smoother position.

"You're welcome." Olive leaned panting against the wall. "Lose a few pounds before you try going walkies again, will you?"

"Ever hear of offering it up?"

"I didn't know I'd need to practice Olympic weightlifting for the offering."

"Sisters, we have guests." Kathryn's voice caused ice crystals to form on the walls.

Barbara Beech nodded at the group of nuns. Giulia escorted her around the wheelchair. Ken Kanning came out of Helena's room. Pit Bull followed, poking buttons on his view screen. The camera bumped into Beech's arm.

Pit Bull backpedaled. "Sorry, Sister." He looked up.

Beech stopped. "Angel?"

"Barbie?"

"Angel?" Giulia and Kanning said.

"Clarence was the name of Jimmy Stewart's guardian angel in *It's a Wonderful Life*," Beech said without taking her gaze from Pit Bull.

"Bull, you must have been adorable in grade school." Kanning's laughter underlay his remark.

"The nuns showed us the movie every Christmas before break." Pit Bull's gaze also remained locked with Beech's.

"Why are you here?" Beech said.

"Sister Agatha asked for me. Why are you here?"

"Ms. Driscoll asked me to visit Sister Agatha."

They both turned on Giulia. "Is this some kind of trick?"

Agatha came to Giulia's rescue with an epic wail. Every head snapped toward Agatha's still-open door. Dorothy dashed from Helena's room into Agatha's. Giulia followed, pulling Beech in the room with her.

The cool, professional head of Eagle Developers with years of successful business deals under her belt did not hide her revulsion fast enough. Her hands slid over her mouth. She backed away from the bed until she came up against the wall. White ringed her ice-blue eyes.

Agatha wailed and moaned and howled, but looked no different tonight than she had for the past several days. Dorothy stroked her head and neck. The howling continued. Dorothy said above it, "I'm sorry. She's having a bad evening after her earlier episode. I don't think she'll come out of it for several hours. We had too much excitement today."

Beech scurried into the hall, looked around in panic, and bolted for the bathroom. She removed her hands from her mouth in time to vomit into the toilet. Ken Kanning snapped his fingers and Pit Bull filmed Beech's toilet worship. Giulia's stomach flip-flopped, but she found a washcloth in the linen closet and soaked it in cool water in the bathroom sink. The breeze from the open window dissipated the smell somewhat.

After several dry heaves, Beech sat on her heels. Giulia wiped her forehead, mouth, and chin, then rinsed the cloth, and Beech took it for a second wipe down. Giulia filled a tiny paper bathroom cup with water and handed it to her. She swirled and spat, then flushed the toilet.

"Thank you."

"Are you all right now?" Giulia realized Pit Bull was probably still filming. Asking him to stop wouldn't cut any weight with Kanning, so she settled for keeping her back to the camera. She leaned over and whispered in Beech's ear, "Pit Bull is filming this."

"Who?"

"Clarence. He's half of *The Scoop.*"

Beech stiffened, but kept her mouth shut. She spent a few minutes at the sink, frowned at her wrecked makeup, and turned to the door. With a large smile she said to the camera, "Clarence, did you get the tattoos to cover up the scars from the beatings your foster parents gave you?"

Filming stopped.

Eugenie maneuvered her wheelchair between Beech and Pit Bull. "You greedy, heartless excuse for a human being! How dare you show your face in our house?"

Seventy-One

Beech looked down in surprise. Eugenie kept rolling her wheelchair forward until she trapped Eagle Developers' CEO against the peeling wallpaper.

Eugenie in full-on rant mode started to spit on hard consonants. "This is our home. We teach the underprivileged. We help the homeless. The few of us too old or ill to work have earned these lousy rooms and substandard health care with decades of hard work. You're a parasite and a thief and a piece of human offal."

She stopped to catch her breath. Beech's mouth was hanging open. Pit Bull's camera was capturing it all. Out of Eugenie and Beech's line of sight, Kanning was all but rubbing his hands together in ratings-induced glee.

Kathryn broke the speechless tableau. "Sister Eugenie. Cease this harangue at once."

Eugenie glanced over her shoulder at Kathryn bearing down on her. "I won't. Someone in this house has to stand up for what's right. Since you don't have the spine, I'll take over the job."

Kathryn took one of the wheelchair's push handles and Dorothy grabbed the other. Together they dragged Eugenie away from Beech. Eugenie fought them by gripping the hand rims and pulling against their backwards motion. "Stop moving me! You have no right to censor me!"

Dorothy slammed on the brake. Kathryn whipped around and put her face nose to nose with Eugenie.

"I have every right." Her low, intense voice stopped Eugenie's diatribe. "I am your Superior. You took a vow of obedience and you will obey me."

She nodded to Dorothy, who unlocked the brake. Together they pushed the chair into Eugenie's room. Dorothy grabbed a thermometer and a blood pressure cuff and closed herself in with Eugenie.

Kathryn walked over to Beech, who had left the wall and turned her back to the camera. "I apologize for Sister Eugenie's outburst. She had no excuse. Please don't think we're all of her opinion."

Eugenie's shout penetrated her closed door. "She sold it?"

Beech produced a smile. "I've encountered her attitude many times. Some people resist change. Nothing could be as bad as the unforgettable moment two years ago when a hoarder poured a bucketful of human waste on me from a second-floor window."

Kanning snickered. Beech rose to the moment. "Mr. Kanning, it's a pleasure to meet you. I don't watch your show myself, but I understand many people enjoy it."

But Kanning was a match for her. "Ms. Beech, please accept my condolences for the loss of your former CEO. Are congratulations in order as well?"

The polite smiles on both sides should've illustrated the dictionary entry.

"Thank you, Mr. Kanning. Everyone at Eagle Developers is saddened by the sudden loss of our founder. The company will carry on his vision to make Cottonwood the showplace of Pennsylvania. As a matter of fact, Sister Kathryn has accepted our buyout offer, clearing the way for Victor Eagle's landmark forward-thinking redevelopment project for this neighborhood. I'm sure your viewers would be interested in the plan. I have the artist's renderings on my phone."

Giulia edged away from the camera group. A few quiet steps down the L-shaped hall and she closed herself into the chapel.

"Florence?" she whispered.

"Who gave permission for a wild party in my house?"

The ghost's loud voice came from behind Giulia. She started, and kicked herself for it.

"Hah. Got you. The living are so predictable."

"At least you're not smoking."

"Oh, you miss it? I won't disappoint you then." A stink of tobacco and burnt paper invaded the room.

Giulia turned on her. "What is in those things?"

For the first time, the ghost looked taken aback. "I rolled my own when I was alive. I liked them simple, so these have dried bright leaf tobacco."

"That's it? How much nicotine is in one?"

The ghost tipped her head sideways and the misty ostrich feather in her hat bobbed to her shoulder. "I don't know." She laughed. "I'm dead. They can't hurt me."

"Well, I'm pregnant and they can hurt the baby." Giulia kicked herself again the second the words came out. "Never give a ghost ammunition," Rowan said. Now look what she'd done.

Giulia braced herself for a blinding fog of smoke from Miss Attitude, but nothing happened. Instead, the cigarette hung limp in Florence's hand.

They stayed face to face for a long moment. Then without warning Florence disappeared from the chapel and reappeared inside Giulia.

Seventy-Two

Giulia felt the ghost's force? Presence? Aura? Ectoplasm? No, ectoplasm was something tangible excreted from a medium during a séance. Whatever the term, Florence Gosnall had invaded Giulia's body.

She shook her brain clear of panic. "Get out of me." She didn't yell, at least not out loud. She thought the words in her Teacher Voice of Imminent Doom. The last thing she needed was *The Scoop* scenting a scoop.

For the longest moment in her life, she fought Florence for her own personal space in the most intimate sense of the phrase.

Giulia pulled on her arms, picturing herself dragging off a shirt with too-tight sleeves.

Rowan had been confident Giulia would find her strength.

She was in a chapel, but nothing overtly Catholic spoke to her.

She reached over her head and yanked her hands from the base of her neck to her chin as though peeling off a wig.

What was her center? Think. God? Family?

Family. She'd do anything to protect her adrenaline-junkie son.

Desperate, panic rising, she spoke within herself. "Zlatan, you and me. Now."

She clenched her stomach muscles, made her hands into claws, and yanked outward from her center.

Giulia's ears popped as she pulled and Zlatan pushed the ghost out of her. The feather reappeared first. The hat brim followed, then the front of the lacy blouse and the skirt, and last the high button boots, all stretching like taffy on a hot summer day. With an inaudible snap, Florence and Giulia faced each other as complete and separate persons.

"How dare you?" Giulia said. Were she a ghost with power over the elements, smoke and flames would be spewing from her own ears right now.

But Florence didn't give her a sarcastic reply. She placed her free hand on Giulia's stomach. "He's beautiful. So small and so perfect." The next second Florence plopped onto the rug.

Giulia gave Zlatan a mental hug. He wriggled for the second time. The joy of feeling him move distracted her until Florence's cigarette relit itself.

The ghost took a long drag. "You don't wear corsets, do you?"

Florence had mastered sarcasm, body invasion, elemental manipulation—and the non sequitur.

"No. My job requires freedom of movement."

Another drag. "I apologize for jumping into you. It was the impulse of the moment." Her lip curled. "The first time I discovered I could fuse with the living it was totally by accident. One of these withered virgins—not the ones living here now—was complaining about the house's design. The longer she whined, the angrier I became. I had to get away from her. She was blocking one of the doorways and I meant to barge right past her, except I went through her. Was I moithered! I saw her bones, her blood, her organs. For the first time since I died, I wanted to puke. The silly cow shivered and said a goose was walking over her grave. How cliché."

She smoked the cigarette into oblivion and stared at her empty fingers a moment. "Watch this." She rubbed her right thumb across the tips of her fingers and a hand-rolled cigarette appeared in her palm. Next she snapped her left thumbnail against her left middle nail in the same motion as lighting a match. A single flame hovered over the tip of her thumbnail. She lit the cigarette and shook the flame out. "Vaudeville would have loved me." She took a drag. "I was apologizing."

"I accept your apology."

"No. You have to know why. I enjoyed my life and I didn't care what people thought of me. I was jailed for marching for votes for women. I went to architectural school in France. I took lovers." She looked around the chapel. "You might think I regret not being alive now, but today I'd be merely one of thousands of talented women. In my time I was daring and clever and exotic. Women were jealous and men were fascinated. When I realized I was with child, I refused to change my lifestyle. I kept dressing to show off my figure and smoked and drank as much as ever. That's why I asked you about the corsets. The baby came much too early and it was horribly deformed and it was my fault. The doctor who came after the neighbors heard my screams did what he could, but I'd been hemorrhaging for hours. I'd contracted childbed fever as well, and I died from the fever and blood loss." Her smile for the first time appeared sad. "The poor dead little baby in the basin was the first thing I saw after I died. If that quack of a doctor had had an ounce of otherworld sensitivity he would've had nightmares from my screams for the rest of his life."

Florence stood and faced Giulia. "Now you've heard my story. I've never seen my own baby's ghost. You'll say he went to heaven, whatever that is. I was never one of those Azusa Street fanatics when I was alive and I'm still not. These snotty virgins whine about God day and night, but I haven't seen a glimpse or heard a peep from their God in the one hundred and six years I've been dead."

"I didn't come in here to discuss religion."

"I'm staying in my house because it's mine. No one is ever going to take it from me, even if I have to put up with nuns in my bedroom for the next five hundred years."

In the back of her head, Giulia recited Jasper's rules. Ghosts lie. Words have power. Ghosts are unstable. Believe.

Florence's death scene could be one hundred percent true. Death in childbirth was all too common in her era. Such a story still didn't mean Giulia was going to roll into a sobbing, motherly ball at the ghost's feet. Giulia's first ghost—no matter how clever, snarky, and fascinating it had turned out to be—wasn't going to make her lose all common sense and detective skills.

"Florence. I came in here to talk to you in private because I have news."

The ghost stopped pontificating and her ostrich feather stopped bobbing. "Do I get three guesses?"

"No." The more time she sequestered herself in here increased the possibility of Ken Kanning searching for her to ambush a sound bite out of her.

"You are a real wet blanket. I'm going to guess anyway." She tapped her chin with her index finger. "Let's see. Number one."

For once, Baby Brain didn't sabotage Giulia and she remembered something called the rule of three. She wasn't exactly sure what all it involved, but without Rowan or Jasper on speed dial, she knew she'd better cut Florence off.

"The Sisters accepted Eagle Developers' offer tonight."

Florence dropped her coquettish stance like *The Scoop* bailing on an outdated story. "Those miserable hags sold my house?"

The ostrich feathers stood straight up. Its hundreds of vanes stuck out in all directions like porcupine quills. Florence's round, handsome face stretched and warped as her pouting lips opened wide, wider, wider. Her skin bubbled and sloughed off in steaming globs. Olive-green mold discolored her teeth. The feather burst into flames. The stench of burned feathers overpowered the stink of mold. Her expanding mouth revealed a seething orange and black vortex deeper than any pit.

Giulia fumbled for one second with the flap of her messenger bag. Then her fingers gripped the holy water flask and it was out, it was free, and she unscrewed the cap and flung its contents in a cross pattern at the thing that had been Florence, her voice cracking on the Latin coming automatically from her lips. "*In nómine Pátris, et Fílii, et Spíritus Sancti.*"

Seventy-Three

The next instant the Gibson Girl returned. No more flames, no more glorping skin, no more pit of bubbling hell in her throat. Water beaded on the ostrich feather and glistened in the lace on her blouse.

"What did you do to me?" Florence brushed at her wet clothes. "You got me wet. How did you do that?"

Giulia wanted to escape. She wanted the security of tough, competent Frank standing at her shoulder. She wanted a shot of Tullamore Dew. She wanted to know if little Zlatan would be born with an Evel Knievel daredevil birthmark. After all they'd been though during this pregnancy, nothing would surprise her.

Since none of her desires could be granted, Giulia settled for giving herself a quick pat on the back for neither screaming nor fainting nor needing to change her underwear.

Rule Four: Believe.

Rule Two: Ghosts are unstable.

Florence shook herself dry. "I said, how did you manage to get me wet?"

Not a rule, but a chance to give the ghost back a little of the ribbing she'd been dealing with a heavy hand.

Giulia said with a smile, "Wouldn't you like to know?"

So would she, but only a fool would undermine her new drop of power.

Florence's clear eyes narrowed. Before Giulia could form worrying theories as to her possible deeper connection with Florence after the whole "let's share our molecules" incident, the ghost showed off a new talent.

The crucifix started to wiggle off the wall. Cigarette smoke surrounded both of them like a low-hanging cloud. The floor lamps rattled. The chairs performed the elephant walk from *The Jungle Book* on their own.

"I will evict you," Giulia said.

The smoke collapsed into the rug. "You're bluffing."

"Try me." Giulia frantically paged through what she remembered of the exorcism ceremony. If holy water affected Florence, then an exorcism ought to. Florence believed, and apparently didn't know enough about the differences between demons and ghosts. Two points in Giulia's favor.

The chapel door opened. "Giulia, who are you talking to? *The Scoop* guys want—" Bart stopped in the open doorway. "What happened to the chairs?"

Ken Kanning and Pit Bull crowded behind Bart. The camera was on.

Giulia bit her tongue hard. Instead of one of Frank's Irish curses, a gasp of pain came out of her mouth. Win.

Lose: Florence went full-on poltergeist. The smoke reappeared. The lamp bulbs exploded. The Bible toppled off its stand. The bronze crucifix launched itself at the group in the door.

Giulia dived in front of Kanning and snatched the crucifix out of the air six inches from his nose.

Seventy-Four

Bart ran downstairs.

For ten glorious seconds, Ken Kanning was speechless.

But all glory is short-lived. He snapped his fingers. Pit Bull refocused the camera and *The Scoop* sprang into action.

"Scoopers, you trust us to bring you important news. This is the big one. Don't take your eyes from the screen. Let the kids go hungry. Lock the cat and dog in the basement. Take the phone off the hook." Kanning backed three steps into the dark chapel, now that the lamps were useless. The camera's spotlight framed him like he was an opera star about to sing a showstopper aria.

"We're here in the Convent of the Assumption, which has just been sold to Eagle Developers. Remember, Scoopers, this isn't fake news. Every word out of my mouth is pure, unadulterated truth. As we entered the chapel to interview the Sisters, chaos greeted our eyes."

He raised his free hand to his shoulder and made a circular motion with his index finger out of the range of the lens. The camera panned left. Its light reached the broken floor lamp.

"We heard the sound of things crashing behind the closed door of this sacred space. Could someone have broken into this house of holy women? We knew that fighting crime is more important than being first with the news, and that our Scoopers would forgive us for missing a story if it meant we saved the nuns from danger."

The light illuminated the overturned Bible.

"This is the chapel tonight. Shattered lamps. Chairs tossed around like doll house furniture. A desecrated Bible. A sacred space poisoned by dark forces."

Bart ran between Pit Bull and Kanning, two light bulbs in one hand and a cut potato in the other. "Sister Fix-It to the rescue." She knelt by one floor lamp and jammed the potato into the socket. With a few twists she unscrewed the remnants of the cap and replaced it with a fresh bulb. Bright white light lit the left half of the chapel as she righted the lamp. She repeated the actions with the other lamp and faced the camera with a huge grin. "All set. I'll get out of your way."

Kanning gave her a thumbs-up. "Our angel of mercy is Sister Bartholomew, whose mission is feeding and clothing Cottonwood's homeless. Who would be so depraved as to try to force these Godly women from their shelter?"

He pointed to the empty hole in the wall above the Bible. The camera's light followed his motion.

"Scoopers, are you sitting down? Don't reach for a snack or a drink, because you'll spill it. I'm about to tell you the Big News. See that little hole up there in the wall? A cross hung there up until a few minutes ago. As you can see, it isn't hanging there now." He whirled around. So did the camera. The spotlight focused on the crucifix in Giulia's hand.

"There is this room's revered symbol of Christianity!"

Giulia froze.

"Scoopers, you're familiar with Giulia Driscoll, Cottonwood's most charming sleuth. Tonight she's much more than that. As you'll see on this replay, when we opened the chapel door, that very cross came off the wall and flew across the room under its own power. It aimed itself right at my head and only the resourceful Ms. Driscoll saved yours truly from a gruesome death." Kanning photobombed Giulia's moment in the spotlight and kissed her hand.

Her innate courtesy stopped her from wiping her hand on her pant leg. Kanning also didn't betray his abiding principle: Hog the spotlight for yourself whenever possible. He took the crucifix from her hands and placed it on the table. The camera deserted Giulia to capture him as he picked up the Bible and made a pass at straightening the wrinkled pages.

"I'm not ignoring the elephant in the room, Scoopers. You're thinking it. I'm thinking it. I'm sure Ms. Driscoll and the good Sisters are thinking it. Say it with me, Scoopers. On three. One. Two. Three."

Giulia had been edging nearer to Florence during *The Scoop* spectacle. At first, the ghost watched Kanning's dramatics with her mouth open. Open the normal way, not the "look into my seething cauldron of hell" way. But as Kanning led up to his big reveal, Florence's temper built.

Giulia could see her in detail now. The skirt and blouse were robin's-egg blue. The lace was ivory and gold and the hat was ivory with blue and white peonies. The ostrich feather had been dyed blue to match, as she'd thought at their first encounter in the cellar.

She'd have to let Jasper know about Rule Number Five: Spending time with a ghost is the equivalent of tuning rabbit ears on a TV to clear the static.

Kanning said "Poltergeist" for his viewers.

Florence shouted, "I am not a cheap circus act!" and snatched up the crucifix. Giulia ripped it from her hands.

Pit Bull said, "Ken," low and sharp.

Kanning took in the eighteen-inch painted and gilded wood figure in Giulia's hands again. He looked over at his cameraman.

"I saw it but I couldn't turn the camera in time," Pit Bull said. "Swear to God, it jumped off the table on its own and Giulia grabbed it in midair."

"I'll make them respect me," Florence said through clenched teeth. The wooden chairs began to rock themselves in a conga line toward Kanning.

Kanning repeated one of the seven words which can't be said on television, with an adjective attached. Several times. Giulia's irrelevant thought of the moment: Someone else likes Cecilia's favorite expression.

Bangs and bumps came from the door. Grumbling words followed. The chairs lurched closer to *The Scoop*. The front half of Eugenie's wheelchair wedged itself in the doorframe. After a last extended squeak, Eugenie squeezed her chair through.

"I did it," she announced.

Seventy-Five

The chairs took five. Pit Bull swung his camera toward the door. Sister Kathryn loomed behind Eugenie like a scytheless grim reaper. Wails from Sister Agatha invaded the sudden silence.

Giulia confronted Eugenie as though *The Scoop* didn't exist. "Did you kill Victor Eagle?"

If Eugenie had been Mrs. Santa Claus herself, her expression couldn't have been more comical. "Of course not. What kind of a Franciscan do you think I am?"

Florence laughed. Giulia steeled herself not to turn toward the ghost. "Then what are you accusing yourself of?"

Eugenie looked over her shoulder at the Superior. Kathryn's posture remained that of Harbinger of Doom. Eugenie shrank into herself. "I sabotaged the gas line in the basement."

"Why?"

"We love this house. It's ours. No one ever wanted it besides us. When Eagle started to terrorize us, I tried and tried to think of a way to make him change his mind." Her words came slower and slower, a guilt-ridden sinner dragged against her will to the confessional. "I don't know when the idea about the gas line came into my head."

Florence chuckled in Giulia's ear.

"The more I thought about it, the more it seemed like a great idea. It wouldn't be dangerous because someone's always in the house. Dorothy or Olive would smell the gas and call 911."

Giulia crossed her arms. "What on earth were you expecting the outcome to be?"

Pit Bull came into her peripheral vision. If Giulia had been more enslaved to vanity, she would've wondered if her makeup was fresh enough for the camera. The last thing she'd expected to be doing when she woke up this morning was providing footage for *The Scoop.*

Eugenie glanced at Kathryn again and slumped deeper in her wheelchair. "We'd make Eagle leave us alone. The gas leak would make the news because of all the emergency responders and the reporters would come up with a sound bite about how unstable old houses are. Eagle would see the news and change its mind about buying our house."

Barbara Beech pushed past Kathryn and elbowed Giulia aside. "You are a waste of oxygen. Haven't you paid attention to anything about what we're doing in this town?"

Giulia could feel Ken Kanning's aura shivering with ratings-anticipation glee. If auras existed. She absolutely was not going to turn around to see. She'd seen more than enough insubstantial things for one day. No, for one month.

Eugenie regained some of her bombast. "You? You're destroying graceful historic architecture and replacing it with hideous boxes. You don't care about preserving the past. All you want is to shove everything old into a dumpster."

Beech glanced sideways at Pit Bull's camera. "Listen to me, you hidebound old woman. Eagle Developers blends the best of the old with the best of the new. For the project involving these two blocks in particular, we're preserving some of the façades as a bridge between the old and the new."

"While throwing poor people out into the street."

"We've done nothing of the sort. Everyone received a fair market value buyout. Everyone including you Sisters."

Eugenie pushed herself up with her arms. "Fair? What was fair about terrorizing us for months? You sent the rats. You sent the teenagers. You hired people to plaster our windows with pornography. When we wouldn't give in your boss finally did his own dirty work and tried to burn us in our beds. You're nothing but criminals in suits and ties."

Beech's belligerent expression melted into bafflement. "What are you talking about?"

Florence cackled. "The fat man dressed in a cat burglar costume was the funniest act I've seen in decades. I wasn't about to allow him to burn down my house. Once the chemicals in his bottle combined, I shortened the reaction time. Duck soup."

Pit Bull pulled the viewfinder away from his eye and checked the settings. He shook his head and resettled the camera on his shoulder.

Frank and Nash stepped without a sound into the hall behind Kathryn.

"Are you responsible for the gas leak?" Giulia said to Florence. Not quietly enough, because Eugenie bristled.

"I already said the gas leak was my fault."

"How did you get downstairs?" Giulia raised her voice enough for Frank to take notice.

Eugenie patted her ample legs. "I have a few surprises left in me."

"I'm asking for specifics."

The not-so-infirm nun made a face at Giulia. "If you must know, these old legs still have a little muscle strength. Sometimes I walk a few steps in my room late at night when I can't sleep. When I decided to make one last effort to save our home, I listened for when everyone was busy, then I scooted on my heinie down the stairs to the first floor and down to the cellar." She swelled with pride. "I walked ten entire steps across the cellar floor to get to the gas pipe."

Florence danced between Pit Bull and Eugenie, pirouetting around the wheelchair and singing. "Take me down to the cellar, Take me to the gas pipe; Unhook the pipe from the thingamabob, Whoops! You're too fat to finish the job."

Pit Bull stuck a finger in his ear and wiggled it. "Ken, I'm picking up something weird."

"Why gas?" Giulia aimed the question at Florence, but made it appear she asked it of Eugenie.

"I whispered in her ear night after night," Florence said. "I told her it was dramatic."

"It was dramatic and attention-getting," Eugenie said.

"Everyone panics when they smell a gas leak," Florence said. "Oh, no! One little spark and the whole place will explode." She produced a cigarette. "I'm the only one in the house who smokes."

"The burners on the kitchen stove have electronic pilot light igniters."

Eugenie and Florence shared the same dumbfounded expression.

"I forgot," they said together.

"What the hell?" Pit Bull balanced his camera on one knee and poked every button on it.

Ken Kanning came over to him. "Keep recording," he hissed. "This is gold."

"I'm getting echoes, and I swore I heard someone singing a minute ago."

"Probably a radio. Forget it. Keep filming."

Beech beckoned Giulia and Kathryn over by the door. "We need to talk."

Seventy-Six

With her phone held out, Beech stood between Giulia and Kathryn.

"The nun in the wheelchair has accused our company of unethical business practices. I won't let such an accusation stand without a challenge, so I logged into our company's system." She gestured to the screen. "Even I don't want to read this Lilliputian document. Could someone go downstairs for my briefcase? My laptop is in it."

"Got it," Nash said.

Beech started. "Who are you?"

Frank held out his hand, "Detective Driscoll, Ms. Beech."

Nash pounded up the stairs, not the least bit out of breath. "Detective VanHorne, Ms. Beech. Here you go." He handed her the briefcase.

"Fine. You can witness the exoneration of Eagle Developers in your official capacity." She sat on the rug in her crisp business suit and booted her laptop. "Is that scandal monger busy elsewhere?"

Giulia glanced up. "He and Pit Bull are focused on their camera."

"Pee-yew." Florence pinched her nostrils closed. "That was a stinker of a pun."

Giulia ignored her.

Beech typed. "Victor and I were partners for years, but he was never able to let go of his lone wolf mindset. Now that I'm in charge, I accessed his private login on the company system."

"His password was easy to break?"

A proud smile flitted across her mouth. "It was not. I'm good." She looked up from the keyboard. "As an instant karma hit for bragging on myself, let me amend. After getting in, I accessed only one-third of his files before I ran into a roadblock the size of the Empire

State Building. I've been working on the block for thirty-six hours."

Beneath the other floor lamp, Kanning and Pit Bull stuck ear buds in their ears and replayed footage on the camera's viewing screen.

A spreadsheet filled Beech's laptop screen. "This is what I was trying to show you on my phone. It's one of Victor's private schemes. Poor word choice, but you can see why."

The four-column spreadsheet listed dates, names, dollar amounts, and an alpha-numeric code.

"The project for which each person was hired?" Giulia pointed to the fourth column.

Beech nodded. "They must be. I haven't yet discovered the key to the code. I've promised myself a bottle of my favorite Prosecco when I crack it and I intend to pop the cork on the bottle tonight." She opened several different files. "No one, not even a nun old enough to be my grandmother, is going to tarnish our reputation." She eyed Kanning. "Let's make it a house party. Victor always said there's no such thing as bad publicity." She raised her voice. "Hey, *The Scoop*. Come here, please."

Kanning dropped the ear buds and palmed the microphone in the two seconds it took him to squat next to her. "In three...two...one."

Frank and Nash faded back into the hall before the camera shone its light on the group around the laptop.

"Scoopers, I'm happy to re-introduce Ms. Barbara Beech of Eagle Developers. We're waiting with bated breath for the news she's just promised us. Hope you're still sitting down."

Beech smiled for the camera. "Eagle Developers is always pleased to connect with the residents of the greater Pittsburgh area. *The Scoop* is giving us a helping hand tonight to dispel some nasty rumors which have reached our offices."

Florence said, "She's good, if you like people who live to pull the wool over your eyes." She floated next to Pit Bull and tickled his chin. "This one is a dandy."

Pit Bull balanced the camera one-handed and scratched his chin with the other. Florence giggled. "I haven't had this much fun in ages."

Giulia spared a moment's attention to hope Florence was still on her best behavior—for her—because of the holy water incident. Now if it would only last until *The Scoop* left the building.

"Kanning, you'll be able to edit out this backstory. I'm working on opening some files our deceased owner put passwords on. As soon as I figure out the access code word, I'll continue my explanation."

"Ms. Beech, we've already started a *Scoop* episode on Eagle."

"I know. You didn't think we were focused on success to the exclusion of everything else, did you?" Her sweet smile rang false. "You will not film my screen. Tomorrow morning I'll provide you with an expurgated version, the kind we use in presentations."

Kanning oozed charm. "*The Scoop* would never expect you to reveal proprietary information."

"I'm glad we're on the same page." Her eyes opened wide. "Wait a second...yes...yes...no, that's the wrong letter. Wait one more minute...Yes." She preened. "I'm better than good. All right, the files I've unlocked in your presence have not been previewed by me, so be prepared for me to shut this interview down without warning. Ready?" A pause for an adjustment to her suit jacket. "In three...two...one." A rearrangement of her smile. "Who better to be here at the reveal of startling information than our home-grown masters of the exposé?" She waved him in.

Pit Bull said, "The angle's not good. Could you turn ninety degrees left?"

As one, everyone on the floor crab-walked a quarter turn. The door was now to the left and their backs were now to the wall where the crucifix used to hang. Giulia eyed the possible angles of sight and gave up on trying to see the opened files while keeping out of the shot.

"I'm opening the first folder now." Her double-click revealed several spreadsheets and Word documents, all with cryptic eight-character names. "This one shares a familiar character string." She opened a spreadsheet with the same four columns as the earlier one. "I spy with my professional eye, a bright yellow comment triangle in the corners of these cells. Viewers of *The Scoop*, Eagle Developers is about to unearth proof of our honorable business practices in real time."

She clicked.

Seventy-Seven

The comment field held a screencap of a handwritten memo. Beech read out loud:

"July 31, contacted Fagin re: Baker St. Irregulars. Will perform usu. symphony for nuns."

Beech frowned and clicked the triangle in the cell below.

"September 5, new Irregular too enthusiastic, solo effort slayed audience of one. May turn to our favor. Fagin will resolve."

Florence's head popped through the laptop screen. "Was this man never taught not to mix metaphors?"

Giulia jerked her head to one side, trying to give Florence a hint to get out of the way of the documents. In response, Florence stuck both hands through the screen and mimed the appearance of someone in the stocks. Giulia saw she could read through her. The answer clicked into place. It clicked for Kanning as well. His quiet exclamation would have been bleeped out of his own broadcast.

Beech, for all her code-breaking skills, still scowled at the screen as she clicked another comment triangle. Kanning snapped his fingers without sound. Pit Bull's lens zoomed in on Beech's face. A second later he detached his eye from the viewfinder. He adjusted the focus on the screen. Looked through the viewfinder again. At the screen again.

Florence rotated her head completely around like an owl and blew him a kiss.

Beech opened and closed three comments in rapid succession. Over her shoulder, Giulia read them as fast as they opened:

Fagin delegated housewarming project.

If you want something done right, you do it yourself.

Will prove to Babs I haven't lost my touch.

Giulia rejoiced—on the inside. Agatha hadn't surprised revelations from Beech, but the CEO had given Giulia what she needed despite herself. Victor Eagle pandered to his own ego by carrying out the bit of terrorism he'd been sure would force the nuns out.

"Stop." She knelt next to Beech. "Do you understand the names and titles Victor Eagle used in these notes?"

"No. They're out of books, aren't they? I'm not much of a reader."

"Ignoramus," Florence said.

Giulia pointed to the first comment. Florence grasped her index finger as though to shake it, but she passed through Giulia like she'd passed through the laptop. The ghost's semi-solid appearance was just that—an appearance. Giulia thought: Is my strength of will stronger than the will of a hundred-year-old ghost?

"Fagin," she said to Beech, "runs a gang of juvenile criminals in *Oliver Twist*. The Baker Street Irregulars are a group of street kids Sherlock Holmes pays to trail people and gather information."

Beech slammed the laptop shut. Florence's head *blooped* through it and re-formed itself. She glared at Beech.

Frank stepped into the chapel. "Ms. Beech, we'd like you to come to the precinct with us to answer a few questions."

Seventy-Eight

Pit Bull backed away to include Frank and Kathryn in the shot. Panic rippled across Beech's face before she schooled it into submission.

"I don't see what interest private memos from my former CEO can have for the police."

Frank's face remained impassive. "A young man in our custody has given up the name of his off-the-books employer."

Kathryn broke the silence. "Then Victor Eagle was behind the harassment to get us to sell the house. I'll never hear the end of this from Olive."

"I knew it! I knew it!" Eugenie aimed both index fingers at Beech as though she was poking out the woman's eyes. "It's a good thing you didn't crawl through our window. You're skinny enough to have made it inside with that bomb."

Whatever Beech might have replied to this was lost in the Wrath of Florence. The new light bulbs exploded. The Bible flipped into the air and its pages erupted into confetti. The window blinds twisted and splintered.

Frank pushed Kathryn into the hall. Nash spun Eugenie's wheelchair and wheeled her out next to Kathryn. Bart hovered open-mouthed in the doorway. Pit Bull's camera tried to capture six angles at once.

"Scoopers, are you seeing this? We have Cottonwood's first genuine poltergeist action caught on video. We've scooped every network. You're our witnesses."

While Kanning stood his ground in the midst of the ghost's hurricane of various missiles, Giulia stuck her fingers in her ears in an unsuccessful attempt to muffle Florence's HULK SMASH hysteria.

"You gibfaced ratbag! You damaged my house! I'll make you pay! You'll never get my house! My house! Mine! Forever! I'll haunt you! I'll torment you! I'll—I'll—burn you alive!"

Florence stopped. The confetti drifted to the floor. The remains of the light bulbs sparked and sputtered. Giulia unplugged her ears, not that it made any difference either way. She squeezed her eyes shut and opened them again. Barbara Beech, the center of the chaos, cowered on the rug clutching her laptop against her like a shield.

Standing over her in twisted glee, Florence snapped her left thumbnail against her left middle nail in her "striking a match" gesture. Giulia yanked out her flask as flames appeared on the tips of all five of Florence's fingers.

"Holy shit," came from Kanning and Pit Bull together.

Giulia flung holy water at the flames. "*Ímperat tíbi majéstas Chrísti!*" They vanished with a unified hiss.

"Scoopers, you saw it. We saw it. Flames in midair. Nothing supporting them. Five of them, like fingertips."

Beech wiped her laptop with the corner of her jacket. "What kind of joke are you pulling, Ms. Driscoll? My Mac isn't waterproof."

"What's on fire?" Olive said.

"Bart, get the fire extinguisher," Kathryn said.

"Someone wheel me downstairs," Eugenie said. "I'm not going to die in this rat trap."

Giulia turned toward the press of bodies in the doorway. "Bart, forget the fire extinguisher. Bring salt and sage and a box of matches from the kitchen. We're cleansing this house."

Pit Bull pushed the camera into Kanning's arms. "Giulia, you just said 'The power of Christ commands' you, right? That's from the rite of exorcism."

"Bull, get back behind this camera."

"In a minute, Ken. Giulia? Tell me what I've been seeing and hearing for the past hour."

Florence walked through Beech, who didn't even shiver, then wedged herself between Giulia and Pit Bull. He took a step back, looking like he didn't understand why he moved.

"What are you going to do?" Florence clutched her hands together.

"I'm banishing the ghost from this house." Giulia spoke to Pit Bull, but the relative heights of the living and dead made it seem as though she was talking to Florence.

Florence bought it. "No! You can't force me out of my own house."

"Watch me."

Kanning hoisted the camera into position. "Scoopers, you're seeing the other half of *The Scoop* right now. Pit Bull, my intrepid chronicler, is conferring with Giulia Driscoll about the incredible events happening in this chapel tonight."

Florence dived for the crucifix, hidden under a snowdrift of shredded Bible pages. She swung it at Giulia like it was a baseball bat. Giulia blocked it with both hands. Pit Bull grabbed it.

"Further proof we have a real, live ghost and it watches Pirates games, Scoopers! Did you see that swing? It would've been a home run for sure, without the perfect double play between the multi-talented Giulia Driscoll and our own Pit Bull." He fiddled with the controls. "Dammit, Bull, where's the zoom on this thing?"

"Bottom left, second button in. Giulia, where's the ghost right now?"

Bart ran up to them with a canister of Morton's, a small plastic jar of McCormick sage, and a glass bowl. "This is all we have. Is it okay?"

"Perfect. Herd everyone into the hall. You, too. *The Scoop* too, please. Pit Bull, I know I can't stop you from filming so I won't try."

"But—" Bart said.

"But—" Pit Bull said.

"What are you talking about?" Kanning said.

Frank barged between Giulia and Bart. "Tell me what to do."

Giulia shook her head. "This is my fight."

He pushed his forehead against hers. "Not when something's attacking my wife."

She put her finger on his lips. "I've got this. It has to be a solo victory or word will get around in the ghost community. Our new business venture will collapse and where will Zlatan's college fund come from?"

He didn't smile.

"I have to press my advantage now."

He turned on his heel and joined Bart as she performed her

sheepdog duties. Giulia poured a wide line of salt across the threshold. "No one cross this."

"Don't you dare," Florence said. "You're not stronger than me. I can turn anything in this room into a murder weapon. I'll suffocate you with cigarette smoke. Watch me."

She created and lit two cigarettes at once. Clouds of smoke swirled around her and billowed through the room.

Kanning's breathless narration increased in volume. Giulia ignored it. She walked into the heart of the cigarette fumes and drew a circle of salt around Florence.

"No!" the ghost wailed. The Bible confetti joined the smoke, creating a blinding whirlwind.

Giulia dumped the sage into the bowl and dropped a lit match into the dried leaves. They ignited. A fragrant line of smoke rose from the burning herb. It knifed through the ghost's cloud, overpowering the cigarette stench.

"Now," Giulia said.

Seventy-Nine

Florence caved.

"No. No, please. Please don't kick me out of my house. It's all I have." She dropped to her knees and clutched Giulia's waist. "I'm alone here. I don't even have my baby with me. Think of you and your baby. Please."

Giulia held the bowl toward the nearest corner.

"No! Wait!" The ghost unlatched one hand and waved it at the doorway. "Bring that Eagle woman in here. We can compromise."

Giulia didn't lower the bowl, but she did acknowledge Florence's existence.

"I mean it. I'm an adult. I can cooperate. You can trust me."

Giulia raised her eyebrows.

"No tricks, I promise. I'm no welsher."

"You're also old enough not to use bigoted expressions." She lowered the bowl and beckoned to the crowd packed into the narrow doorway like multiple teenagers squeezing into a telephone booth in the 1950s.

"Ms. Beech, would you come in? Please cross over the salt line without breaking it."

Beech peered at Giulia, at the room, at the smoking bowl, at the camera. "You people are a bunch of fruit loops." She didn't budge.

"Pit Bull, would you replay the five flames footage?"

"Got it." He retrieved the camera and held down a button on the viewing screen. "Here it is."

He angled the screen toward Beech. Her stiff face slackened into astonishment. Without another word she took two exaggerated steps over the threshold.

Florence hissed at Giulia, "Tell her the house has to stay."

"Not without some explanation." Giulia set the bowl on the rug, the smoldering herb scenting the room like a precursor to Thanksgiving dinner. "Ms. Beech, now that you've seen the video evidence you may not be surprised to learn this house harbors a ghost."

In the doorway, Kanning reached new heights of histrionics. Olive kicked his shin. "Shut up."

"The ghost designed this house and has been bound to it since her death."

"Her?" Beech said.

"Yes. She's asked me to negotiate a compromise between you."

Beech's gaze roamed around the chapel, landing on Giulia's face. "I don't see a ghost."

"Are you questioning my veracity?"

Barbara Beech, survivor of Catholic grade school, responded to Giulia's Sister Mary Regina Coelis voice as intended.

"No, not at all. I didn't mean anything of the sort. What does she want?"

"For you not to tear down the house."

"Well, but, you've seen the drawings. Only a few of the best-preserved façades will be kept. All the houses are too old and unstable to make them worth repairing."

A pause. Giulia said, "The ghost will describe to me the designs relating to the weakest places in the house and the most efficient way to effect repairs." Another pause. "She offers to let you use her presence as a draw for adventurous tenants." Giulia crossed her arms and said to Florence, "Define adventurous."

Florence leapt to her feet. "Have you ever seen those ghost hunting TV shows? The nuns watch them. Fans of that nonsense will eat up what I can do with my cigarettes. Harmless tricks only, I promise."

Giulia relayed the proposal.

Beech imitated Giulia's posture. "Is this for real?"

Florence lit a cigarette and puffed smoke at Beech. The new CEO of Eagle Developers lost every speck of pigment in her face. Kanning leaped the salt barrier and caught her as her knees buckled.

Florence laughed. "These office types have no guts."

Beech wrested herself out of Kanning's arms. With steady hands she straightened her suit and smoothed her hair. "Thank you, Mr. Kanning. Ms. Driscoll, I apologize for doubting, but you will admit negotiating with ghosts was not a course offered when I received my MBA."

"Certainly."

"Your ghost won't be able to sign a contract."

Florence huffed. "Tell the gutless wonder I was making business deals before her grandmother was a gleam in her great-grandfather's eye."

Giulia relayed the message without the epithet.

Beech managed a thin smile. "As a fellow professional, I applaud her force of character. We women of business have to stick together."

Florence laid her hand on top of Giulia's. "Shake on it for me."

Beech peered at Giulia's hand. "I still can't see her. How are we...wait. Ms. Driscoll, my office will contact you by the end of the week to discuss retaining you as intermediary for this aspect of the project."

Florence elbowed Giulia. "This is the beginning of a beautiful relationship."

"You watch classic movies as well as ghost hunting shows?"

Florence fluttered a hand at her bosom. "Humphrey Bogart is every girl's dream. If only he'd haunt with me."

Beech looked from Giulia's face to several indefinite spots in midair. "Your ghost watches TV? My marketing people will be all over this."

Giulia said to Florence, "Eagle Developers will have my number on speed dial if the truce is broken."

"You outrage me, madam." Florence struck a pose. "I am an upright woman."

"Assisted by the corset. Ms. Beech, please confirm you have my direct line."

Beech held up her phone's contact screen.

"I said I'd behave." Florence pouted. "Anyway, you have to come back to show me the baby. If only it was a girl, you could've named her Florence."

Giulia signaled Frank. He herded everyone out of the room,

including *The Scoop.* Kanning cracked his shoulder against the door frame as he tried to walk and watch the camera's replay screen at the same time.

When she had Florence to herself, Giulia found the cap to her holy water flask and held it up without screwing it on. "Do you think I'm naïve enough to believe everything you said just now?"

Florence froze in the act of conjuring a fresh cigarette.

"You've played tricks on everyone in this house except Steve."

"Well, but—"

"You showed us what you're capable of when you're angry."

"I was provoked—"

"You showed me how easily you allow yourself to be provoked." Giulia covered the mouth of the flask with her index finger and tipped a drop onto it.

Florence lit the cigarette with a trembling hand.

Giulia balanced the bead of water on the tip of her index finger. "Do you expect me to blindly trust you because you made a few blithe promises under pressure?"

The cigarette burned unheeded. "Well, but, the baby...and the house..."

"And the little fact that you murdered Victor Eagle."

"I did not!"

The denial surprised Giulia. Not the actual "no" but the ghost's voice and body language. Instead of snark and a figurative nudge to bring Giulia in on the joke, Florence exuded shock.

Giulia didn't give in. "You admitted you accelerated the chemical reaction in his plastic bottle."

"I did, yes, but his number was up no matter what. In my day a child would've known not to put a match to a stack of dried paper layered with insect carcasses and desiccated rodent droppings. He would've gone up like a torch no matter when his explosion happened. I made sure he did as little damage to my house as possible."

Giulia weighed her explanation. It tallied with Florence's only true obsession, the house. She might not be against a spot of murder, but not if the spot of murder destroyed her house. Giulia was relieved. As long as Victor Eagle's ghost didn't show up at the office one day for any reason whatsoever.

Florence crushed the cigarette in her long fingers. "Are you going to renege on the deal?"

Giulia wasn't about to cede an inch of her power and turned hard eyes on the ghost. "I don't make promises lightly."

"Are you implying I do?" Florence bristled.

Giulia stopped a potential hell-throat before it started. "I'm here to make sure all promises are kept."

Florence crossed her arms. "More rules?"

"Let's call it insurance." She dripped water in a half-circle around Florence. The ghost cringed. Giulia had been right. For all the folklore Florence had picked up while lurking while the nuns watched TV, she didn't know that ghost rules weren't necessarily demon rules.

"Now," Giulia said, "we'll discuss the real terms of your continued residence here."

Eighty

Rules in place, Giulia joined everyone else in the wide hall by the invalids' rooms. Steve the Chihuahua was shamelessly begging for attention.

Frank said to Bart as Giulia arrived, "The report came back on Victor Eagle. It confirms he miscalculated the timing on his chemical arson attempt and, in layman's terms, blew himself up."

Bart clutched his sleeve. "Does that mean we're no longer under suspicion? All of us? Me too?"

Frank smiled at her. "Yes, all of you."

Olive hugged her. "I knew it."

Dorothy stuck her head in Helena's room. "Did you hear that?"

Frank took Giulia back into the chapel, away from *The Scoop*. "If this keeps up I'm going to die of a coronary before I turn forty."

"As long as you don't haunt me." She leaned against him. "Tonight was more extreme than I expected."

"You think?" He squeezed her. "The protective instinct is strong in the Driscolls. You're messing with generations of genetics."

"Don't crush Zlatan. We'll discuss genetics and adaptation tonight. I have some fascinating stories to tell you whenever we get home."

"I need several beers."

"Sure, tease the pregnant woman. Come on, let's get back to the hall before Kanning realizes we're gone."

As soon as Frank reappeared, Kathryn put her hands on Eugenie's shoulders. "Detective, what about this one's tampering with the gas?"

"Tampering with a gas meter is a criminal offense." Frank eyed the stairs. "We'll have to bring the Sister to the precinct, but it's more than likely she'll be released on her own recognizance."

Eugenie shrank into herself. "You're arresting me?"

"What did you think would happen?" Kathryn beckoned to Frank. "Is this necessary?"

"Our apologies, Sister, but yes. Sister Eugenie isn't a flight risk, so it's a ninety-nine percent chance we'll bring her right back here."

Olivia cackled. "Hear that, Eugenie? You're not a flight risk. That's rich."

Frank turned to Barbara Beech, who just happened to be sandwiched between himself and Nash. "Ms. Beech, your presence at the station is also requested."

The executive lost her business façade yet again. "What? You watched me experiment with passwords until I unlocked Victor's hidden files. Then you saw with your own eyes I knew nothing about any reprehensible practices initiated by him."

"Ms. Beech, we were also auditors as you explained how you had already unlocked certain files and chose to complete the process for *The Scoop*'s camera."

"The time stamps on those files will prove I had nothing—"

"Ms. Beech, persons in the pay of Eagle Developers have committed acts of vandalism and intimidation."

"And murder." Olive's voice was shrill. "I heard Ms. Driscoll read that coded memorandum off the computer screen. Poor Matilda didn't have a fatal heart attack out of nowhere. The thug he called Fagin scared her. Or somebody that Fagin told to do it."

Diane said in her quiet voice, "Olive was right all along." She said to Frank, "Detective, Sister Matilda was walking our dog when the incident occurred. If he can be taken to the person in custody, he may recognize the person's scent."

Frank's face betrayed no reaction. "Thank you, Sister. We'll keep it in mind."

Beech's angry voice took on a shrill undertone. "Detective, it's likely Victor Eagle had an assistant within the company to effect these reprehensible acts. That assistant was not me. I pride myself on my integrity, which reflects on the entire company. Our legal department will work with you to root out any unprincipled employees and bring them to justice."

"Ms. Beech, it is our duty to advise you that the evidence in our possession indicates high-level complicity within the company. You are welcome to have a lawyer present during your statement."

"You're damn right I will." Beech's long nails beckoned *The Scoop.* "Clarence."

Pit Bull's camera sprang into action.

"Eagle Developers will fight this accusation of complicity in illegal business practices and we will win."

Ken Kanning's voice replied, "Scoopers, we promise you that we will not be outdone in rooting out corruption and crime in our city. Stay tuned next week for developments worthy of Perry Mason."

Frank said to Kathryn, "We'll send transport for Sister Eugenie."

Nash stepped closer. "Ms. Beech, we're ready to leave."

Beech stalked downstairs between Nash and Frank.

Olive stage-whispered, "Isn't that called a perp walk?"

Giulia stared at her.

"What?" Olive said. "I like to watch cop shows."

Florence appeared at Giulia's side. "Don't cross that business owner. She's the vindictive type. I'll make sure to play nice with her, especially with you as my keeper."

She sat on the hall floor, her dress ballooning around her. Steve's little legs dodged and leaped everyone's feet as he ran to her. Florence rubbed his ears. The dog flopped onto his back and presented his belly. The ghost obliged.

Ken Kanning's voice intruded. "If I didn't know better, I'd swear someone's rubbing the Chihuahua's belly. Scoopers, are you seeing this?"

Kathryn took charge. "Gentlemen, Sisters, Giulia, it's been an eventful evening. May we offer you a glass of wine to toast our new adventure?"

"Not Giulia," Bart said. "Wine and babies don't mix."

Kanning and his microphone teleported so close to Giulia she could smell his scented hair goo. "The intrepid Giulia Driscoll will soon have an able assistant in her ongoing fight for justice." He parked the microphone on her stomach. "Let's see if we can share the new Driscoll's heartbeat with our faithful Scoopers."

Giulia stepped back before she committed on-camera mayhem.

"Mr. Kanning, you watched tonight as I gained the goodwill of an unpredictable and violent ghost. You realize I could call in a favor if I chose?"

Florence stood. "As long as it's to annoy the loudmouth and not the cute one, I'm happy to oblige."

A precise cloud of cigarette smoke covered Kanning's head. From within, violent coughing distorted his silken voice. Pit Bull kept filming.

"I'm okay. I'm okay." More hacks. "Giulia, tell your ghost—" Kanning could well be coughing up a lung from the sounds— "I apologize."

"See?" Florence said. "The beginning of a beautiful friendship. The detective and her ghost."

"You are not my ghost," Giulia said.

"Are you sure?" Florence could also be coquettish.

Giulia's phone rang. She stepped away to take the call.

"Giulia? It's Jasper. Can you come by the shop tonight, no matter how late? Rowan did another reading and she says unless she's a talentless hack she saw every ghost in the tri-state area headed your way and they all want to talk."

"And we know she's not a talentless hack." Giulia sighed. "I'll be there."

She hung up. "Sister Kathryn, could I trouble you for a cup of coffee? It's going to be a long night."

Alice Loweecey

Baker of brownies and tormenter of characters, Alice Loweecey recently celebrated her thirtieth year outside the convent. She grew up watching Hammer horror films and Scooby-Doo mysteries, which explains a whole lot. When she's not creating trouble for Giulia Driscoll, she can be found growing her own vegetables (in summer) and cooking with them (the rest of the year).

**The Giulia Driscoll Mystery Series
by Alice Loweecey**

Novels

NUN TOO SOON (#1)
SECOND TO NUN (#2)
NUN BUT THE BRAVE (#3)
THE CLOCK STRIKES NUN (#4)
NUN AFTER THE OTHER (#5)

Short Stories

CHANGING HABITS
(prequel to NUN TOO SOON)

Henery Press Mystery Books

And finally, before you go...
Here are a few other mysteries
you might enjoy:

FIXIN' TO DIE

Tonya Kappes

A Kenni Lowry Mystery (#1)

Kenni Lowry likes to think the zero crime rate in Cottonwood, Kentucky is due to her being sheriff, but she quickly discovers the ghost of her grandfather, the town's previous sheriff, has been scaring off any would-be criminals since she was elected. When the town's most beloved doctor is found murdered on the very same day as a jewelry store robbery, and a mysterious symbol ties the crime scenes together, Kenni must satisfy her hankerin' for justice by nabbing the culprits.

With the help of her Poppa, a lone deputy, and an annoyingly cute, too-big-for-his-britches State Reserve officer, Kenni must solve both cases and prove to the whole town, and herself, that she's worth her salt before time runs out.

Available at booksellers nationwide and online

Visit www.henerypress.com for details

IN IT FOR THE MONEY

David Burnsworth

A Blu Carraway Mystery (#1)

Lowcountry Private Investigator Blu Carraway needs a new client. He's broke and the tax man is coming for his little slice of paradise. But not everyone appreciates his skills. Some call him a loose cannon. Others say he's a liability. All the ex-Desert Storm Ranger knows is his phone hasn't rung in quite a while. Of course, that could be because it was cut off due to delinquent payments.

Lucky for him, a client does show up at his doorstep—a distraught mother with a wayward son. She's rich and her boy's in danger. Sounds like just the case for Blu. Except nothing about the case is as it seems. The jigsaw pieces—a ransom note, a beat-up minivan, dead strippers, and a missing briefcase filled with money and cocaine—do not make a complete puzzle. The first real case for Blu Carraway Investigations in three years goes off the rails. And that's the way he prefers it to be.

Available at booksellers nationwide and online

Visit www.henerypress.com for details

BONES TO PICK

Linda Lovely

A Brie Hooker Mystery (#1)

Living on a farm with four hundred goats and a cantankerous carnivore isn't among vegan chef Brie Hooker's list of lifetime ambitions. But she can't walk away from her Aunt Eva, who needs help operating her dairy.

Once she calls her aunt's goat farm home, grisly discoveries offer ample inducements for Brie to employ her entire vocabulary of cheese-and-meat curses. The troubles begin when the farm's pot-bellied pig unearths the skull of Eva's missing husband. The sheriff, kin to the deceased, sets out to pin the murder on Eva. He doesn't reckon on Brie's resolve to prove her aunt's innocence. Death threats, ruinous pedicures, psychic shenanigans, and biker bar fisticuffs won't stop Brie from unmasking the killer, even when romantic befuddlement throws her a curve.

Available at booksellers nationwide and online

Visit www.henerypress.com for details

CROPPED TO DEATH

Christina Freeburn

A Faith Hunter Scrap This Mystery (#1)

Former US Army JAG specialist, Faith Hunter, returns to her West Virginia home to work in her grandmothers' scrapbooking store determined to lead an unassuming life after her adventure abroad turned disaster. But her quiet life unravels when her friend is charged with murder – and Faith inadvertently supplied the evidence. So Faith decides to cut through the scrap and piece together what really happened.

With a sexy prosecutor, a determined homicide detective, a handful of sticky suspects and a crop contest gone bad, Faith quickly realizes if she's not careful, she'll be the next one cropped.

Available at booksellers nationwide and online

Visit www.henerypress.com for details